THE PATH TO THE LAKE

SUSAN SALLIS

ISIS
LARGE PRINT
Oxford

First published in Great Britain 2009
by
Bantam Press
An imprint of Transworld Publishers

Published in Large Print 2009 by ISIS Publishing Ltd.,
7 Centremead, Osney Mead, Oxford OX2 0ES
by arrangement with
Transworld Publishers

British Library Cataloguing in Publication Data
Sallis, Susan.
    The path to the lake
    1. Husbands - - Death - - Fiction.
    2. Widows - - Fiction.
    3. Village communities - -Fiction.
    4. Large type books.
    I. Title
    823.9'14–dc22

ISBN 978–0–7531–8466–0 (hb)
ISBN 978–0–7531–8467–7 (pb)

Printed and bound in Great Britain by
T. J. International Ltd., Padstow, Cornwall

THE PATH TO THE LAKE

To my family

Prologue

The lake was finished in the spring of 1922. These man-made lidos were being created all over the country, but on the Somerset coast they were particularly popular because the tide-fall exposed rocks and mud, which made the sea inaccessible to swimmers until it was high on the shingle. Man-made lakes collected water each high tide and could be drained and cleaned annually. They could be made deep enough for divers, and shallow enough for children. There could be sun terraces and proper changing rooms and deckchairs and model boats and pedaloes. And if the lie of the land was right, they were relatively cheap to create.

George Jackson was one of the masons employed by the local council. He lived in Cardiff, and took digs on the Somerset side of the Bristol Channel with Mrs Stevens down on the Pill — which was what the Somerset people called their little harbours. The night before the Grand Opening he took her daughter, Nellie Stevens, on a tour of the site. She had viewed it from above as it took shape, but to walk on the carefully cambered surface seemed to her to be terrifying. She did not understand how anyone could commit themselves to the sea, even when it was filtered and tamed into this enormous cavernous space. She clutched George's arm and as they stumbled towards the far wall in what would be the deep end, she kept her head tilted upwards towards the stars. He was carrying a galvanized bucket, but he managed to pat her hand indulgently and ask her again whether she had brought the birthday present with her. They reached the far wall, four feet above her head, and she leaned her back to it and looked the way they had come. "Told you I had, George. How many more times?" She was breathing quickly, as if they had run the length of the deep hole. The diving tower was silhouetted against the night sky. It was taller than the headland. No one would dare to climb to the top and dive off, surely?

He put down the bucket and followed her gaze. It was the biggest project he had carried out so far. He was deeply pleased with it.

"Folks are going to be happy here, Nell," he whispered. Sound was odd at this depth, and the sibilants carried around the wall, leapt over the closed sluice gate and completed the circuit. "And we had something to do with it."

"You did, you mean." He had no idea how this place affected her; she was cold with fear. It was like a gigantic tomb.

"I did it for you, Nell. You know that. And your birthday present is going to make it ours. Proper-like. No one will know it's here, 'cept you and me. How many folks has their own private lake, our Nell?" He was laughing. "Come on now, how many?"

She looked into his face. He always made her feel special, but this business about a private lake — what was he on about now?

He turned her around and put both her hands on the wall and moved them around. She squeaked. The wall was rough. He stilled her left hand when her arm was at full stretch, took the forefinger and gently pushed it. It went into a hole a little bigger than itself. She squeaked again; supposing there was a spider? She did not actually mind spiders, but everyone else did, so she squeaked again just in case. He was laughing in her ear now, her head was full of him.

He reached into her pocket and took out the so-called birthday present, put it into the palm of her left hand and wrapped her forefinger around it. Very gently he adjusted their mutual grip and inserted it into the hole which he had made especially for it the previous night. "Fits perfect," he murmured. He lowered their hands, kissed her again and took the wet linen cover from the bucket. "Won't take but a minute," he said as he reached inside and then up again and cemented her birthday present into place.

He stepped back and looked at it. She looked, too, and saw again the Victorian door knob, and felt again the pang of disappointment that it had not been a ring. But she loved him, and she said, "It looks very . . . important, George."

He was delighted. "That's just what it is, Nellie-girl. Important. The door to our lake. When I found that

there door knob I wanted to put it on our first cottage."
He sighed. And then seemed to shake himself. "But
there, this is our lake, and there's our door to prove it,
and all the people that come here and laugh and splash
about and don't know nothing . . . they will be our
guests! And you understand that, Nellie." He was
kissing her crazily, and laughing in her ear again, and
she wanted to tell him about getting wet cement on her
summer dress, but she did not. She suddenly saw it all
through his eyes. Just for a minute. And she knew it was
the most romantic gesture in the whole wide world.

CHAPTER
ONE

November 2005

The little bungalow crouched in its laurels at the top of the hill, a full two miles from the old marine lake, less than that from the pier. It seemed to be completely isolated, but it was almost within the grounds of the Elizabethan manor, which had long been sold and converted into a nursing home. From the sandy road leading to the manor it looked like what it was, one of the many one-storeyed bungalows put up without planning permission between the wars. But this one seemed to be in the wrong place. Surely if you wanted to live by the sea you would build your bungalow or chalet within reach of the Victorian pier or marine lake? Certainly not on the top of one of the outcrops of the Mendips, so steep that before the advent of the motor car the lord of the manor had stables two miles away on the moors and harnessed four horses to his carriage for his journey home.

But when you walked along the side of the little bungalow, you could understand the reason for it. The garden dropped away to a sheer cliff; below that lay the town and to the right was the sea. The view was breathtaking. The gulls and crows and sweeps of starlings flew beneath as well as above.

The Venables bought it in 1996. Vivian Venables taught in a primary school twenty-five miles further down the coast, but the motorway made light of the distance, and though she did not like the drive during the holiday season it was worth it to come home every evening to the peculiarly insubstantial dwelling at the very top of Christmas Tump, and watch the sun drown itself in the Bristol Channel. The weather often came over from Wales, and was a constant interest. She loved to watch the prevailing south-westerlies bend the trees into the land so that it looked as though every leaf, every blade of grass, had been groomed with a curry comb. The thunderheads piling up after a hot day would make her heart pump with excitement. The short daylight hours of winter became precious; at weekends she would sit in the window with her knitting and become part of their gentle fading.

David worked from home; the second bedroom was set up as his studio, and in between "earning a crust" — as he called his cartoons — he would take a sketch book into the garden and block in views which would be developed later into unusually vivid watercolours. There was a great deal of sky to be seen from the Tump, and as he wryly pointed out to Viv, not many people wanted to hang a skyscape above their fireplace.

"Just you wait and see!" she told him. "They'll be queueing for them after your first exhibition." But David was happy with the way things were. He loved being at home, keeping house and garden "going", working in his studio most of the day, and painting the sea and the sky when he found time. He had worked for the same national newspaper for many years, and had built a reputation for genuinely funny cartoons that were also political comments. Until he met Viv he had felt he was marking time; one day he would have accumulated enough money to give up his day job and become a "proper artist". In the last ten years, though in other ways he was still waiting, contentment had soothed away any sense of dissatisfaction surrounding his work. It had led him to Viv and his life here. What more could he ask?

His father lived in a village in a fold of the Mendip range, where he had retired from his job as a curator in the Bristol museum the same year David and Viv had married. He was proud of his son, and professed himself "tickled pink" by his amazing ability to capture on paper the very essence of a person with a few slashed lines. But he could not take this skill seriously as a career — certainly not as a profession. He rarely saw it as inspirational; if he had been forced to describe it, he would have called it a knack. Until Viv arrived. She changed everything.

For one thing, David was thirty-seven when he met her, and she was thirty. Neither of them had had any permanent relationship before, indeed had gone out of their way to avoid it. They had fought against this one. David had told her bluntly that he was happier to be on his own: he could not remember his mother and had been brought up in a masculine household, well able to cook and clean, encouraged to speak his mind. Viv had smiled with relief. She had also lost her mother as a child, and had been frightened of her father, who was crazy with grief. She had left home as soon as possible.

She was a great admirer of David's work, and when he showed her some of his abstracts she felt honoured. He wanted to move to what he called the "flat lands" so that he could begin to paint sky, and she helped to set him up in a studio in Bridgwater because she had been teaching there for almost ten years and knew it well. And then, because he had told her right from their first meeting how much he needed space, she left him to it. It was a shock to find him waiting by the school gate, asking plaintively what on earth the difference was between stewing beef, shin and skirt. As he had been looking after himself for the last twenty years this was obviously some kind of ruse. He admitted as much, and then told her sheepishly that work was not going very well and he needed to establish a proper routine, and if she popped in after school it might help. She looked at him and burst out laughing.

"What is it you need? An organizer? Cook?"

He frowned. "I don't know. I do know I moved down here so that I could see more of you, not less."

"But I explained to you that there could never be anything between us. I can never have a — a — relationship. And you said the same thing." Her face flamed.

His frown deepened. "I know all that, but we were wrong. We were talking about our sexual impotence. We have a relationship, Viv. We are friends." He took a breath, and said emphatically, "We're such *good*

8

friends, Viv. If we lived next door to each other or in a block of flats, we'd see each other every day. Can't we do that? We'll work together. You have your lesson plans and your marking. Surely you need someone to talk to about your work? I do. When I was in Bristol and we got together once a week, it was marvellous. Really helpful. And I hoped — I thought — we could do it on a daily basis, so I moved."

So though she laughed again and shook her head, she got into his car and went back to his flat. He was a good man; he was himself. Because he had no armour surrounding him she thought he needed protection. She never dreamed he needed protection from her.

The daily visit was established immediately. As soon as school was over each day, she went to his flat. For her it was like walking into sunlight. She had thought that most men had something of her father in them. She learned that David's gentle humour was part of him. Gradually, very gradually, she relaxed into this wonderful, guilt-free relationship. In spite of her own armour, it began to develop and grow.

After a walk to Crooks Peak during the summer of 1995 he said casually, "I saw this bungalow today. On the top of one of the hills that drop into the sea further up the coast. It would be half an hour's drive to school."

She said, "Do you mean . . . live together? In a bungalow? Buy a house together?"

He said, slightly surprised, "Well, yes. We're together most of our free time, anyway. And this house is . . . well, special."

She looked at him, then away. She was a long, rather angular woman, with brown, shoulder-length hair which she wore "done up" for school; her face was bony, eyes blue. David had done many sketches of her. The first one showed a typical blue-stocking with glasses on the end of a long nose. The last, dashed off a week ago, was just a face, classically beautiful, framed and emphasized by a coif. She had not recognized it. When he told her that was how she looked when she was thinking, she said, "You see me as a nun?"

And after a considered pause he had nodded. "One of you is a nun. Yes." And after pausing herself, she had simply nodded.

She referred to that sketch now.

"Nuns don't live with men friends, David."

He grinned suddenly. "They do. I saw a film once. Deborah Kerr, I think it was. Might have been Virginia McKenna. Looked a lot like you — good facial bones, very slim. She was a nun, and she fell in love and renounced her vows and married whoever it was. Can't remember his name."

She cut in quickly. "I don't look a bit like those two. I'm that first sketch you did. The blue-stocking."

"You're that, too, and other things, it's confusing. But very interesting." He leaned sideways trying to engage her averted gaze. "Viv, there was another film. About a bloke and a woman who were terrific friends for years and did not realize they were also in love. And when they did they got married and were wonderfully happy."

10

She sighed. "I saw that one, too. They were married about a year, and then he died. In fact they got married because he was dying." She lifted her head and looked at him suddenly. "My God. You're not ill, are you?"

He held that look. His own eyes were grey and very steady. He whispered, "No, but I think I will be if you don't agree to buying this house and living with me."

She tried to get it back to being light. "Which one do you want, nun or blue-stocking?"

"I'm afraid I want all of them."

She became very still. "You don't mean all this."

He said again, slowly. "I want all of them."

"But you know — I thought you understood — surely you *understood*?"

"I understand. I have shown you that I understand. When I spoke of mutual impotence I meant . . . I understand."

"Then why change anything?" Her voice was nearly querulous, and she brought it down a notch. "Living together . . . it will change the status quo —"

"Yes," he said, flatly and unequivocally.

She felt her eyes filling with tears. She said, "Then . . . no."

He leaned towards her and saw her hands clench by her sides. He cupped her thin face, held it still, kissed her, then whispered, "See? We can do this. We can be good friends and loving friends." He held her hand very gently.

When he leaned away, smiling at her, she said, "You would be willing to accept that kind of relationship? Always?"

"Unless you tell me otherwise."

Her voice was still controlled but very low. "You know I will never change, David. You say you understand. Perhaps . . . you don't."

"I think we are talking about sex. About sleeping together. Cohabiting." He was smiling, cajoling her. He leaned close again and she leaned away from him. He said with emphasis, "It doesn't *matter*, Viv. Not to me. There are so many kinds of love. We know most of them. Do we throw all of them away because we cannot have that one, that particular one?"

She said nothing, and after a while he stood up and went to the kitchen and made tea. He stirred sugar into hers and passed it to her. She looked up and smiled through the steam.

"That nun. Oh, and that blue-stocking." Her smile widened into a grin. "They both love you." She lifted her shoulders. "There are no sleeping beauties underneath them, however. No glamorous princess waiting to be woken with a kiss."

"I couldn't cope with a princess. Or glamour."

They both laughed.

He said, still laughing, "Viv Venables. It sounds good."

"I don't think we should marry." She put her tea down carefully. "Face facts, David. You might want children. Meet that princess. It would be so much simpler if we didn't marry."

"No it wouldn't. The bungalow needs a married couple. And I thought *you* understood. I cannot father children, Viv."

12

Flustered, she said, "Oh my God. It's all about a house!" She threw up her hands in mock horror and nearly knocked her tea over.

He looked at her and made her look at him. Grey eyes and blue eyes. He said, "Would it make it easier if I told you I had only five years to live?"

She laughed, but then checked both of them. "Don't say things like that, David — I'm serious. It's tempting fate."

They had their five years and more. David's father had a stroke and moved into Tall Trees, the nursing home just above their bungalow. They visited him often, and he sometimes walked down on Sundays for lunch. He used two sticks and was stubbornly independent. He still thought Viv was "tops" as he put it, but also he thought she was the reason he was not sharing the bungalow.

Sometimes she caught him looking at her from beneath a frown. She asked David to find out what was wrong, and he talked to his father. Nothing came of it. But subtly something changed in the marriage. And then, very unsubtly, everything changed.

She could not tell David what it was. She could not tell him that at forty years old she was pregnant. They were still loving friends. She had learned over the last ten years that David was indeed impotent. He never told her why, and she could never ask, but as her trust in him grew until she was part of him in every other way, she knew that they would never be able to become physically one. He had married her on her own terms.

And gradually she understood why. It became part of her love for him; she took the responsibility for their friendship on to her own shoulders. They shared all thoughts, fears, joys . . . except the one. So she could not tell him that she was pregnant. And it therefore followed that she was unable to tell him that in order to save her marriage she would have to have an abortion.

It was 18 November and a late half-term, so she had been home all week. She took the car out of the garage on to the sandy road. He came out of the front door and raised his eyebrows at her through the window. She wound it down.

"I need a few things. For Christmas. Thought I'd dash into Bristol."

He pretended that was all right and nodded. "I'm coming. Wait until I get my jacket."

He trusted her not to drive away without him, although she had been shutting herself off for two or three weeks now. It was his trust that made her wait for him. She thought of that often, later.

It was when they were driving down the combe that separated country from city . . . it was then that it happened. There were hairpin bends and woods either side. She remembered nothing about the event. She assumed there had been a fault in the steering. It seemed to become loose between her hands. After that, nothing.

She was cut out of the driver's seat by the firemen. David, still strapped into his seat, was found against a tree. He was dead. She was hospitalized until just before Christmas. Nobody ever mentioned a baby.

14

A few weeks after it had happened, David's father staggered down to the bungalow and washed up the breakfast things, then went into the bedroom and made the bed and folded David's pyjamas and Viv's nightie. On the way back to Tall Trees he collapsed, and a few days later he died.

Vivian's story

2006

I came out of hospital in December some time. I don't remember anything about the accident and very little about the hospital. There was an inquiry — something official — about the car. Nobody ever told me what it was all about. I came home. Everything was neat. People rang up. Some people came with flowers and fruit as if I were ill. Someone showed me the headline in our local paper from November: "Local couple in crash tragedy". It seemed to be about someone else entirely.

A couple of the nurses from Tall Trees came and told me they could do with help with the flowers, and now that I was alone perhaps I would be interested. When I said something about David's father they nodded and said they understood that the home held sad memories too, but if I could not bear it then I should join the local bereavement group, because it was not good to be isolated up here like I was. They did not realize that isolation was all I wanted. I wanted the white silence; I wanted the void; I wanted whole sections of time to

15

pass without me knowing it. It was when time was marked out by visitors and phone calls and the need to eat or put on other clothes or wash my unwanted body . . . it was then that everything became unbearable. It was when I had to think. I could not think. The pills helped. But not always. And when it became unbearable, I ran. A woman at the bereavement group suggested writing it all down, but that didn't work. There was nothing to write down. That was what I wanted, and that was how it was. Nothing. The woman said to write down what I saw when I ran. But I saw nothing. I heard nothing. I felt nothing. That was the whole point of it.

But then, months later, something happened. Something that frightened me, jolted me out of my void and into something else . . . I did not want to forget it. It was something I had to remember, and I had to remember it properly, as it happened. So I started writing it down. I made myself into an observer. I observed. I recorded.

It was another of those nights. End of September. I had forgotten to take the pills. I focused on my watch and saw it was two o'clock. I had got into bed almost two hours earlier, listened to the World Service without hearing anything, and was now rigid with the effort of not thinking. I knew I wouldn't sleep until it was light.

I got up and twitched the curtains aside; the garden was lit theatrically by moonlight, and I stood there and fought for emptiness. It was often easier at night because of the darkness, but the moonlight was too bright. Much too bright.

I dropped the curtain angrily, holding my head, screwing up my eyes. I had various methods of controlling thought, but when it was really bad like this, action — frantic action — was the only cure I knew. I turned towards my clothes — thrown over a chair last night — and dragged on the jogging bottoms and top, stuffing pyjamas in anyhow, adding a knitted cap pulled well down over lank brown hair, opening a drawer for gloves, finding none and slamming it shut. There was absolutely no need to hurry, but I grabbed keys and ran down the hall as if I had a train to catch. The mirror reflected me running towards it, tall and skinny, lank hair still in its rubber band, empty eyes and bony face registering exhaustion. The grandmother clock gleamed for an instant, it was ten past two.

At first my body had difficulty in keeping up with my legs. I live on the Tump and all roads go down to the sea very steeply. My arms pumped, reaching in front of me as if I could brake myself against the thin night air. My legs leapt in huge giant leaps; I could not slow them, not even to turn right into Easter Lane. And then, as the road levelled slightly into the series of hairpin bends leading to the sea one way and the village the other, I managed a decelerating jog — and finally came to a stop just before the next bend. My lungs were pumping like mad; I stopped and hung on to a wall retaining a terrace. I was so hot I thought I might explode; I whipped off my hat and stuffed it into a trouser pocket, unzipped my top and let the cold light beat on my pyjama jacket. I did not allow myself the inevitable question — what on earth was I doing there at that time of night? Had I done so, the answer would have been obvious. I couldn't sleep; my thoughts were getting out of hand, and I was doing something about it. But it would be another four hours before it was light enough for me to allow myself a morning jog . . . I was like a drinker only allowing themselves refreshment after the sun reaches the yardarm . . . or something similar. So I could not ask myself that question. Sometimes an addict has to break their own rules.

My body cooled, and my breathing slowed, and I started running again to the next hairpin bend. Down another level, across the road, plunging down the donkey path and landing up on the tiny promenade opposite the bandstand. And there it was: the silver sea, the dark shapes of land thrusting into it, lights here and there. A pocket-book resort; ice cream and coffee and a posh Italian restaurant, and the daddy-long-legs pier striding out, much as I had giant strode down. And all lit by that moon. It looked totally artificial.

If I had wanted to take my mind off whatever it had been on, then I couldn't have done better than come to the side of the sea, where everything declared itself to be unreal: a stage set with an expert lighting technician sitting around somewhere, unobserved in a box. I had made model theatres like this when I was ten, cardboard cut-outs in cardboard shoe boxes, lit cunningly with a couple of torches. The brilliant thing about them had been their very limited life. Someone trod on them, or they had simply fallen to pieces when my mother caught them in the vacuum. Then they went into the incinerator, and I made another. Even better. No broken hearts; a pang, maybe. My mother had been alive, then.

Could I make another? That was definitely not the right question. The right question was: did I want to make another? And I knew the answer to that.

I walked slowly over to the Victorian railings that guarded the drop down to the rocks, and stared over the gleaming mud towards the islands, very black lumps in the midst of all that silvery movement. That's what painters couldn't get: the constant movement. They could come near to it, especially if the viewer stood well back. Too close and it became clear it was a static sea. No such thing. Art could not even begin to imitate life. Once life was gone there was nothing and art, literature, music . . . they were all rubbish. Rubbish, rubbish, rubbish!

I was gripping the railings, shaking them with each repeated word.

Below me, half-way down the slipway, part of the darkness shifted slightly. Someone was trying to sleep in one of the boats, and the whining gripe of the railings had disturbed them. I turned, walked quickly away from the view of the beach, and then went into a jog again. The bandstand was left behind, and there was the huge secondary loop of the bay where the amusement arcades, crazy golf, tennis courts and playing fields grouped themselves in the shadow of Becket's Hill. And in the darkest arm of the hill was the lake: an artificial lake, the sharp angle between the bay at Becket's Hill cut off by concrete and fed every high tide by the sea.

I hadn't meant to go so far; the run back up the zigzag of roads and lanes to the Tump would take three times as long to climb as it had to descend. The lake was a mile away, maybe more.

But for some reason, I wanted to see it. The moon could not reach it; it was dark and full of secrets. I rammed on my hat again, not breaking the rhythm of the jog; I started a pattern of breathing. The promenade narrowed to a path, all on the level. I pumped my arms. There was no space anywhere for a single thought. On my right the railings flicked by, and on my left the occasional overflowing litter bin would be lit by a surround of broken bottles glinting in the moonlight. The sea was sibilant, tide well out. The bulk of Becket's loomed closer; the hill itself was clothed in trees almost all the way to its summit. The top rose bald and unadorned. Becket's assassins were supposed to have stood there and looked out to sea at the islands and possible refuge.

Darkness closed in, the railings became a wall, the path divided and went into the woods on my left and led to steps on my right, and I stopped, almost collapsing on to the wall, panting, closing my eyes while I concentrated on breathing.

When I opened them the blackness had graded itself into black and very black. I stayed where I was, leaning on the wall at the head of the steps, staring down at the water. Here and there a ripple would pick up a reflection of the moon, and when my eyes became accustomed to the darkness I could just make out the concrete blocks that had been the foundations of the old diving boards, and the broken bases of the changing huts. The expanse of water had been divided by "causeways" of rocks: a shallow paddling pool, a boating lake, a deep water area for swimmers. We'd always set up our deckchairs behind the diving area, where the sun was trapped after midday. We'd wallowed in its warmth whenever we could, then swum for half an hour or more before towelling off and collapsing into the chairs again. And then the picnic stuff had come out.

I was so exhausted that the memories ached instead of screamed. In any case it was hard to fit them into this black hole beneath me. Retrospectively, it seemed to have been filled, always, with sunlight. The row of changing huts had been rainbow-painted; Mrs Bartholomew, who was in charge of everything, had run a very tight ship indeed. No running or jumping or changing on the promenade, and certainly no pushing or shoving or throwing clothes about. Her voice was not exactly stentorian, but everyone could hear it, and nobody ever disobeyed Mrs B. She was a champion swimmer, and a top-rate first-aider. When she was there, all was absolutely well. But she wasn't there any more, and neither was anything she had so carefully looked after.

I took a deep breath and went towards the steps. I had let myself remember without becoming frantic; up to a point I was in control — as Mrs B had been in control. Why hadn't I run here before now? Because it was derelict and unwanted? Yet that was the kind of place I could relate to. Even so, I had to steel myself . . . dare myself to go down those steps and walk that wide promenade alongside the paddling pool. I was on the top step; I dared myself again and the voice inside me was high and hysterical as usual, but with another note. Challenging? I moved down two steps.

The little promenade, as it had been called, was so full of blackness that it became another dimension. I touched my toe from the last step on to the slimy flagstones, as I had touched bottom when I'd jumped off the edge of the deep end. Then, I had bent my knees automatically and straightened them immediately — a reflex action, a living being making for the light. Now, I could not do that. I gripped the handrail hard and put both feet down solidly, and stood there looking into and at the blackness, smelling it, tasting it, cold and somehow heavy.

After what seemed a long time, I moved away from the handrail towards a glimmer of light, which was the moon reflecting on the rock pools beyond the lake wall. That had been the deep end, where the diving tower had stretched its single arm over the steps. Neither tower nor steps were there any more, but the blackness was just a little less black here, and I could see things moving in the water, and gradually identified them as beer cans, plastic bags and what looked like orange peel — all tangled into a mat with seaweed. I looked back to the steps leading to the top path. They had disappeared into the blackness, too. I had scuffed and foot-felt my way right around the paddling pool and up to the sheer

22

wall that dammed in the sea water at every high tide. There was nowhere else to go unless I wanted to walk along the top of the wall to the boating pool and then the sand pit, and I could hear Mrs Bartholomew's voice saying sternly, "Anyone who walks along there risks their lives and the lives of others. Therefore anyone making such an attempt will be banned from the lake for the rest of the summer." Not that I would have tried it, anyway; I have a fear of heights.

So I had to go back the way I had come, shuffling through dried seaweed and other unidentifiable rubbish through the dense blackness to the steps. Then I supposed I had to go home. I did not want to do that.

What happened next is difficult to explain. I was standing above the wrack of litter, looking down, seeing now with accustomed vision the inevitable movement of all that trapped fluid, and I felt the faintest of pressures in the small of my back. Just sufficiently strong to let me know that I had jogged twice as far as usual, yet insistent enough that I took a small step back from the edge. And then it became stronger. I resisted it but was forced to take half a step forward again. And then quite suddenly it was a small shove.

I am pretty certain I could have withstood it, turned to my right and walked back into the darkness. But I didn't. I let it push me into the water, and so that I could avoid the tangled mess of rubbish edging towards the wall, I gave it impetus and leapt forward and over the wrack and smashed the calmness of the lake with a knees-up bomb. That's what the children called this kind of entry. A bomb.

There was no time to think. I didn't reach the bottom; for a short while my jogging stuff and pyjamas held enough air to send me to the surface like a cork, and I struck out wildly before they could absorb enough water to become a dead weight. And for some reason I did not immediately turn and swim through the wrack to the edge — maybe four strokes — I made for the other side where the wall dividing the deep end from the boating lake showed a clear silvery line of moonshine. A long swim for me at the best of times. This was certainly not one of those.

Half-way there I had to tread water while I kicked off trainers and struggled out of jogging bottoms and then top. I was exhausted. I lay on my back and did my thing with breathing again. Also I looked back into the blackness of the hill. Someone had pushed me in. Was that why I had not turned and gone back? I couldn't see a thing, of course. But there had been that pressure; and surely — surely — the pressure had ended up in a definite push?

I rolled on to my front and began the very gentle sort of breaststroke that would eventually get me to that wall. I talked to myself. No panic. You're fine. Just do it slowly, then you haul yourself up and bump or crawl along to the shallows of the paddling pool and wade out. All right, so you have to go back into the blackness and find the steps up to the top, but if someone actually did this thing, they'd hardly wait around. They'd be clambering through the woods of Becket's Hill right now. You just have to jog home — bare-footed and pyjama'd — and get under a very hot shower. And forget all about it. The chap you disturbed in the boat on the slipway . . . it could have been him getting his own back. He's got no idea where you live. At least it stops you thinking about the past. This . . . here and now . . . has to be dealt with. And there is absolutely no need to panic.

But I couldn't help it. Now and then I felt myself trying to scramble through the water, convinced I had made no headway whatsoever. And then I'd take in a mouthful of the black water, and though it was salt it was not quite the salt of the sea. The lake had been derelict for so long, it was full of rubbish. I cleared my throat and spat vigorously and then had to do the breathing again.

Eventually I reached the wall. I was almost exhausted. I managed to push myself up and out of the water high enough to get the fingers of one hand on the top of the wall; it was incredibly rough but for a few minutes it provided a respite. Then I had to let go and my pyjamas tore against the armour of dead shells and flints below water level. I felt myself weeping with terror and frustration. I tried — three or four times — to get a better handhold on the wall. When at last I did I could not hold my body weight for long enough to begin to move myself along the wall by hand. I tried to use my feet to scramble up the ragged surface but soon fell back helplessly. I floated again, calming myself somehow, pushing gently with one hand towards the paddling pool. The panic now was about my own strength. It was ebbing fast.

My hand, gingerly trailing the roughness of the wall beneath the water, felt the protuberance and curled around it cautiously, waiting for more sharp edges to lacerate the skin. But it was smooth. My hand gripped hard. The protuberance was perfectly round. The shape and size of a door knob. It was a door knob. Set in that ghastly wall about two feet below the level of the water surface was a door knob. And I gripped it very hard. That was what door knobs were for. Gripping. My hand gripped it and my floating body came to a halt and swung itself into a vertical position held completely steady by the hand and the door knob.

It was such a relief to be free of that wall and yet supported by it. I just hung on for a while, not even asking myself what I could do with this tiny respite. There was a sense of peace suddenly. No more struggle. I let my legs swing out behind me, my head only just clear of water. It was perhaps two feet beneath the surface. If my hand had not swept downwards at just that point, I would not have found it. I closed my eyes, smiling. I knew I was going to be all right.

However, it was not easy. I had to get a foot on that smooth, small protuberance. Then I had to stand up using the wall to keep upright. The pain of my own skin tearing with the ragged remnants of pyjama top was awful. What was worse was the possibility of the door knob suddenly pulling out of the wall. It felt rock solid, but it could have been rusted through or simply shoved in by some joker during the past eighty-odd years since the lake had first been excavated, and now, with my weight on it, shove itself out just as easily. But as I heaved myself on to the top of the wall and saw the moon still shining brightly on the amusement arcades and the crazy golf . . . it was still there. I collapsed on to my side, and when I began to shiver in the early morning air, I knew I was still alive, and I actually stood up on the wall, and with Mrs Bartholomew cheering me on, I walked to the paddling pool and then waded through the mud to the base of the steps and climbed them.

It was almost light when I got home, but I had seen no one and I prayed that no one had seen me. My feet bled on to the doormat. I showered and rubbed cream into them, and dealt with my hands too, then fell into bed and slept properly for the first time since it had happened. Almost a year ago.

When I woke I was different. I thought — for almost a year I had thought — that I wanted to die. Yet, when I was offered death in the early hours of that day, I had chosen to live.

CHAPTER
TWO

Investigations into the accident, if accident it was, got nowhere. Before he died David Venables senior mumbled something about Viv being very depressed at the time, and a small rumour started . . . but was quickly squashed. Though they were a very private couple, it was well known that they were idyllically happy. The few people who had seen some of David's skyscapes dismissed the couple as arty-farty types; others thought of them sentimentally as "the folks who lived on the hill". But only the few who had watched too many documentaries about conspiracies entertained the thought of a suicide pact. And when the local computer expert was called to the hospital to retrieve some "lost" files, and was able to confide to his wife that Vivian Venables had been just about pregnant at the time of the accident, she put two and two together and decided that they had been keeping an appointment at the gynaecology department. Any thought of suicide was discarded. Almost. It reared its head when old David Venables collapsed and died in December. There was talk of him not being able to face his daughter-in-law, blaming her for the death of his son. His friend, John Jinks, who was in the next room, revealed this when he told the matron of the home that poor old Venables had spoken of not being able to face "one more day in this hell-hole". Mr Jinks was well known for stirring things up at Tall Trees. And though officially old Mr Venables had had a coronary, everyone knew he had died of a broken heart.

Before Viv was fully conscious, she repeated the word "steering" several times, and the investigators tried hard to find something that would point to a sudden failure of the mechanism. It was impossible. The car had plunged down the side of the combe, ricocheting from tree to tree, rolling at one point, righting itself on a shelf of the cliff and then hurtling on and into an ancient beech that shed the last of its leaves like confetti over the steaming crumpled mass of metal. It was a miracle that four weeks later, Viv Venables came out of hospital and, at her own insistence, returned to the single-storeyed house buried in laurels and conifers. She had successfully suppressed all memory of the accident; though as she rarely spoke to anyone, gradually discouraged all callers, and never replied to letters or phone calls, it was impossible to know what she remembered and what she did not. In the following months, while the sun shone relentlessly and drought warnings became a part of daily life, people accepted that she was dealing with the tragedy in her own way. In spite of the drought, the foliage grew around the bungalow until it was like a beleaguered castle in a fairy tale, but Viv was certainly no sleeping beauty. She had never been overweight, but when people saw her jogging very early in the morning, they reported seeing "a bag of bones".

"She doesn't seem to have a relative in the whole world. It would have been better if the old man had hung on till she was conscious," someone said in the Becket's Head after one of these rare sightings.

"He still thought she were going to die. It was touch and go," someone else put in. "Anyway, it's against nature to outlive a child — that's a well-known fact."

"But he loved her like a daughter," someone else put in. "He might've guessed she would need him."

"He had no choice in the matter, I reckon. He was knocking on, for Pete's sake!"

"Bit funny somewhere, though. *I* reckon a lot been hushed up there," said the first voice lugubriously.

It had been hushed up so successfully that Viv never even asked about her father-in-law. Someone must have told her that he was dead, but she never called at the nursing home to collect his things. She had no idea where his remains were. They told her that David's ashes were in a crematorium in Bristol, where he had lived as a young man. His father must have arranged that. She told herself she was not interested.

It was that evening that she had started to run. Everyone called it jogging but they knew she simply ran as fast as she possibly could. Someone called her the Gingerbread Woman. Nobody could catch her.

Vivian's story

It was almost three o'clock by the alarm on the cluttered chest of drawers. I had slept more than eight hours and a grey light filled the bedroom. It was raining, a soothing window-wash, therapeutic. That fierce, uncaring sunshine had gone at last. I lay very still and listened to the rain dripping from the overhanging eaves outside, and registered that the guttering wasn't taking it and I had better get someone in to clear out the accumulated rubbish of the past year. Then I remembered the ladders, which must still be in the garage. I could clear out the blasted gutters myself.

But first, the chest of drawers where the tube of antiseptic cream I had used on my cuts and grazes was unstoppered and leaking everywhere. One of our many radios was behind the clock, unused, probably containing batteries leaking like the tube of cream. There was a clutter of photographs, mostly lying on their faces, but one of my mother smiled at me encouragingly. How she would have hated the mess in here! She had died when I was ten years old, but by then I had known her almost as well as she knew me. She was a natural home-maker.

I rolled out of bed, clutched a dressing gown around myself and made for the bathroom, where the tattered remains of my pyjamas still lay on the floor; they were horribly blood-stained. I smiled. Amazingly, the terror of last night had gone. As I had plodded on bleeding feet back up the zigzag of bends to the top of the Tump, I had been forced to face the fact that I had been given a choice. I could have let myself die; it would not have been suicide in the true sense of the word. An opportunity had offered itself quite outside my own volition: a small shove into oblivion. The alternative . . . a door knob. I knew my smile was rueful, to put it mildly; my early morning jogs so often took me along the unfenced coastal paths, where a step to one side would probably be the last one in this life. And I had not taken it yet. And I had not taken it last night when it had been quite literally thrust upon me.

I splashed water on to my face, gathered up the rags on the floor, and made for the kitchen and tea. While the kettle boiled I sat at the table and made a list which started: clean house, clear gutters, mow grass. Then I poured boiling water on to proper tea leaves in a proper teapot and inhaled the steam. And the front doorbell rang its infuriating ping-pong. I smiled again.

It was Mrs Hardy. Hardy by name, hardy by nature. Everyone else had got the message that I wanted to be left alone. Not Mrs Hardy. She was red-faced from the hill, and held up a hand before I could say my usual piece — that it was nice of her to call but I would prefer to be on my own.

"No trouble. On my way to work. Evening shift." That was what she always said, too; she worked at Tall Trees, set in its own grounds where the road to the Tump degenerated into a track. My father-in-law had died there and had always said if Mrs Hardy hadn't been married already he'd have made an honest woman of her.

She rummaged in her bag. "Brought you a few apples. Maybe p'raps you could pick some blackberries on one of your rambles. Makes a lovely mixture, blackberry and apple." She found the apples and hauled them out, waiting for me to say thank you but no thank you.

I wanted to cry. I said, "That's so kind, Mrs Hardy —"

She looked up, alarmed and then shocked. "My dear Lord! The state of you! You had a fall, didn't you? Them blessed jogs you takes, and so early every morning, too. I says to Hardy, I says, that girl could lie there for hours before anyone found her."

I shook my head, almost laughing, but crying, too. "Have you got time for a cup of tea? I've just made a pot."

She was seriously worried now, and saw it as an emergency, so, though she did not have time, she made it and followed me into the kitchen. Her eyes flicked around, then settled on the tray with the teapot and milk jug — as civilized as it possibly could be.

I poured and we drank together. Conversation consisted of exclamations from her and reassurances from me. She ended up on her knees with a roll of kitchen paper and the vinegar bottle, dabbing at my feet.

"Vinegar or salt water, Mrs Venables. I always says, vinegar or salt water." She glanced at the drying rack and reached up for socks. "Salt water this morning —" She tried for a grin. "Now vinegar. So you've had both. Can't go wrong, can you?" She eased the socks over my sore feet. They were stinging like mad, but I knew they would be all right; nothing to do with vinegar and salt water, everything to do with Mrs Hardy.

I said suddenly, "Do you remember Mrs Bartholomew, who used to be in charge of the lake?"

Mrs Hardy laughed. "There isn't nobody within a ten-mile radius of this place who don't know Mrs Bartholomew. Right tartar. But good and fair."

I almost asked her about the door knob but that would have meant confessing to my . . . my what? My adventure. And she was late for work, too.

She wanted to take my shopping list, but I shook my head. I had repudiated all offers of help for selfish reasons. Now, there were other reasons. I didn't know what they were, but they were imperative. Just as I had taken the car across country to the all-night garage in the early hours for milk and bread, eggs and cheese, so I would continue to do so. Different reasons. I would work that out later.

She hovered anxiously by the front door.

"If all your rambles gives you comfort, well, you got to do them. But be careful. Remember the winter is coming on. Not good for you to get wet and cold. Night after night."

I walked with her to the front gate. I had let the conifers grow wild — Mr Hardy had been volunteered to keep the garden down and I had simply shaken my head. The small bungalow was almost buried in foliage, a stranger would not know it was there; I certainly could not see who was passing. That might have given me a fleeting satisfaction yesterday; today I lingered by the gate watching Mrs Hardy climb on her bicycle and then turn right and disappear among the rhododendrons. Perhaps it would be good to ask Mr Hardy to take down the conifers to hedge level.

I returned indoors and cleared the tea things, made my bed, saw to the chest of drawers, then went into the cobwebbed garage and hauled out the ladder. It was five o'clock, two or three more hours of daylight.

At eight o'clock I wheeled the trolley into the living room. It held a plate of scrambled eggs, another pot of tea, and a small dish holding one of Mrs Hardy's apples, baked and oozing sultanas, collapsing within its own skin. Rather like me, I thought, grinning with the basic satisfaction of having actually accomplished something. I wanted to eat; I wanted to see what the weather forecast was for tomorrow. If it prophesied rain it would give my satisfaction an edge of smugness, because the guttering around my little bungalow was clear of mud and weeds and would do its job however much rain arrived. I could not remember feeling like this.

The forecast was good. That was OK because I could mow the grass. I went on watching, marvelling that the television was still working perfectly after almost a year of hibernation. Of course I had heard — somehow — some of the things happening around the world. The floods earlier in the summer had made a teaching colleague homeless and she had written to tell me about it. There had been a plane crash somewhere; it had been headlined on one of the piles of newspapers in the garage on the Bristol road. A building society had closed its doors, and people had massed outside, shouting, some of them weeping. Somewhere in my head I had registered these things and then rejected them with everything else. I had told myself that the one lesson to be learned was that nothing really mattered. Someone — somebody who meant well — had said to me almost a year ago that I should get through just one day at a time. One minute had been too much of such pseudo-wisdom and I had turned away yet again.

Now I watched a young mother being interviewed about the possible abduction of her baby. She wept. I wept. I wept for *her*. I was actually weeping for somebody else. I thought of Mrs Hardy and her kindness, and I wept again. I went out in the darkness and stared at the roof . . . at the gutters . . . my gutters . . . and believe it or not, I wept.

That night I slept for twelve hours. The next day I walked to the top of the Tump, where brambles crouched around the wall of the nursing home. I picked blackberries and stewed them with the rest of the apples, and when Mrs Hardy called I handed her a plastic box of the mixture. For a moment I thought she was going to weep. I asked her whether Mr Hardy still had his chainsaw, and if so, would he be able to take the hedge down to shoulder height?

She nodded solemnly. "Course he would, Mrs Venables. And only too glad to do it. It's a sign, you know."

"A sign?"

"A sign you're looking out." She smiled at the obviousness of her remark, and added, "Letting the outside world back in."

I smiled, too. I had known exactly what she meant, but it did not help when the six o'clock news showed that the young girl who had wept to the world yesterday had been arrested today for murdering her own baby. I sat in front of the flickering television and put my hand to my throat. It was a terrible world; did I really want to "let it back in"?

The next morning, just before dawn, I jogged slowly down the three levels of sandy roads to the beach and then, as light silhouetted the pier, I turned and ran fast along the path to the lake.

It took about fifteen minutes, during which time the edge of the sun sent a weak path of light along the sea towards Becket's Hill. The forecast had been right: it looked as if it was going to be a lovely day. Even so, that light, which should have continued into the lake's corner, seemed to bend and wander into the sea towards Devon and Cornwall. The lake was still black and impenetrable.

I stood for a long time at the head of the steps leading down to the little promenade, getting my breath, staring down until my eyes could distinguish the concrete blocks, the old pump house. Gradually, black became grey and there were the dissecting walls between paddling pool, swimming pool, boating lake. And crouched on the cruel, flinty wall that had lacerated my feet and hands not very many hours ago, was a figure. Man or woman I couldn't tell, human most certainly. The hump of a hooded sweatshirt was there, the sharp crook of knees as he or she hunkered just out of reach of the water. I stayed very still.

For what seemed like a long time, the two of us did not move. I had no idea whether he — or she — knew of my presence. My approach could not have been heard; I was wearing old tennis shoes, and though the tide was now coming in fast, the waves weren't exactly crashing on the rocks, but even so the ebb and flow of constantly moving water would have covered my gentle jog. I did not think my silhouette would be visible against the woods of Becket's Hill either. But I did not trust my luck; I could see the figure down there and he could probably see me. I knew by then he was male. As the light filtered around the lake, I could see that the arms supporting the long lean body were too muscular for a woman. The sleeves of his tracksuit fell over his hands, and the hood hid his face, but he was male. My memory remembered one of those invisible hands in the small of my back.

Very slowly indeed I bent my knees and began to drop out of sight behind the wall. Once there I moved back to where the path forked to the left and disappeared into the trees of Becket's Hill. I straightened and jogged into their sanctuary. The path was carpeted with leaves and pine needles and was pleasantly springy. It swept around the back of the lake and emerged from the trees facing west; a perfect view of the islands. I stopped for breath again and looked over my shoulder. The lake was below and behind me; I couldn't see it for trees. I moved to the edge of the path, sat down and slid carefully from tree to tree until there was space for me to look down on the water. It was like the old days, the whole corner was bathed in sunshine. Mrs Bartholomew had called it a "regular sun trap".

There was no one in sight. Not on the causeways, nor the little promenade, nor the steps up to the path. I stared until my eyes ached. If he'd left immediately I plunged into the trees, he would still be visible going back to the amusement arcades and then the bandstand. Unless, of course, he had followed me up into Becket's Hill.

I took a breath and held it so that I could hear above the sound of the water. Nothing. I let it go slowly. But I did not begin to move myself up on to the path again. My feet were braced against a tree beneath, one of my hands clutched the branch of another tree level with my face, the other hand was flat on the leaf mould. It was through that hand that I felt a footfall. I dropped my head sideways on to the ground, vividly recalling the old cowboy films when the Indians had put their ears to the railway lines to listen for oncoming trains. Muffled yet clear enough to identify, the pad of someone walking the path above me came through the earth and rock of Becket's Hill. I glanced upwards; I was well hidden. I stayed still, breathing with the top of my lungs. The sounds were louder and then passed over my head. Where the path turned to the west and levelled off, they became closer together. He was jogging now.

He was trying to catch up with me.

I glanced at my watch: almost eight o'clock. The village would be stirring now, day staff for the nursing home passing my gate to relieve Mrs Hardy, perhaps. Here, a mile from the village clock, the amusements and ice cream kiosks were closed until mid-morning. Becket's Hill cut us off from the farming communities along the water meadows. And once my follower rounded the next part of the hill, he had a clear view of the footpath as it led down to the tiny disused harbour. He would know that I had taken to the trees. He would probably give up. But he might not.

Very carefully and slowly I began to slide downwards again. From tree to tree, negotiating the rocky outcrops nearly all the time, I lowered myself to where the trees ended in a wall of brambles, and then there was a sheer drop back down to the little promenade and the lake.

I put my ear to the ground again and heard nothing. But with my face against the ground I could see two or three distinct holes in the low-lying brambles. They were big; too big for rats surely? Perhaps a fox — or a badger? I kept my eyes on them and saw no sign of life, and decided they had been made by children in the school holidays. And then I heard those footfalls returning and told myself those tunnels were most definitely made by children. By which time I was already sliding into the biggest one.

How long I crouched there I have no idea. I kept my ear to the ground but heard nothing at all, no sounds of sliding as the man saw my tracks and followed me down the almost vertical face of the hill. He could have jogged on for all I knew, or climbed upwards through the trees to the bald summit. And then, when I was on the point of pushing myself out of my burrow, the padding sounds resumed, slowly at first, then accelerating into a comfortable jog. I was frozen again; this man had been waiting in complete silence for sounds of movements. He must have suspected my presence in some way; perhaps he was a kind of tracker, like those old-time Indian trackers in the films. And I had been on the point of shuffling out of my hole and giving myself away. In a kind of nervous reaction I pushed myself deeper still, and then my feet came up against the retaining wall and I could see light where the schoolchildren — if it had been them — had made a kind of lookout over the lake and the tennis courts behind, sweeping right round to the bandstand and the pier. Somehow I got on to my knees, and ignoring the brambles clawing at hair and clothes, put my arms and chin on the top of the wall and took all this in. It was the perfect watch-tower. I saw my pursuer emerge from the trees on to the path above the little promenade. He had the hood of his sweatshirt well over his head, and he appeared to have pulled the sleeves over his hands. I watched, fascinated, as he pumped along the level path. He was the perfect jogger, his rhythm and movements perfectly coordinated. He began on the long straight length taking him beyond the tennis courts to the crazy golf and then the amusements, leaving the lake to itself. And then he stopped. He seemed to listen for a while; he was too far away for me to see him in detail, he seemed to be concentrating on something. And then, slowly, he turned towards the lake and kept turning until he was facing me. He could not possibly have seen me framed in brambles at least a quarter of mile away. But after a while his arm went up above his head in a kind of salute. And he turned and disappeared.

I should not have told Mrs Hardy. She had been on a day shift and was on her way home, so had more time to spare. She wanted to tell me that Mr Hardy had really enjoyed the blackberry and apple for his last night's supper. She had made him eat three slices of bread and butter with it to make it last. He would pop up on Saturday afternoon and see to the hedge, and he had a spare door-chain from another job which he would fit on my front door if I agreed.

I thought about it and nodded, and Mrs Hardy looked surprised again.

"You had any trouble with callers?" she asked, trying to sound casual.

I shook my head, but then found myself telling her about the man down by the lake.

"I got it into my head he was following me." I sounded apologetic. "Of course, no such thing. Must have made me a bit nervy. But . . . well, I wouldn't mind the added security. And if the chain really is going spare . . ."

"Course it is. D'you think he might have followed you home?"

"Not for a moment, no. Just made me more . . . aware. The house is a bit cut off. You know."

"Remember the staff up at Tall Trees. When the weather's decent there's always someone wheeling one of the residents down to look at the view and get some fresh air."

"I know. Perhaps I'm being silly. Mr Hardy's got enough on his plate —"

"You ain't being silly, and Hardy will be only too pleased to think he can do something for you. He always says, 'How's that girl doing up there?', and when you sent him down that fruit he was that delighted. And will be even more when he can do the hedge and the door." She looked at me, still frowning. "What about reporting this to the police?" I shook my head violently and she sighed. "I knew you wouldn't a'course. But it dun't sound quite right. And now you're doing so well, Mrs Venables, we don't want you going backwards, like."

It was very good that I was touched and not irritated by her concern. But I wished I hadn't mentioned the man. Policemen always needed descriptions, and I had not even seen a face beneath that hood, nor hands below those sleeves.

But I had heard the footfalls; I had definitely heard the footfalls. So it could not have been . . . a ghost.

CHAPTER
THREE

The Hardys had lived in the small seaside town all their lives, and were completely content to continue doing so until those lives were done. Michael Hardy, known by his old school friends as Mick, had done a long carpentry apprenticeship with his uncle, and had inherited his reputation and customers when he had retired. Mrs Hardy said he would do twice as well if he could develop a bedside manner, but she accepted that this was a biological impossibility for her Hardy. He would occasionally burst into a conversation, but kept to monosyllabic grunts and comments if he could. "Nice day" disposed of the weather. "Decent timber" or "rotten wood" dealt with the materials of his trade. When Mrs Hardy told Vivian Venables that she and her husband had talked things over, it meant that she had talked and he had nodded or grunted assent. He was honest, painstaking, turned his hand to anything, and was an excellent carpenter. That was what counted to her and to his many friends, customers and acquaintances.

She was the same, though not trained to be anything except full of common sense. She had taken a job at Tall Trees when their son was found to be unusually clever and they saw that in the future he would need help to go to university. She turned out to be a born carer. Half-jokingly, half-not, most of the male residents had asked her to marry them the minute Hardy threw her out. She always laughed, not so much at the marriage proposals as at the thought of Hardy throwing her out. Old David Venables had suggested that she should do the throwing out and then marry him. She had laughed again, then said, "Hardy and me . . . we're like peas in a pod. Couldn't do nothing without him." She nodded. "Like your boy and his wife, I reckon."

He had said nothing. She was used to male silences, but she noticed this one and registered it. When he and his son died within a few weeks of each other, she was unexpectedly angry. She talked to Hardy about it.

"Silly old fool! Coronary, my foot! Let himself go, that's what he did. He could surely have hung on till she came out of hospital. She's got no one now, no one at all."

Hardy grunted, and she smiled and put a hand on his shoulder as she poured tea. "What should I do without you, love? You always understand."

He cleared his throat and said, "You. She's got you."

"She wouldn't have let me get near her, Hardy love. It was only because she had a bit of an accident, like. Scraped her feet and legs something awful. Did her good in one way, though. I persuaded her to let you do something about them conifers in the front. And perhaps fit that old chain on her front door. That all right with you, love?"

45

He grunted. Then suddenly he took the teapot from her, put it on the stand depicting Brunel's suspension bridge over the Avon, and pulled her on to his knee. "It will stop you worrying about our Tom and Della, won't it?" he said.

She held his head to her wrap-over pinafore and whispered, "I hope so, my love."

They stayed very still, and shared the usual thoughts about their son. He was an only child, and they would have loved him however he had turned out. The fact that he was clever and hard-working amazed them, but made little difference to their feelings. He "made his own way", and eventually combined his father's practicality with his mother's instincts for caring and became a doctor. He joined a big practice in Cheltenham, and within two years had met and married Della.

As Mrs Hardy had said so often, Tom had married Della for the wrong reason: because she needed him so desperately. She had been no more than a skivvy for her parents, and Tom had rescued her from that and given her status and self-respect. And he would have stayed with her for the rest of his life had he not met and fallen in love — "prop'ly this time" — with the practice nurse at his local health centre in Cheltenham.

He tried to talk to Della. But it was a situation beyond words because he knew exactly what he was doing to her. Even so, he was aghast when she overdosed on her sleeping pills and ended up in hospital. And it was there that she was told she was pregnant, and lucky enough not to have lost her baby.

46

So Tom went back to her and was "doing his best".

Hilda Hardy sighed deeply. "I'd feel easier if I could hate Della. Or be angry with Tom. Or blame that woman — Elisabeth."

"Elisabeth Mason," Hardy murmured, which showed he had followed her thoughts as usual.

"But it's not no one's fault really. It just happened. Poor Della can't help being hopeless. And Tom can't help feeling really sorry for her. And . . . I s'ppose he can't help falling in love again."

"It's the first time, my maid. He weren't in love with Della. But he's stuck with her now. So he'll have to fall out of love with Elisabeth Mason double-quick!" He leaned back, exhausted by so many words.

She stared for a while longer, then sighed again and kissed his forehead. "I think you're right, Hardy," she said.

It cheered her up to go to work. There was always plenty to do, and the residents were appreciative, and the home was a little world on its own, sealed off from big worries of the big world.

When she cleared the supper tables, there was some kind of discussion going on around John Jinks's chair. It was not his usual chair, which had arms on which he levered himself up and into his wheelchair. She assumed he was complaining about this. She had told him only the week before that he would get a gold medal for complaining if the Olympics would allow it as a sport. She sailed across the dining room with her trolley, relishing the thought of crossing swords again.

He was that sort of man; as she said to Hardy that night, he brought out the worst in everyone.

But this time it was nothing to do with the seating arrangements. She pointed out to him that a chair with arms was vacant right next to him.

He looked at her sourly. "So it is. I'm not blind, thank you. I can't get myself close enough to the table — the arms block me. Thought I'd try this chair for a change. Won't be bothering again. If I drop food someone must clear it up. That's why I'm paying such an exorbitant fee to the owners of HH!"

"HH?" she queried unwisely.

"Hell Hole," he answered back, smiling happily. "I understand they called the place Tall Trees, which of course would be TT. Teetotal. That's true, as well. So the whole thing would be the TTHH. Teetotal Hell Hole. Suits it well, don't you think?"

She almost grinned back at him, but said quickly, "If the armless chair is your choice, what's all the fuss about?"

"I'm trying to put these old fools straight on one or two things. It's like collecting water in a colander, of course."

"Of course." She winked at Esmé and Winifred. "We're well known for improvising, Mr Jinks. Aren't we, ladies? I expect if there was nothing else around we would be quite capable of collecting water in a colander."

It was too petty for words, but at least they were speaking to each other.

Esmé's face was very pink. "He says that Mrs Venables is running away from her own guilt. How can that be, Mrs Hardy? What a terrible thing to say about someone who cannot defend herself because she has simply forgotten the whole tragedy!"

Winifred added severely, "I always thought women were supposed to be the catty ones — until I met Mr Jinks here."

"As if you could simply *forget* something like that!" Mr Jinks ignored Winifred's sideswipe. "You *want* to forget it. Of course you do. But you can't. So what do you do about that? You run."

Mrs Hardy stopped feeling part of a valuable social confrontation and wished she could give Mr Jinks a sharp clip on the ear. At last, after almost a year, she had been allowed into the little house and had helped poor Mrs Venables. Mrs Hardy knew a lot about grief.

She bent down to look at the old man crouched over the supper table, bald as a coot, miserable as sin, trying to stir up a row as an antidote to boredom, and her indignation fell away; an enormous sadness engulfed her. She said, "If we had a leg and an arm missing, if we was suddenly only half a human being . . ." She looked into the colourless eyes so full of bitterness. ". . . maybe we'd think it was impossible to run ever again. Mrs Venables puts us right, don't she, Mr Jinks?"

She stared him down, and at last he said bitterly, "I know things about that woman that would turn your hair from grey to white!"

And at last she burst out laughing. "I reckon you are right, Winifred! Men certainly can teach us a trick or two when it comes to being catty!" She swept the linen napkins on to the trolley and picked up the water jug. "Now, I think *Coronation Street* is starting. Why don't you wheel Jinx here into the lounge and help yourselves to coffee?" She made it obvious she was using John Jinks's nickname, which nobody ever did — at least to his face — and his scraggy eyebrows climbed at least half an inch up his forehead, but then two of the nurses arrived and hoisted him into his chair, and the ladies followed willy-nilly. Winifred actually winked behind his back. Mrs Hardy smiled. She hated it when they sat in the lounge or around the dining-room tables and stared glumly into space.

Vivian's story

A week went by and it was October. I made tea for Mr Hardy, mowed the grass and did some weeding. He took the mower to service it, tamed the front conifers into a hedge, fitted a chain and some bolts on to the front door. Word got around, and the phone rang a lot, and people came to the door. I worked in the garden and told myself that if it was urgent they would come to the side gate and call down to me. I never answered the phone, anyway. I intended to have it taken out, but like a fool mentioned this to Mrs Hardy, who almost threw up her hands.

"Dun't do that, my girl! What if you fell and broke a leg? Or someone broke in — not that that is possible now, of course, what with Hardy putting the bolts on as well as the chain. But you never know when you might need to ring someone. I could be up here with you in five minutes. Hardy would get out the van." Mr Hardy used his van to carry his larger tools; people rarely got into it. Mrs Hardy's assurance was meant as a sign of his regard for me.

The phone seemed to present another choice: if I was injured should I get the phone off the hook somehow, and dial for help? Or simply lie in the hall and wait? It was all so hypothetical: I wasn't going to fall and break my leg anyway. So in the end I did nothing about the phone — except ignore it. It rang less and less. By the end of October it was silent again, and the doorbell ping-ponged just once a day when Mrs Hardy came or went from Tall Trees nursing home.

The clocks went back, and evenings began at tea-time, but mornings were earlier, and my jogs took me further than the bandstand and home. I took the path past the amusement arcade one Sunday morning. It was six thirty and almost light, and in an hour's time I could return home to the sound of the church bells. I still liked church bells. But I hadn't come this way since September.

The little promenade was not deserted: two men and two girls, wet-suited and helmeted, were launching canoes. Their laughter echoed around the lake, and I stood watching them, and hearing other laughter from another time, and for a moment or two I smiled reminiscently. One of the girls threw back her head at something that was said and saw me. She went on laughing, and waved. I waved back, but then I had to move on; to stand there staring at them wouldn't have been right. So I went along the left-hand footpath, through the woods, and into the empty west face of the hill. I wasn't keen. I simply did it without thinking, and didn't even glance to my right where I had slithered down the steep slope to the bramble burrow. Back then it had been an ordinary working day, not a Sunday. No canoeists or dog walkers. The path began to slope down towards the little harbour — or the Pill as it was called. The tide was out, and the enormous flat pancake of mud gleamed slightly. Boats were on their sides; nearer the land where the shingle started, one was propped either side so that it was upright. It was being painted by two men in overalls and Wellingtons. My spirits lifted. I lengthened my strides. The sun was out, and the forecast had been good. The men had six hours for their paint to dry, then the tide would lift their boat up and off the props. They worked steadily.

I passed the small boat store where the local yachts were stored, their long masts sticking out from the wall, making the whole thing look like a gigantic pincushion. A breeze came from the south-west and halyards clanked. Someone had said once that man and sea made the perfect orchestra.

Someone.

I stopped in my tracks, shocked into stillness by that word. Someone. Was that what it had come to? I could not use his name? It was David. His name was David.

And as if at a signal, from the bald crown of Becket's Hill came a man, running, slipping, sliding down towards the path. His sweatshirt had a hood which was up, and too-long sleeves dangled over his hands. He must have had feet because I could hear them slithering on the dew-wet grass.

I was a long way ahead of him and on the flat, too, but I ran like the wind, past the cemetery and then away from the sea and into the village. And as I started up the hill the church bells rang out. They were reassurance. I stopped trying to run, and hung on to the wall at the first of the hairpin bends. There was no one in a hoodie behind me. A cyclist was making for one of the half-a-dozen churches; a woman emerged from one of the dozen pubs and threw a bucket of water along the pavement, and then tackled it with a broom. I started to walk slowly home.

November the fifth came and went. Mrs Hardy reported "fine shenanigans" on the summit of the Tump. "We all got up in the top storey of the home and had a grand view. Old Jinx said as how your dad would've loved it. Remember they was good pals?"

Of course I remembered. But I mustn't remember. Just as I mustn't remember Someone. When I remembered Someone it was as if I summoned him. I certainly did not want to summon my father-in-law . . . who was most definitely not my dad. I could remember my dad. He did not actually unbuckle his belt to teach me stuff, simply because he did not wear a belt. He wore braces and a tie, and reminded me often that he was a white-collar worker. But that did not stop him beating me with whatever was to hand.

I said, "How is Jinx?"

"Not so bad that he couldn't enjoy the fireworks and the bonfire." She paused, then added, "You could pop in and see him sometimes. P'raps."

"I don't think he'd want to see me."

Jinx, or Mr John Jinks to give him his proper name, possibly knew everything there was to know about David and me. He and my father-in-law had been good friends, especially after they both moved into Tall Trees. I was pretty certain that my father-in-law had told him . . . most things.

And it was obvious that Jinx had told Mrs Hardy he did not want to see me. She shook her head. "Silly old fool, he is. You could break through that if you was to try."

I said nothing. After a bit she stood up to go. She never stayed long, but she never missed a weekday. I hadn't noticed the days of the week before she started to come in; now weekends were barren days.

As if she could follow my train of thought she said, "The new Harry Potter's on at the cinema. Fancy us going on Saturday? They got a matinee so we could both be home before dark. And I'll be in good time for Hardy's tea. What d'you say?"

Saturday was the anniversary. Had she remembered?

"That would be nice."

"See you down there. Make it by two o'clock. There'll be a queue."

"Yes. OK." I felt a little thrill of excitement.

It was great. The queue was very long, but it was mainly composed of children, and I didn't know anyone at all. I was surrounded by noisy life that demanded nothing of me. I had taught part-time at a school twenty-five miles away; I never ran into any of my old pupils.

Mrs Hardy made a face. "Forgot how rowdy they are. Manners they certainly ain't got."

I laughed delightedly, and she raised her bushy brows. "I 'aven't seen you laugh for over a year." So she had remembered. I glanced at my watch; it would have been a year ten minutes ago, as we joined the queue. That was why she had chosen a matinee performance. Mr Hardy would not have missed his Saturday tea if we'd gone later. The matinee would bridge the actual time of the accident.

We settled in our seats; the noise was now excruciating, and there was a great deal of movement within our row as best friends demanded to be next to each other. Big cartons of popcorn were fitted into holders on the arms of the seats. We could not imagine how we would be able to hear the film. And then the lights went down and with them went the voices. It was as I remembered from childhood. The magic still worked; they were rapt.

So were we. I hadn't expected to feel entranced, I had thought that objectively I might enjoy the film for the unexpectedly traditional boarding-school atmosphere bound up with the fantasy element. There was no such analytical approach to this film; you either went with it helter-skelter, not knowing whether it was good, bad or indifferent; or you stayed outside. Mrs Hardy and I went with it willingly, in my case eagerly. Already I planned to go to the bookshop before it closed and buy a copy of this particular story. Something was happening the whole time, and you had to hang on to find out what it was.

When we emerged on to the shallow steps of the cinema I could not believe it was still just about daylight. I thanked Mrs Hardy profusely, and she blushed and blurted that she would have loved to ask me to tea, but Saturday night tea was Hardy's favourite, and they always had it by the fire with the football highlights on the television. I leaned forward suddenly and pecked her cheek — and then instantly regretted it, as she put her hand up as if I had slapped her. I said quickly, "I want to go to the bookshop anyway. Then I'll start reading while I have my tea by the fire, too." We walked back together as far as Smith's. I would have loved to have talked about the film, but she told me what she was cooking for tea and then asked me what I was having.

"I don't know . . ."

"Promise me you'll have a boiled egg. I do remember you saying to your dad once, that your favourite tea was boiled egg. Promise."

I promised. "He was my father-in-law, not my dad," I went on. "My dad would have given me what for if I'd wanted something cooked for Saturday tea."

I laughed as I said it, but she was silent.

When we parted outside the shop she said soberly, "You en't 'ad it easy, 'ave you, Mrs Venables?"

"I've had it very good a lot of the time. Like most people, I expect."

But I knew she did not agree with me. It seemed to me that she was happy all the time. Her contentment was built around a good fire and sausage and mash. Perhaps she had never known the sort of happiness I had had, and perhaps hers was the right sort; the only sort. I was determined to make my own contentment as good as hers. I grinned. "Looking forward to the boiled egg!" I called as she crossed the road and turned to wave. It was the best of beginnings.

I got the book and laboured up the vertical hill to the start of the hairpins. Then held on to the wall as usual to get breath for the next three stretches. Ahead of me a woman in the navy-blue uniform of Tall Trees nursing home was doing the same thing, and with better reason because she was pushing a wheelchair. I caught up with her. "Let me give you a hand," I offered. "These hills were not made for wheelchairs."

She had no breath to thank me, but nodded and smiled. We took a handle each and started to shove. Even with two pairs of hands and arms it was hard work. I panted something about the weather and she said, "Typical November." And that was it until we reached the Tump, where the road levelled off to the nursing home. Then she gasped a laugh and put a hand to her side.

"Really good of you. I don't think I could have managed that today. We went for a posh tea in the hotel, and I ate too much. You told me I was eating too much, didn't you, Jinx?"

I stared down at the back of a head, capped and swathed in scarves. I had not recognized him, and he had not recognized me. He said in that blunt, aggressive way he had, "Well. You were. Weren't you?"

No, he didn't realize it was me. I'd only said a few words. This was the opportunity Mrs Hardy had mooted: a chance to make friends with Old Jinx again.

I tried for a sympathetic chuckle; he'd never recognize a chuckle. I so rarely indulged in them.

He grunted, "Let's push on, nurse. It's cold on my chest."

I put my gloved hand over hers and smiled, and she said, "Good night, Mrs Venables. Good to see you out and about again."

I froze where I was, half-turned to go through the gate. Jinx twisted in his chair and tried to see me through the November murk. He said loudly, "A year ago today, wasn't it? Long enough to ease your conscience?"

I said nothing. The nurse said, "Stop sounding like a crabby old man, Jinx! We've had a lovely afternoon — don't spoil it!"

Then they were gone.

I was determined I wasn't going to let anything spoil my lovely afternoon, either. I boiled my egg, made up the fire and opened my new book. Then I switched on the television and watched some of the sporting highlights. Then I washed up, and had a shower, and got ready for bed, and tried the book again. Then I banked the fire, and put the guard round, and went to bed, and lay rigidly between the sheets for hours. Then I got up and put on a lot of clothes, and left the house. The clock in the hall showed three twenty.

I ran.

Sunday was long and uneventful. I tried to spend most of it in the garden. The year's neglect had not yet been made up, and I was still at the stage of pulling out the old rubbish and composting it. The thick stems of golden rod were tougher than the hollyhocks. Two echiums standing sentinel either side of the bottom arch were still upright, and I marvelled at their intricate design, which enabled bees to use them so efficiently. They were like high-rise flats, economic of ground space yet providing accommodation for hundreds. I wondered why they had proved unpopular with humans when bees loved them so much. And then I thought of the twin towers in New York, and the horror of being trapped in any high-rise accommodation. And at last I gained enough determination to cut off the fifteen-foot-high plants and lay them in the trench next to the kidney beans. Then I drew off my gloves and put them in the trug, gathered the secateurs and loppers, and climbed the first of the stone steps which led up the steep garden to the back door of the bungalow. I hadn't slept last night, I had worked most of today; surely sleep would come early tonight? And tomorrow Mrs Hardy would drop in and perhaps leave me some of her placid contentment.

CHAPTER
FOUR

When Mrs Hardy got home from the cinema there was no time for sausage and mash. The situation with Tom Hardy and his wife Della had suddenly worsened. Della had been taken into hospital that afternoon in an effort to control her soaring blood pressure.

"No need for you to panic, my maid." Hardy had cut sandwiches, and now bundled them inexpertly into some foil wrap. "He rang through less than an hour ago. Nothing you could've done if you'd been here. I told him you'd stay a couple of nights and cover the visiting."

She nodded. She had already stuffed her night clothes into a holdall, but still stood there feeling helpless. Then she said sadly, "He won't be able to leave Della now, will he? He can't leave her to look after a baby on her own."

"She might go back to her mother."

"Tom couldn't let that happen. Mrs Leach — Althea — she was always odd, but since her husband died she's much worse. Poor Tom. And poor Della, too." She looked at her husband and gave a gusty sigh. "What a mess, Hardy."

He returned her look wryly. "I'll go on doing out his room, anyway. You never know when he might want it."

She nodded. Then she telephoned the matron at Tall Trees, told her about Della, locked up the house, and they left.

Hardy's van, discreetly grey rather than metallic, bumped its way in front of the Victorian pile of the original hospital in Cheltenham, and Hardy began a long search for a place to put it. The car park was full as usual, and eventually he drove the van into a space reserved for doctors. It had been a poor drive: very dark and full of spray from lorries and cars. Even Mrs Hardy had not been able to find words to speak. Their silence was a pall of anxiety.

Once parked, they put their heads down against the rain and hurried into the maternity unit. Tom was expecting them, and there he was, standing in a corner of the foyer talking to a woman in a white coat wearing a stethoscope around her neck. Otherwise the rows of chairs were empty; visiting time had started.

"He looks terrible." Mrs Hardy hung back, holding Hardy's arm.

"Just cos his sweatshirt is — is —"

"Ripped. His sweatshirt is ripped. And his hair is on end."

"His hair's like yours."

"Thank you!"

"I mean curly. Black."

"Mine's grey and not curly any more. And his hair ain't seen a comb in days."

Tom turned and saw them, and held out his hand. "My parents," he said to the woman with the stethoscope. Then to them, briefly, without any expression, "There has to be an operation. A Caesarean. But the blood pressure needs to be down. A bit." Tom was like his father, he stated facts only.

They both smiled at the woman. Mrs Hardy turned to Tom. "Where are you living?"

Tom flicked her a look from his dark eyes. "At the flat. I have to. Della is just . . . so frightened."

"'Tis only right," Mrs Hardy said stolidly. "I'll stay there. Dad will have to go back. Work."

It was agreed tacitly. They went in to see Della. She was huge. She was weeping. Mrs Hardy realized she had rarely seen her not weeping. But at least she had something to weep about now. Mrs Hardy had always been "good" with her. She held her gently and told her how wonderful she was, and at last she calmed down.

Hardy drove the three of them to the flat in Bath Road. They picked up fish and chips on the way there, and sat eating them glumly. Mrs Hardy spoke of Harry Potter and Mrs Venables, and Tom said bleakly, "You're not still seeing that woman, are you?"

"Don't speak like that, our Tom." His mother gave him one of her looks. "She's making progress." Just for a moment she considered telling him about the ghost of Mr Venables shoving her into the old lake not so long ago, but then decided against it.

Tom said indifferently, "Good."

Hardy left them just before ten o'clock. Mrs Hardy made up the spare bed and went to bed. Just before midnight Tom went out on an emergency call. He was not back the next morning when she got up.

By Thursday they were both exhausted. And then came the operation.

Vivian's story

Mrs Hardy did not come the next day. I told myself she must have dropped in while I was running, so I did not venture out at all on Tuesday. She did not come.

On Wednesday I ran very early, and when she had not ping-ponged by the time it started to get dark, I rang her number. Mr Hardy answered.

"Good of you to ring, Mrs Venables. Not much news as yet. Blood pressure under control . . . dun't know what that means zackly, but it's got to be better than if it's not. Once they're happy with that they will do a Caesarean. That's what they said this morning."

My mind was jumping around crazily. First of all it sounded as if Mrs Hardy was in hospital with blood-pressure problems. But she certainly was not having a baby.

I said tentatively, "The baby wasn't due for a while, then?"

"No. We was called on Saturday night." He paused, then said, "She's a bit on her own, you see. Della. Tom's wife."

My wits were all over the place, but I had enough sense to ask, "Can you give me the address of the hospital, Mr Hardy? I can send flowers or something."

63

He gave me the address of a maternity unit in a hospital in Cheltenham. I stared at the wallpaper in the hall. Almost an hour's drive up the M5. And Mr Hardy did not like people in his van. So I would have to do it myself.

I put down the phone and went on staring at the wallpaper. I was so wrapped up in fighting off memory . . . and all the time Mrs Hardy . . . faithful Mrs Hardy . . . had been dealing with her daughter-in-law's pregnancy . . . job at the nursing home . . . and me.

I put my head against a faded paper rose and groaned aloud. After thinking what, if anything, I could do, I glanced at my watch, saw the shops would still be open, and got out the Yellow Pages. I rang an Interflora agent and had a long conversation about flowers, discovering that carnations were best, because they survived hospital heat so well, and then something stopped me before I placed my order. I put the receiver down very gently.

After another boiled egg, I got out some notepaper and began to write to Mrs Hardy, care of Cheltenham hospital. Then I realized that my Mrs Hardy and her daughter-in-law would have the same name. I frowned into the ashy fire-place and geared my letter to the two of them. I remembered the daughter-in-law's name. Della. I rolled it around my mouth, and suddenly a stupid teenage sort of joke flipped into and out of my head. What a good job neither of them had been christened Laurel! I was ashamed of the sheer superficiality of that thought, when the whole situation was so big and serious. Yet, as I finished off the little

64

note to them both I must have been dallying with it still, because I realized that I had no idea what Mrs Hardy's first name was. Just supposing . . . I pushed the notepaper into an envelope and sealed it briskly.

The next morning, which was Thursday, I woke at eight thirty. Too late to run. I drove out to my all-night garage, filled the car with petrol, and bought chocolates, fruit, magazines and flowers. Then I got on the M5 and drove to Cheltenham.

It took ages to find the hospital; I was not used to busy towns and one-way systems and street signs offering schools, colleges, pump rooms and . . . at last . . . hospitals. Cheltenham Spa had sounded genteel, a backwater for retired army officers and teachers. It probably offered those things, but it was also a bustling town full of shops and churches and enormous municipal-looking buildings and a statue of Neptune with water coming from him somewhere. The beautiful Regency Promenade flashed by just outside the driving limits, and there was a car park. I drove into it thankfully and asked the attendant for directions.

He considered my question then asked his own. "Can you walk?"

I thought of my morning jogs and nodded. He said, "Then you'd do better to leave the car and do it on foot. It could be as much as a mile, but if you drive you'll have a job to park." I was fed up with driving round and round the edge of the town, so I nodded again and he proceeded to give me directions.

"You never been to Cheltenham before?"

"Yes. But my husband always drove, and I sort of concentrated on the view. I haven't seen anything I recognize except just a bit of the Promenade."

"That's cos the planners are all mad," he said calmly. He pulled pen and paper from his pocket and wrote down the directions and a few useful landmarks, told me to reverse them when I came back to the car, have a nice cup of tea in Bath Road, a nice walk down the Prom, and a nice sit-down in Imperial Gardens. "Get the feel of the place. Better on foot." Which was rich coming from a carpark attendant. Or perhaps not. He pulled a face when he saw me take flowers and two polythene bags from the back of the car. I told him they weren't heavy. He said, "You'll need to sit down on the way back."

It was all good advice. The still, grey day was ideal for a walk. Cheltenham really was a garden town, and leaves were everywhere underfoot as I walked past the town hall and obediently turned right into Bath Road. I had always loved dry winter days, and though as a child I had lived in a run-down part of Bristol, there were lovely areas close by. I had shuffled through leaves along Cumberland Road to cross the footbridge for school in Bedminster. The smell of early winter was the same there as it was here. I felt myself enjoying it.

Bath Road was an area of small shops; there was a big restaurant — one of a chain — on the other side of the road as I turned to walk up a hill, but then single-fronted shops in between the original Regency houses with their canopied porches and wrought-iron verandahs. Second-hand bookshops, probably ideal for students, a window full of model trains, the top pane plastered with hand-written advertisements, for sale, wanted . . . and then a tiny cafe, steamed-up windows, a delightful smell of sausage rolls. Then a line of houses, all brass plated. Solicitors, agencies of all kinds, a dentist at the end.

I crossed the road at the lights and turned left. I could see the Gentlemen's College and its sweep of lawns over on my right. I remembered going there for a cricket match. Someone had had tickets. David. Not Someone, David.

It seemed to be getting dark and I glanced at my watch. One forty-five. Surely visiting would be at two? Mrs Hardy would be prompt; I knew she would be prompt. It began to drizzle, which explained the poor light. I tried to protect the flowers; for some reason everything was getting heavier. Then the bulk of the original hospital appeared on the left, and I wended my way through the packed car park, and eventually found the maternity unit.

It was bright and modern, a very young offspring of the sooty, established Victorian building not so far from it. The reception area was unnaturally quiet; double doors were labelled "The Wards" and next to them a large clock showed the few people waiting that visiting time was not quite yet. I looked around frantically for Mrs Hardy but she was not there. I needed Mrs Hardy. I sat down on the edge of a chair and waited. My hair dripped on to the collar of my fleece. Bags and flowers dripped on to the floor. Someone asked me brightly whether it was raining, and I nodded. I noticed

67

suddenly that everyone seemed to be smiling: the nurses who constantly crossed and recrossed the floor looked from one to another with smiles all over their faces, and the waiting visitors responded and then kept on smiling. The visitors were nearly all women of Mrs Hardy's age. Of course. They were mothers and now grandmothers. It was a weekday afternoon when fathers and grandfathers would be at work. It was visiting time for all these new grannies. I found myself smiling, too.

I stopped when the doors were opened, and everyone got up and went through them. Where was Mrs Hardy? She was my key to seeing the other Mrs Hardy — Della. I did not know where Della could be. Perhaps she wasn't here at all, perhaps she was at this moment having her Caesarean. I bit my lip. That would be why my Mrs Hardy was not waiting to visit her.

I began to gather up bags and flowers; I would leave them at the tiny desk in the corner of the room and go home. I had no right to be here, anyway. My motive had been selfish as usual: I had wanted to see Mrs Hardy.

I was half-way to the desk and another smiling nurse, when the outside door opened violently and a young man entered at full speed. I stepped aside and he shot up to the desk. I knew before he opened his mouth that this was Tom Hardy. He was sturdy like his father, capable-looking like his mother. He wore jeans and a checked shirt. No top coat but he wasn't wet. He must have left his donkey jacket in his van after the last job. Hedge-cutting, tree-lopping?

He said, "My wife — is she still OK? And the twins?"

His smile was brief, but the nurse reflected and amplified it.

She said, "Yes, doctor. Everything is fine. Mrs Hardy's mother did not stay long."

He interpolated something that sounded like "good job".

"Mrs Hardy is very comfortable and the babies are in the nursery if you want to go through."

He waited for no more; he obviously knew his way around. He was through the doors before she had finished speaking. She looked at me and her smile went from ear to ear.

"There's something about twins, isn't there? Especially when it's a complete surprise — she absolutely refused to have a scan. And a doctor's wife, too!"

She laughed, and so did I, though I felt easy tears behind my eyes. I swallowed and laid my bundles on the desk next to the telephone.

"Actually, these are for Mrs Hardy. I didn't know that all this had happened. I didn't know . . . anything. I'm so pleased everything is all right."

"Oh, do take them through. She will be so pleased to see you."

"She doesn't know me. I'm a friend of her mother-in-law. I won't interrupt anything now. But I am so glad to hear the news."

I turned and left quickly. It was no longer raining and I felt light without the flowers and the bags. Physically light; light-hearted, too. I wanted to find a seat and sit down and think about everything that had just crashed in on me. The successful operation through the night . . . dear Mrs Hardy being right there for her daughter-in-law. And Della's mother — somehow for all the complicated reasons there must be — not there. And then, twins! Surely Della's mother was pleased about the twins? I wished I had asked their sex. I pondered on the alternatives, girls, boys, one of each. And then names — certainly not Laurel! I found myself smiling. How wonderful this was! Mr and Mrs Hardy had twin grandchildren. Lucky, lucky twins.

All this hypothetical thinking was exhausting, and anyway I had now reached the town hall, and on my left the grey November light revealed the gentle beauty of Imperial Gardens. I walked down one of the paths, and sat on the first seat I came to, and went through the whole thing again. The fact — the series of events — that had somehow made me part of this wonderful whole, almost overwhelmed me. I had been so closed in, so tightly bound-up in not remembering, not thinking, and now suddenly I could think, I could open up to all this. It was wonderful. And Tom, Mr and Mrs Hardy's son, was a doctor! It was just marvellous.

I was cold. I stood up and walked the length of the gardens, past the cannon guarding the Queen's hotel, and into the lounge. It was warm, spacious, calm and quiet. The waiter who came to me was charmingly French, and when he brought me tea in a silver teapot we talked about the weather. It wasn't a bit trivial, it was full of meaning and depth. I was happy yet I wanted to cry. I wondered whether I was going mad. Or whether I had been mad and I was walking back into sanity.

Eventually I left and retraced my steps to the top of the Promenade and then walked down there looking at the shops then up at the trees, then across to Neptune still dripping water. Then I went back to the car park, chatted to the attendant, and thanked him again. And drove home. It was dark when I took the last hairpin and reached the Tump. I walked through the house switching on lights. Then I found a wine glass and a bottle of red wine I hadn't known I had. I poured a glass, opened the French window to the garden and looked across the town and over the sea to Wales. I lifted my glass. "To the Hardy family, young and old," I said aloud.

Down in the darkness of the garden, where the steps led to the fig tree and the echiums, I could have sworn someone said amen. But probably after my long day and the wine, I was slightly drunk and could have said it myself.

CHAPTER
FIVE

In the two years of Tom's marriage, Mrs Hardy had imagined that, although the relationship was obviously not ideal, Della had been the perfect housewife and had looked after him . . . perfectly. She was the same age as he was, and until she met him she had looked after her parents to the exclusion of everything else. In Mrs Hardy's opinion she had been no more than a slave. It was to escape these parents that Della had seized on Tom and clung to him like a limpet.

It turned out that Della's "training" had slipped since Tom liberated her. Her cupboards were almost bare. When Mrs Hardy wanted to make cheese sauce there was no milk, no plain flour nor any other kind, certainly no cheese. After searching the cupboards in vain, she found a cardboard packet of salt in the fridge, along with a loaf of bread and a slab of butter. She did better with the chest freezer, which she eventually found in the garage. It was packed with ready meals. Mrs Hardy stared in dismay. It was as if Della had left a diary for her to read.

Exasperated at first, then almost tearful for her daughter-in-law, she set herself a daily regime: she cleaned and cooked during the morning, and visited

Della in the afternoon. Tom was working as the local emergency doctor and his area covered half the Cotswolds as far as she could tell. He rang her now and then for news of Della: "I'm at Bourton-on-the-Water", or "I've stopped at a pub for a sandwich somewhere between Cranham and Painswick." On Monday afternoon, she was the first to know that there were two hearts beating inside Della's womb. She let the doctor tell Tom that night, when he visited.

While he was gone she telephoned Hardy and said, "I dun't know what to think. She'll never manage two babies."

But Tom's unemotional face was transformed when he got back to the flat that night. He looked like an eight-year-old again as he said to her wonderingly, "Two . . . two of them, Ma. Can you believe it?"

Mrs Hardy said flatly, "No." She felt mean; she should have rejoiced with him. But she was exhausted with the physical effort of housekeeping, and the emotional slog of supporting Della.

In the early hours of Thursday morning the phone rang. Tom drove them to the hospital and talked to the woman doctor while his mother held Della. The situation had gone suddenly wrong, and an emergency Caesarean was the only answer. It was a race between life and death. There was no choice. Tom talked to his wife and she nodded, not really understanding, but, as always, willing to be told exactly what to do. She clung to her mother-in-law while they waited for the pre-med injection to take effect.

73

The operation was a success. By ten o'clock it was safely over and Della was in bed very peacefully asleep. Mrs Hardy sat by her while Tom inspected his children and reported back. He wanted to take her down to the nursery, too, but suddenly she did not feel up to it.

Tom put an arm around her and helped her to her feet.

"Dad's here," he said gently. "He wants to take you home for a bit. Let's go and find him."

It was so good to see Hardy she almost wept, but Mrs Leach was also sitting in the waiting room, and her tirade and accusations put tears right out of the question. Hardy ignored her and swept his wife away. Tom followed them, and told them he would probably take a couple of calls while Della was asleep, and return that afternoon. Then he would telephone them at home.

She did not argue; she made no attempt to reply to the stream of accusations coming from the other woman. She hung on to Hardy with all her strength, and it was only when he tucked her into the van that she spoke.

"We should stay with Tom," she said.

"He can deal with Mrs Leach. And she is Della's mum, they must get on." He manoeuvred the van out into Bath Road and headed for the motorway. "Just come home for an hour or two, love. You could do with getting away from it all for a bit."

"Oh Hardy . . ."

"I was took to the nursery. They look bonny. Boy and a girl. Lovely."

74

"Oh *Hardy*! I never went to see them! I should've gone! Oh, Tom will never forgive me!"

"Don't be daft, my maid. Tom will have enough on his plate. And he'll go out to wet the babies' heads — double dose, I reckon."

They were already approaching Gloucester. She subsided. "We'll be back for visiting tonight," she said. "An' everything will be all right now. Perhaps her mum will take to dropping in now and then."

"That's right." He sounded like she sounded herself when she was talking to Della.

She smiled for the first time that day. "Sorry about . . . back there. I was that anxious for her. Sat on her bed and just willed her to stay alive. When that dear nurse said she'd come through all right and the babies were all right . . . Anyway, my love, I'm all right, too. An' like I said, everything will be now. An' if her mum does keep in touch, it could be more — sort of — normal. If you know what I mean."

"I know, my maid."

Tom phoned later that afternoon, after they had eaten together and she had lavishly admired the way Hardy had kept the house so neat; especially the kitchen. She had sighed and said they had better get going back to Cheltenham and at that moment the phone had rung. Tom sounded exhausted but euphoric. "They're perfect. All those fingers and toes . . ." She was too ashamed to tell him she had not seen the babies. "Oh Ma, they told me how good you were with Della. Thank God you were here. Dad, too." He took a breath. "Just over four pounds each, scruffy dark hair and the way they squint at you and frown and . . . look like real people. Della's mother says they remind her of a pair of marmosets!" But he laughed. "Knowing her she could have likened them to something much worse!" He cut through her protests. "Listen. That friend of yours was here. Left flowers and fruit and Lord knows what. Say thanks, will you?"

Mrs Hardy frowned, then made a sound. It was Mrs Venables, of course. Hardy must have phoned her. Even more surprising. She made more sounds.

Tom cut through them. "Ma. Listen again. There's no need for you to come back just to look after me. If you could spare a couple of days when Della comes home it would be really good. But until then perhaps you should save yourself." He laughed. He sounded great. And he was a doctor, so he would know if everything was all right. Mrs Hardy smiled gratefully.

She slept well that night. When she woke, Hardy had left for work; it was getting light. She lay there and thought about her grandchildren. And then her son, who was clever but sometimes still a schoolboy. And then her daughter-in-law, who had "let herself go". Mrs Hardy knew what she meant by that phrase, but she saw, too, that it could mean something far more literal. She shivered in her warm bed.

Then she thought of Mrs Venables and how she had "let herself go", yet had never really let herself go.

And then the phone rang. And everything changed again. Tom was on call, and would get to the hospital as soon as he could. Mrs Leach was unwell, but would also come as soon as she felt up to it. The Hardys arrived before either of them and went straight to Della's room. She was propped on pillows, white and suddenly fragile. The life-giving drip stand was pushed aside by a nurse. "She's been waiting for you . . ." she said.

Della held up her free arm to her mother-in-law. Hardy stood at the foot of the bed and put one of his enormous hands on her feet.

"Hang on, hang on, dear girl . . ."

"Mum . . . I'm scared."

Mrs Hardy looked at her husband in sudden agony, and he said, "We're all scared, my maid. Just do as Mum says. Hang on."

The nurse tapped the bottle, which was dripping blood through transparent tubes into Della. And Della hung on until at last Tom took his mother's place. Then she seemed to sink into herself.

Mrs Hardy said much later to her husband, "When Tom arrived . . . she looked . . . different. Didn't you think?"

He nodded sadly. "She settled herself on his shoulder like a bird on a nest."

She nodded, not surprised by this. And then Hardy said even more sadly, "It's like that Mrs Venables, isn't it? She's got her husband with her for the rest of her life. And our Tom's got Della with him for the rest of his."

Vivian's story

It was the weekend. I did not run on Saturday. I was making visible progress in the garden, and I saved my energy for clearing up around the fig tree. There was no sign at all of anyone having been there, but I was drawn to it somehow. The tree itself could do with some kind of pruning but figs are strange things and only fruit properly every two years. A specialist's job. Mr Hardy.

I put the phone in my pocket when I went into the garden. Mrs Hardy had not phoned, but Hardy had sent two messages from her. The first had told me that everything was fine, and the twins were just lovely, and my flowers were lovely. The second had been . . . odd. It had mentioned the weather and the difficulty of living in a flat without a garden for the washing and the dustbins. I had not phoned back because Hardy was working in the day and then driving up to Cheltenham most evenings, and I thought he had enough on his plate. But if he rang again I was determined to be on the other end of the phone. Of course, it did not ring.

As the afternoon quickly waned into dark grey I went back inside, lit the fire, pulled the coffee table close to it, and went into the kitchen to cut bread and butter. On the table was a battered old door knob. I stood very still where I was and stared at it. I knew it. And I knew where it had been last September.

To make assurance doubly sure I went slowly towards it, touched it with my forefinger, felt it to be slippery. It was still muddily wet. When I picked it up, the shape of it fitting into my palm confirmed it was the same one. I checked that the front door was bolted and the side gate padlocked. None of the windows were open, because it was one of those damp, misty late November afternoons. No one could have wrenched that door knob from its cement housing; no one could have put it inside my bungalow. Yet it was there.

I got the car out and drove as if the devil was behind me. The door knob was on my lap, and at the first of the hairpins it rolled on to the floor; I tried to kick it under my seat, the car veered slightly, and I swallowed and said aloud, "Control yourself, for goodness' sake." It was four o'clock by the digital clock on the dashboard, but I needed the headlights. At the bottom of the hill Saturday shoppers were beginning to turn for home. A council lorry was parked inconveniently, and I had to wait while they repositioned it and extended a ladder towards a street light. Then I turned towards the sea and drove as far as I could towards the lake. I parked next to the ice-cream stall in the amusement arcade, foraged for the door knob and crossed the grass to the footpath. It was bitterly cold, the sea air wrapped me damply, I hadn't stopped for gloves or hat, and the fleece I had worn all day for gardening had no hood. I ran along the path and stood above the lake, my breath like smoke in front of me. The lake was empty of water; the sluice gates were open; the little promenade was waist-high in rubbish of all sorts. There was a bright yellow digger where the diving boards had been and a barrier tape across the bottom of the steps. The smell was atrocious.

I stared for ages. They were going to clean up the area. Why? Were they then going to replace the "amenities" and get the whole thing going again . . . deckchairs, paddle boats, changing huts, springboard . . .? And the door knob two feet below the water line of the big pool . . . was it still there or was it in the pocket of my gardening fleece? I clutched at it. I had to know.

I ran down the steps, ducked under the tape and stood on the small area of the little promenade not stacked high with muddy, oozing rubbish. I edged past the enormous mechanical digger. No one was inside the cab; I could see a packet of cigarettes and a newspaper on the seat. I side-stepped past that, and then over the concrete bridge with the housing for the boards, and reached the retaining wall. I looked down. This was where I had been "helped" into the water almost two months ago; dammit, I had told myself often that the push had been all in my mind, but I knew, standing there, looking ten or twelve feet down to the mucky sludge on the bottom of the lake, that I had most definitely been pushed. I glanced around me, checking no one was within arms' length this time. It was too far to fall now that the water had gone. The only way to reach the wall which separated paddling pool from swimming pool was to walk along that retaining wall. The tide was somewhere else; the drop down to the rocks and pebbles of the sea-bed must be twenty feet. Mrs Bartholomew would have had a fit if she had seen me edge on to the wall's broad top and begin to walk oh-so-slowly along its length. But she had not just found a door knob on her kitchen table.

Half-way down that stone wall, I got a steady, proper balance and stopped long enough to stare at the end of the swimming pool and scan its length and breadth for a door knob. It was a ridiculous thing to do: the only way to complete this stupid, stupid task was to keep moving. There wasn't a chance of spotting something as small as a door knob in the muddy, flinty darkness of the empty pool. And I had lost momentum.

Somehow I got going again; my heart was racing and I was beginning to feel sick with the effort not to look to my left and see that sheer drop and the rocks beneath me. I reached the right-angled turn with a sob of sheer relief, then I crouched and straddled the wall which divided the paddling pool and the swimming pool. The drop on my right was still dangerously deep, but on the left it was barely six feet. I sat there for some time, just breathing and telling myself I was all right. It was such a crazy thing to do I was incredulous at myself. I could have come tomorrow or the next time it was sunny . . . brought the binoculars and stood up on the path searching the wall through them. And here I was, smeared with the rank mud that was everywhere, and it was almost dark, and the fire I had lit an hour ago would be dead again and . . . I realized I was nearly exhausted.

I began to bump myself along the wall; I could have walked along it easily, but I needed to be able to lean right over and search that rough surface every two or three yards. It wasn't difficult, but for some reason I was sobbing.

A shout came from behind me just as I was convinced the door knob was no longer cemented into the wall but was in my pocket. I straightened up with enormous relief. I'd done it before I could be hauled ignominiously "ashore". A man in the bright yellow waterproof jacket of a council workman was coming down the steps, lifting the tape, running close to the wall past the heaps of rubbish towards the children's pool. I started to bump forward to meet him.

"What the bleedin' 'ell d'you think you're doing, lady?" He started along the wall to meet me. "You saw the bleedin' tape — Christ, I only leave the cab two minutes to go to the toilet and when I get back . . ." He held out his hand. I grabbed it and hauled myself to my feet. We both staggered back to the little promenade. He kept ranting and it was like music in my ears. I gathered he'd got a case of the runs from eating parsnips the night before, and he shouldn't even be here, but it was a decent contract, and if he got it finished before the next crazy woman came along it would all be worthwhile. He was blessedly ordinary. He stood next to one of the odorous heaps and pointed a stubby finger to where the little prom ascended gently to the old sandpit. I had forgotten all about this entrance; it had been fenced off but of course the digger had had to come down to this level somehow. He said shakily, "Sorry to go on. But you could have been badly injured, and I'd have been hauled up for it. Now just go

82

home like a good lady and make yourself a cup of tea. We'll forget all about it."

I'd found out what I'd come for, and made apologetic noises as I turned away. But then I turned back. "What is happening here? Is it going to be demolished?"

He looked exasperated. "They don't tell me nothing official, only what I got to do. It were drained last week, and I got to get the muck out and trailer it over to the landfill." I waited and he added, resigned, "The word is that it's just a clear-up and repair job, then they'll put down the sluice gates, let it refill and be a natural feature. No money for a proper re-fit."

"Do you know anything about it? When it was built?"

"Twenties, I believe. The old squire paid for it, then handed it over to the town. We could do with a few more like him."

"Yes." I smiled, loving the way he made all these things so ordinary. I nearly showed him the door knob, but he was in no mood for anything more. "I'm sorry to have caused so much trouble. It's just . . . you know . . . a spot of local research. There's a story about a Victorian door knob being implanted in the wall of the swimming area and I wondered whether it was true."

"There's nowt there now, lady, I would have seen it. You want to talk to the old district engineer. I think he's still alive."

I stopped in my tracks and looked round again; but my lovely ordinary yellow-jacketed digger man was walking carefully past a mound of weed and driftwood topped with a beer can.

I knew full well the "old district engineer" was still alive. His name was John Jinks and he was living in Tall Trees nursing home at the top of Christmas Tump.

CHAPTER
SIX

It was more than a week before the Hardys came home. Mrs Hardy had the exhausted look of someone who has been in a war zone, Mr Hardy was grimly silent. She said, "I cannot believe it is only a fortnight since Mrs Venables and me saw that Harry Potter film." He said nothing; he hovered over the kettle, waiting for it to boil. He had tried to tidy up before he went to Cheltenham to pick up his wife, but realized now that he had no idea where the tea caddy was.

She said, "Now I know how that girl feels."

Unexpectedly he knew at once that she was talking about Mrs Venables, and he said decidedly, "No, you don't. We got new things to think about. I'll have to finish Tom's attic room a bit quick. You'll have to get stuff in. We got the babies to think about. She hasn't got nothing like that."

Hilda Hardy shook her head but said, "You're right. We can look forward. She can't do that."

He found the tea caddy in the fridge and made tea. She sat opposite him. He poured two mugs of tea and pushed one across to her. He said, "It's Tom, isn't it? He looks like a zombie."

"Yes. He doesn't seem to realize what has happened. He's on the go all the time. He told me yesterday he has signed up for a mother-and-baby course."

"Nothing wrong with that. Good luck to him."

"Yes. But there's Della's mother. He knew she would blame him. He blames himself. But he thought . . ." She frowned painfully. "He thought she would . . . *grieve*. Like we grieve. More still p'raps. Maybe."

She paused and they both thought about it. Hardy had nothing to say. She added, "They never were like us. She didn't even tell Della when her own dad died. Tom didn't know. We didn't know." She sighed. "No. They never were like us."

He spoke with conviction. "They weren't. And that's for sure."

She hugged his arm. Then said as if changing the subject, "There's still the other woman, too. What was her name?"

"Elisabeth."

"He went to see her a couple of times. I couldn't . . . bear that."

"We've known about her, my maid. He's always been honest and open with us. And din't we — you — always know Della weren't the right wife for him? So, there could be a chance for our Tom with this Elisabeth." She said nothing, and he waited for her to drink, then said, "I know you too well, my maid."

She lowered her head, in acknowledgment. "It's always the upbringing at fault, Hardy. I thought we'd brought up Tom to be loyal and faithful. And he chose to marry her. And he told her about this Elisabeth ... tis no wonder Della's blood pressure was high."

"We didn't spoil him," he said stubbornly. "We never had the money to spoil him. And if he hadn't worked his way through the medical school, we couldn't have afforded that, neither."

"But he hasn't been faithful, Hardy. Not for very long, at any rate."

He was silent while she finished her tea. Then he drank his. Then he said, "He might not've been faithful in that sense, Hildie. But he were loyal. Soon as he knew she was expecting, he was back with her. And he would have stayed with her. You know that — you said it yourself."

"I do know that." She spoke in a low voice. "Oh, Hardy. There's so much to do, and we're not youngsters any more."

He stood up. "I'd best get on, then."

"And I had, too." She pushed back her chair and stood with him. "I'll pop out and get some nice steak and kidney."

Just for a moment they clasped each other.

Vivian's story

It took me a whole week to garner the courage to face John Jinks. I wasn't sure how much my father-in-law had told him. It was obvious he knew enough to dislike me and to blame me for what had happened ... perhaps he was right. I could not remember things properly any more. Perhaps I had been running for too long . . . the Gingerbread Woman had escaped the past.

Anyway, it was Sunday afternoon and I was sitting opposite Jinx in the very public, very large sitting room at Tall Trees. I had suggested the small parlour upstairs, but he had rebutted that by asking me aggressively why the hell I thought he had insisted on a ground-floor room when he'd come to this god-forsaken place ten years ago. Hadn't I noticed he was sitting in a bloody wheelchair?

I did not point out that the lift was quite large enough for his chair, and I was capable of wheeling it down the hall. He wanted to be angry with me, and I wanted his cooperation, so I smiled as if he'd made a joke, and asked whether I could fetch some tea for him. A nurse had wheeled a large trolley just inside the door, and people were going back and forth pouring themselves a cup and taking cakes as if they were starving. Pretty soon there would be no tea and no cakes left for Jinx.

"I'll have mine when you've gone," he said tersely.

I took that to mean hurry up and say what you have to, then go. I plunged straight in.

"I'm after some information about the old lake next to Becket's Hill."

He had been staring at my hands in my lap; I knew they were dirty. I'd been in the garden again, and I might have forgotten to wash them. Now, suddenly, he looked up sharply and narrowed his brownish eyes at me.

"What sort of information?" he asked.

"Did you have anything to do with the plans or the building?"

"Building started in 1922, and I guess it was mooted and plans drawn a couple of years before that. I was born in 1922." He spoke levelly.

That made him eighty-four. Father-in-law had been ten years younger.

I pressed my lips together in disappointment, then made to stand up. "Thanks anyway." I tried to smile humorously. "You can have your tea now. Sorry to have bothered you."

He leaned out of his wheelchair, grabbed one of my wrists and pushed me back down. "I was in charge of the maintenance after the war. It came under public works. I was responsible for public works."

I sat there for a moment collecting myself, rubbing my wrist. I could hear him breathing.

"You emptied it now and then and did the necessary repairs?"

"It was emptied and cleaned every spring ready for the summer. Not much in the way of repairs. Mortar here and there. We cranked up the sluice gate a couple of feet — didn't want to wash away any of the sea-bed just there because of the retaining wall, so we let it out slowly. Took two or three days. Then I had men with yard brooms and hoses. Took them another two or three days, but you could have eaten your picnic off that lake floor by the time they'd finished. Pride in the job in those days."

There was a pause while we both thought about his words. I heard an angry, embittered old man; I expect he heard a proud craftsman.

I said, "This sounds crazy. Did you ever notice a door knob about half-way down the wall of the deep pool where it divides off the boating lake?"

"A *door* knob?" He stared at me as if I was mad. "For God's sake stop fidgeting with your hands all the time! Did you say a door knob?"

I fished in the pocket of my mac. "Yes. In fact, this door knob." I put it on the small table next to his chair, which already contained his spectacle case and a newspaper. It started to roll on to the floor, and he grabbed it.

"Bloody table. None of them level." He looked at it then gave it back to me. "No," he said.

I waited for something else. I knew there was something else. His brownish eyes were still on the knob, which now lay in my lap. He cleared his throat. "It's brass. Corroded of course." I nodded. "How did you find it?"

I was going to lie, then realized there was no point. I told him about being pushed into the water, and thinking I might drown, and finding the door knob.

He said quietly, "Bloody hell."

"Yes."

"You must have imagined the push. But it made no difference why you were in the water. You were there. And you had to get out."

I said quietly, "I saw the man who did it. He chased me up into Becket's Wood a couple of days later. I hid and watched him when he came back. He spotted me and sort of waved. Or saluted. I'm not sure."

He came straight to the nub of it all. "Was it David?" he asked.

I tried to laugh. "How could it be?"

He stared directly at me. "Why not? Because you killed him? Don't murder victims come back to haunt their killers sometimes?"

I gasped and put my hands to my face.

He said quickly, "I know it wasn't your fault. Sorry. I've got a lot of time to sit here and think about it all, and I can't help . . . sometimes . . . wishing he'd never met you."

I half-sobbed, half-groaned. "Oh God . . ."

"You think it was him, don't you?"

"I couldn't see a face. Or hands. But he had feet. I could hear them thumping the ground. I put my ear against the earth and I could hear his footfalls quite clearly."

"Right."

Another long pause; I wondered whether I should leave.

He said, "How did you get the door knob? You didn't go back and dig it out, did you?"

"No. I found it. On my kitchen table." I had been looking down again, my hands still shielding my face. "I was gardening. The bungalow was locked, side gate too. I don't know . . ."

"When was this?"

"A week ago. I got the car out of the garage and drove straight down to the lake. It's being cleaned again. It's empty but there's still plenty of mud. It stinks to high heaven. There's no door knob there any more. This is it."

He said, "So you came to ask me about it."

"I'd forgotten the lake would have come under your jurisdiction. The man who was driving the digger mentioned it."

Another pause. My hands started up, turning and twisting the door knob this way and that.

He said, "See if there's any tea left. Pour yourself a cup and bring a plate of cakes. I need to think."

I stood up, put the door knob very carefully on to his table and crossed the room to the trolley. The nurse appeared with hot water and I put about a cupful into the teapot and poured tea like black treacle into two cups. All the fancy cakes were gone, but there were buttered buns on the bottom tray, and no one had touched those. I took the whole plate and went back to Jinx's corner and was rewarded by a tiny smile. He shovelled two spoons of sugar into his tea and we both tucked in. I knew he would always dislike me, but even enemies sometimes form a cautious alliance. He wiped his mouth on his handkerchief — there were paper napkins all over the place — and said, "I reckon it's something simple. Trivial. Like carving initials on a tree. Something like that."

I nodded. "Could be. But why would anyone bring it all the way up the Tump and somehow get into my bungalow and leave it on the table?"

"Don't fool yourself, woman. You pocketed it that night, or the second time you went down."

I flushed. "I think I would remember. It was firm enough to take my weight — save my life, perhaps — I would have had to go down there with tools and chip away for ages. There would be signs now of damage on the wall. There's nothing."

"So what do you think? David chiselled it out and brought it up as some kind of token?"

"You think it was put there in the first place as a token, so that's not such a ridiculous idea!" I could feel my face grow hot.

"So you do think it was David's ghost? You do think that he tried to polish you off, just as you polished him off? Then brought you a bloody love-token?"

"Don't keep accusing me of — of — that. You admitted yourself that it's not true. I was in the car with him —"

"And you wish it had been you, don't you? Your conscience has been at work ever since, and now this scenario is taking place. Put two and two together, Mrs Vivian Venables. You and I are the only ones who know your real state of mind. No other car was involved. The investigators could find nothing wrong with your car. It careered off the road and into a tree. Full stop."

"You think I did it purposely?" I could feel tears on my face; they were hot.

"I think you are forgetting — deliberately forgetting — something in this particular equation. Perhaps you are also forgetting that I am now the only other living person who knows about it."

"I have to go —"

He made no attempt to stop me, this time. As I tried to find a place on the table for my cup and saucer, he said in a low voice, "Your friend Mrs Hardy has told me how you run. Every day you run like a crazy woman around the town, along the coast, into the Mendips. You can't run for ever. Is that why David brought you the bloody door knob? To force you to stop and face up to it?"

I grabbed the door knob and thrust it into my pocket. I heard him sigh sharply. Then he said, "No fool like an old fool, I suppose. I ought to let you run yourself into the ground but . . . see if Juniper Stevens is still alive. She was born that year, 1922. See if you can get anything out of her."

I barely heard him. I was almost through the door when he called out, "If you stop running long enough, come and let me know."

I ran down the Tump, and through my own gate set in the middle of the beautifully trimmed conifer hedge. I locked the front door behind me and went straight into the kitchen and put the door knob carefully on to the table. If only I had not gone to see Jinx I could have explained away what was happening now. Somehow. It need not have been anything at all to do with all the terrible business of this time last year. It could have been my special Someone trying to reassure me that he understood. Understood everything. And that I could . . . maybe . . . stop running, and have boiled eggs for tea, and be interested, really interested in dear Mrs Hardy's twin grandchildren. The enormous effort I had to put into not remembering that moment of consciousness as the firemen started to cut me out of the car and I knew that I was alive . . . the effort was exhausting in itself. I put my hands over my face and gasped for air. The only thing to do was to run. I went back into the hall, put on my mac, unlocked the door and . . . went.

It was ten o'clock when I got back, and I had reached that state of numbness that would get me through the night. The light was flashing on the answer machine and I ignored it while I hacked bread and cheese and made tea. Then I had a shower and put a hot-water bottle into the bed. And then, in case it was Mrs Hardy, I pressed play. It wasn't until her voice spoke that I realized it was getting on for midnight.

She said, "It's me. Mrs Hardy. That was a lovely thing you did, taking those flowers and presents to Della like that. I knew they was from you and I could tell her as much that very evening. So she knew." There was a pause; I could hear her breathing and it was ragged. She cleared her throat and went on strongly, "I wasn't intending to tell you, Mrs Venables. You got enough unhappiness. But you might hear from someone else at the nursing home and wonder why I didn't let you know. Poor Della died on Friday. Her mum was with her. It was something to do with her blood pressure. Tom thinks it was his fault." There was another pause. I realized she was giving me time to pick up the phone, and of course I hadn't been there. She coughed again and said quickly, "I'll try to slip in soon.

95

We're all right here. Don't worry. Take care of yourself."

She was gone.

I went to bed, and at last I wept properly. Not for myself, or from fear, or guilt of any kind. I wept for Mrs Hardy and her husband and her son and the twin babies who would never know their mother. The strange thing was that just when I thought I had better get up and make some more tea or something, I fell asleep. It was past nine o'clock when I woke to hear the front doorbell. I knew it would be Mrs Hardy. I didn't bother with a dressing gown. I opened the door in my pyjamas and gathered her into my arms, and wept again.

CHAPTER
NINE

It was Monday morning; six o'clock and very dark. Mrs Hardy made tea and took it upstairs, then brought it down again because Hardy never drank tea in bed unless he was ill. "And I en't ill, my maid, nor can afford to be, with the Lammertons needing their roof tiles fixed after last week's storm."

They sat — crouched — elbows on table, tea held in both hands. "It'll soon warm up," Mrs Hardy said irrelevantly. But he nodded.

"You could've laid in a bit this morning." He looked at her. "Not very comfortable at Tom's place, was it?"

"It was fine. I couldn't find anything and the cooker was difficult. But I gave the whole place a good clean. Funny, I always thought Della was a good housekeeper."

"She was on her own there so much of the time. She needed someone to tell her what to do and when to do it."

"And she was pregnant, too . . ." They glanced at each other. They knew it was unfair to hand all the guilt to Tom on a plate, yet, for the moment at least, there was no way they could criticize Della.

Mrs Hardy sighed sharply. "Anyway, it gave me something to do. I couldn't be at the hospital till two o'clock." She sighed again. "I would have liked to have done some cooking, though. I could have left Tom a couple of tins of my rock cakes. He always liked my rock cakes. I remember when he came home from university and nearly ate us out of house and home, I told him his stomach was like a colander, and he said to make him a batch of rock cakes cos they'd fill holes in colanders any day of the week!" She sighed gustily. "Should've told old Jinx that one, when he was on about colanders."

Hardy smiled and said gently, "Why don't you go back to bed, my maid? It's not seven o'clock yet."

"That's fine. I want to leave early so's I can pop in to see Mrs Venables before work."

"You're not going to work?" He was appalled. "You only came home Sat'day!"

"You heard me phone Matron. They're short on the morning shift. An' I got a shopping list as long as your arm. I can do it on the way home, pop it in my bicycle basket and be back before dark." She leaned over and touched the back of his hand. "I got to keep going, Hardy. You know that. Tom didn't want us there. He needs to be . . . separate for a bit. Just a day or two. Then he'll come here, and as soon as possible he'll bring the twins down . . . Says he'll be glad of us at the funeral."

He looked down at her fingers; the wedding ring was worn down to a thin band. After a while he nodded.

Vivian's story

We sat at the kitchen table and Mrs Hardy made the tea; I couldn't seem to staunch my ridiculous tears. She wiped her eyes now and then, but she didn't break down properly again.

"I know now why you kept such a stiff upper lip all that time last year," she said, setting mugs on the table and putting milk and sugar within reach. "There's so much to think about, so much to do. When this happened I wanted to see you — be with someone who knew what loss and grief was all about. Didn't mean to upset you like this. I'm real sorry, Mrs Venables."

"Don't be." I had another go at clearing my nose, and was reminded of father-in-law, who had trumpeted like an elephant into his enormous handkerchiefs. "I'm sorry to be so — so — weak. I just cannot believe it, somehow. You and Mr Hardy . . . I really don't know you, yet I feel so close to you. You've been a faithful friend all these months . . . I didn't even realize your Tom was a doctor . . ." I kept stopping and blowing again. "So wrapped up in my own unhappiness . . . all that joy and now . . . this."

"Joy. You're right. It was joy." She poured boiling water into the pot and her glasses steamed up. "And some of that has got to still be there. We got to get in touch with it again. Cos of they twins, and cos of Tom." She rubbed at her glasses as she came to the table with the teapot. "Oh, we're happy enough, Hardy and me. And we've had our joyful moments. Course. But babies are different. They bring work and trouble by the

shed-load. But on the other side of the scales is the joy."
She looked at me. "You was cheated out of that, Mrs
Venables, wasn't you? I did hear you was pregnant and
lost it in the crash."

"Do most people know that?" My voice sounded like
something from the Wailing Wall.

"Some. They reckon the coroner knew and that's
why you was never called nor nothing." She pushed a
steaming mug towards me. "People are mad, aren't
they? As if you would do a thing like that deliberate,
baby or no baby." She sipped her tea and then
de-steamed her glasses again. "It was a terrible thing to
happen to you. And what happened to Della was
terrible, too." She sighed. "She threatened suicide when
Tom left her. If she'd known . . . dear Lord."

I could imagine what Mrs Hardy's neighbours and
friends would make of this. Tom left his wife when she
was pregnant, and she died in childbirth.

I said quietly, "Poor Tom."

She looked up and saw that I was no longer crying,
no longer wailing my words. She said, "Damage is
done. Della's dead and Tom is coming home."

I thought about this and nodded. "What about the
babies?"

"Della's mum isn't up to looking after twins." Mrs
Hardy looked down into her tea. "It's for the best. Tom
needs those babies more than ever now. He's done so
well, Mrs Venables. So well. We knew he was a clever
lad, but . . . he's a doctor. A *doctor*! Everyone proud of
him. And then, along comes Della and falls in love with
him, and she's having a rotten time at home, and he

100

makes her happy, but then he also — somehow — makes her dependent on him so that she don't think she can live without him. And he marries her. And then, can you believe it, *then*, he falls in love. And not with Della, neither." She swigged the rest of her tea and took the mug to the sink. "Poor Tom. Della, too. Said she couldn't live without him — and she couldn't, could she?" She was crying now. Washing up fiercely and crying the same way. "But her death isn't Tom's fault. She would have died whether he loved her or not. I made them say that in front of him. Don't know whether he took it in or no." She dried her hands and drew on her gloves.

I took my cup to the sink and washed it. I said, "How will you manage? Two babies and Tom to look after?" I wasn't shocked. Just like me he was responsible for the death of his . . . spouse. But the woman he loved was not dead.

"He says he'll stay at home and see to them himself. He's got no idea. It'll take both of us. I was going to retire from the nursing home, anyway."

I said, "I'll help you." Then I held my breath, terrified I'd stepped out of line. Mrs Hardy had been patient and kind with me for a whole year. Had that given me any right to shove myself into her affairs? And why was I trying to do so — was it some kind of therapy for my own grief and guilt?

She pushed the cuffs of her gloves under the sleeves of her coat and said nothing for ages. I still held my breath.

She said, "Let's take it gently. Tom might not want anyone to help him, not even his mum and dad. But . . . p'raps it could work. If he gets a job here — and he will want to work — well, I could do with an hour off here and there." She gave the tiniest ironic smile. "I'm nearly sixty, you know."

"And I'm forty-one." I grabbed at the chance to lighten everything. I went to the door with her and we cheekpecked each other. "I bought the book. You know, the film we saw last month."

Mrs Hardy smiled again. "I enjoyed that. We'll have to do it again. Gets me away from the sport on the telly."

"Me, too." And I laughed. And after a surprised moment, so did she.

I spent time in the garden, and thought about the young man who had rushed past me in the waiting room of the maternity unit so recently. A much-loved, clever son of ordinary, probably rather bewildered, parents. They would not have pushed him, but he would still have wanted to make them proud. And the local school here, how they would have loved this boy! What a credit to their teaching! They would have pushed him all right; nurtured him, coached him, pulled every string they could. He would never have felt alone, and even when he landed up in Cheltenham he was only fifty miles from home and all that support. And then there had been Della, who had adored him, who had been unhappy at home and had needed him desperately. So he had married her.

I wasn't trying to find parallels; I didn't want to think of myself as another Della. I had found the strength to leave Dad and his symbolic belt a long time ago. Once Mum died there had been no doubt in my mind that I would leave home as soon as possible, and I always felt Mum had made it easy for me. Dad would have put every possible obstacle in the way of university, but he thoroughly approved of having a teacher for a daughter. I got a place at Bristol, and was well established ten years later when David came into my life.

No parallels at all. Nor with Tom Hardy. I had not fallen in love with anyone else. I had not.

Nevertheless I understood that Tom would always carry a weight with him now. I also understood that he was not free to run as I ran. He had two babies.

It started to rain, and I stood for a few more minutes, face upturned, licking the drops from around my mouth as they fell. I still did not know the sex of the twins, just as I would never now know the sex of my baby. I wondered for a dreadful second what would have happened if that baby had lived. I gasped and fled indoors.

I had assumed that Mrs Hardy would not stay to do her shift, but would hand in her notice and go straight home. But the bell ping-ponged after lunch, and there she was, looking much better for her morning on duty. She was due for a visit to the hairdresser, and the overgrown curls refused to be contained within her headscarf. I could see she might have been really pretty when she first met Mr Hardy.

She said, "I wasn't going to bother you again, but that Mr Jinks has been yapping at me since his lunch. He has to be fed, you know, else he won't bother. He told me you been to see him Sunday."

"Well, yes. It wasn't a good idea —"

"It was my idea. And I think it was good. He hasn't been so chatty for ages." She followed me into the kitchen, but shook her head when I picked up the kettle. "Got to get home in case Tom's arrived. Though I think Hardy would have phoned me at work . . . don't know." She looked at me sadly. "I don't know anything any more. Everything has gone from my grasp." I could see how awful that must be for her; she had always been in control.

She said, "I know he's a cantankerous old fool — Mr Jinks, I mean — but underneath it all he has got a heart. I think he was sorry for some of the things he said to you."

I swallowed. "Did he tell you what he said?"

"Not really. Just said he'd been a bit 'straight'. So I can guess. But he did mention old Juniper Stevens. She lives down by me, you know. One of they cottages by the river. With her daughter and son-in-law. She's knocking on a bit, early eighties, but she's still with it. They — the daughter and her hubbie — want her to come to Tall Trees, and she could do worse. Old Jinx wants you to talk to her. I could mention it to her, if you like."

I was going to shake my head very definitely, but then I didn't. Mrs Hardy wanted to be helpful; it was her nature to be helpful. I said that would be very kind of her. I found myself telling her a bit about the wretched door knob. To my surprise she was interested. Taken up by it. She looked like my staunch Mrs Hardy again.

"How did it get on the kitchen table, then?" she asked, her eyes wide.

"I've no idea. But it's definitely the same door knob I used to lever myself out of the lake that night. D'you remember, I was all scratched and bleeding and you bathed my feet with vinegar?"

"Course I remember. I thought it was a fall — well, it was a fall!" Her eyes widened still more. "And it just appeared here, like that?"

"I know. It sounds crazy. I've been through it dozens of times, and I hadn't left a window open or anything. Jinx thinks I've gone mad of course —"

"You're not mad — I'd put money on it," Mrs Hardy said staunchly. "It's obvious, innit? That door knob is a symbol. It saved your life. And it must have been put there by your David. So he brought it to you to show you that. Oh, my dear Lord . . ." She sat down abruptly.

I had thought that, too. But I said, "I don't think he did put it there. We used the lake a lot when we were courting, and after we were married. We used to set ourselves up with deckchairs and picnics and stay as long as the sun shone. I'm sure he would have told me about the door knob if he'd known about it."

"He must have known. But he didn't think it was important. Maybe Juniper told him?" She shook her head. "It's something, most likely simple, and we can't see it . . . did he propose to you proper-like?"

I swallowed, remembering. It hadn't been proper-like, not really. We had been planning a very private affair for about a month. Something my father couldn't spoil. But then David had asked me to marry him as if we hadn't been talking about it for ages. And he had got down on one knee, only half-jokingly, and produced a ring, and slipped it on my finger. It had happened on the little promenade, with moonlight rippling across the surface of the lake. It had been past midnight. Long past midnight. Somewhere around the same time of night as I had found the door knob two months ago . . .

Mrs Hardy said sharply, "He did, didn't he?"

"Well, sort of. It was a bit of a joke, really."

"He didn't think so."

"I don't know. It doesn't make sense."

"He's using that blessed door knob to tell you something." She was more like her old self. My problem was occupying her thoughts, ousting the terrible things that were happening to her family. "And Mr Clever-clever Jinks reckons Juniper Stevens can give the answer, does he?" She screwed up her face, considering. "He's a funny one, is that man. Enjoys stirring things up now and then. Used to stir up old Mr Venables, now he's doing it to you."

I felt the usual sick terror. I said, "Let's leave it, then. I don't see that it can help with what is happening now."

She gave me another of her searching looks, then nodded. "All right. Don't fret yourself. Just take in

106

what has happened. It — it's wonderful, really. And if ever you want to see old Juniper — lovely name — then let me know."

"And will you let me know if I can help out with the twins? That would be really wonderful!" I smiled. "D'you know, you haven't told me whether it's two girls or two boys or one of each —"

She too smiled. "It's one of each. No names ready or anything. Tom couldn't care less. But Hardy and me, we wondered about Michael for the boy. Hardy's name is Michael. And now I'll put it to Tom, Joy for the girl. It's beautiful, isn't it?"

"Yes. Yes it is." I went with her to the gate, marvelling at her resilience as I watched her bicycle make its normal bouncing way down to the first of the hairpins. I went on standing there, noting that the rain had come to nothing, but a wind was working itself up from the north-east. I did not like winds, they seemed to blow right through me as if I didn't exist. They made me feel like my father had always made me feel, as if I was nothing. I hurried indoors, and then out to the garden again to put away my tools. The prunings and their leaves were already blowing around everywhere, and I almost ran around the lawn gathering them up and thrusting them into the compost bin. I stood in the shelter of the tool-shed and watched the afternoon darken into early evening. "Michael and Joy Hardy," I murmured experimentally. "Joy and Mike." And then, slowly, "Della Hardy. Oh, Della, I am so sorry. I wonder whether you had a choice and you opted for death?"

I pushed away that morbid thought and locked the tool-shed and climbed the steps on to the patio and into the bungalow. Still shocked by my own thoughts, I laid a tea tray, cut bread and butter, and carried it all into the living room. The fire was laid, but for some reason I did not light it. I went back to the kitchen to make the tea. There's a long mirror in the hall, sited so that you can check your appearance on the way out of the front door. I watched myself walking towards it, and thought there was something wrong with my appearance. I went closer to see my face. And David was looking out of the mirror and into my eyes. I knew he was a figment of my imagination; but he was smiling and there wasn't a mark on him. His skin was clear and slightly tanned, as it always had been. And he was saying, "It's all right. You must know by now that everything is all right." But the mouth in the mirror did not move. His voice was low, it was his voice, but he was not speaking.

I was wearing the old fleece I wore for gardening; I grabbed a woolly hat from the hall stand, put keys in my pocket and left. I don't know where I went. I was back at the house as the clock in the hall struck ten. The mirror reflected me. Just me. Unkempt, haggard, even. Just me. I made tea and took it to bed. It still worked. The running. I could run from almost anything. Even David. My dear David. The man I loved, and yet had betrayed and then killed.

About four o'clock in the morning I went to sleep and dreamed about Della Hardy.

CHAPTER
EIGHT

Things moved quickly for the Hardys. The next day they drove to the flat in Cheltenham and began sorting out. Tom came home at lunchtime and they ate the pea soup his mother had brought with her. Then he took them to the maternity unit and they visited the twins. The babies were both asleep, their eyes sunk in surplus skin, cheeks and mouths already filling out. Tom said, "They're going to survive. They've already stopped being miracles, and they're babies in their own right."

Mrs Hardy glanced at him; he had changed. The enthusiasm had gone, and he was looking at the two small babies as if they did not belong to him. Too clinically. He went on, "I've been practising with dummies, but very soon now I'll be able to manage the real thing. Bath them and change them . . . normally."

Hardy said humorously, "Don't reckon anything will be normal again with them two around."

"I don't mean we can go back to what we were, Dad." Tom smiled, then suddenly stopped smiling. "I don't want to do that, anyway. But our lives should be normal for people who have babies. Chaotic probably. But normal."

Mrs Hardy nodded, as if he had said something profound. "You're right there, our Tom. Mrs Venables has offered to give us a break now and then for a few hours. We'll manage, I reckon. But it will be . . . chaotic." She told them about the names, and Tom described how to feed twins at the same time, head to head. Then they all went back to the flat, and decided which things should be kept, and which sold.

On the way home Mrs Hardy said, "Love . . . do you believe in ghosts?"

Hardy frowned into the snake of headlights on the north-bound carriageway of the M5, and was glad he was driving south.

"Don't reckon I do," he said, at last.

"Not even . . . not ever?" she persisted. "What if I died? Don't you think I might be able to come back now and then just to . . . see you?"

"Ah . . . that might be different." He turned his head sharply and tried to see her in the darkness of the car. "You en't ill, are you?"

She laughed. "Course not," she said. And crossed her fingers beneath the pile of bags on her lap.

They went up three times more during that week. They worked on rearranging the house by the river to accommodate three more people. Mrs Hardy took a great deal of stuff to the charity shop in the village. Even so, the little house was still crowded.

At the end of the week they felt they were as ready as they were ever going to be. "They'll be here for

110

Christmas," Mrs Hardy said, her voice a mixture of pleasure and apprehension.

Hardy had just come in from his final trip to Cheltenham. He put a big box on the kitchen table. "Just ran into Juniper's girl. They persuaded old Juniper to go up to Tall Trees. She's incontinent. They couldn't manage any longer."

Mrs Hardy opened the box and peered inside; it was full of Tom's medical equipment. She said, "I'm really sorry. She didn't want to go. I'll walk up and see her tomorrow. Help her to settle in, perhaps."

Hardy nodded and sighed. "I knew you'd say that."

Vivian's story

A week went by. Mrs Hardy did not drop in, the phone did not ring. I kept the door knob on the kitchen table, and looked at it each morning, half-expecting it to disappear as mysteriously as it had appeared. The weather was awful: gales in the mornings, quietly exhausted afternoons, evening darkness with no visible sunset, the gales whipping up again in the night. Everything became difficult once more. I didn't want to run because of the weather, and I could not get out in the garden, same reason. I knew the Hardys were having a difficult time, and I wanted to help them but was frightened of overwhelming them. Christmas was drawing inexorably closer, but I did nothing about it. This time last year I had returned home from hospital and barricaded myself into the bungalow to avoid all the callers. It was a life-saver to discover my strange predilection for running; I had worked on that to the exclusion of everything else. When I got too weak to run I realized I was not eating properly, and began my midnight forays to all-night garages and motorway service stations. Christmas must have come and gone somehow. This year was different. This year I was noticing how the days went by and what happened in them; I recognized I had choices about what to do. One of the obvious diurnal conditions was the weather. I had not noticed the weather last winter, yet this winter I found I did not want to run in driving rain — so I chose not to. Just as I chose not to contact Mrs Hardy because . . . because I was more concerned with her welfare than my own.

I drifted into the kitchen and picked up the door knob. Then I moved into the living room and peered out at the thrashing shrubs and the grey pall, beyond which was the sea and the little huddle of houses on its edge. As darkness swallowed up the fog of rain, small lights appeared twinkling crazily around the base of the Tump. They were Christmas lights. I put on my anorak and got the car out and drove down to look at them. Of course, that was what the lorry had been for on that Saturday two weeks ago: the council workers had been stringing up the Christmas lights. And now they were switched on.

I drove around the village half a dozen times, watching the lights as they fought with rain and wind to say . . . whatever they were meant to say. "Christmas is a-coming," I suppose. It was December, after all. I glanced at the cinema doorway where people were queuing with their children to see a Disney film. "Matinee, Saturday, 9 December" announced the advertisement.

Just over two weeks until Christmas day.

I drove down to the bandstand and past the wispy string of fairy lights along the promenade. The fog was thicker here, yet two women were trudging slowly along by the railing as if it were a lovely summer afternoon. I slowed and wound down my window. One of them was crying, and hobbling, almost falling over, the other was trying to soothe her. The one who was doing the soothing was Mrs Hardy.

I stopped the car and leapt out. They were both startled; Mrs Hardy recognized me almost immediately and looked relieved.

"Someone up there has sent you, Mrs Venables. Just caught this one trying to jump over the blessed railings — tide's in, she wouldn't have lasted but a few minutes!"

"Oh my God!" I took the woman's other arm.

She started to wail again. I made out the words "There's no point —"

Then Mrs Hardy said, "It's that Juniper Stevens old Mr Jinks told you about. She's not been well, and her daughter has got her a place at Tall Trees . . ." She turned to her companion and bent over. "I'm just telling Mrs Venables, here, that you don't fancy coming to see me at the nursing home!" She tried to make it sound jocular, pretending to take umbrage, but Juniper Stevens could see nothing funny in this situation, and wailed again.

Mrs Hardy said to me, "Could you take us up to your place for half an hour, my dear? Get her a cup of tea and calm her down, then I can ring the home and her daughter. They're sure to have reported her missing by now. I told them I knew where she'd be, but of course they have to cover themselves."

I opened one of the back doors, and between us we got the woman inside. I grabbed a rug from the parcel shelf and tucked her up, then fastened her belt over the top of the rug. She could barely move, but it seemed to comfort her, and she stopped wailing and started to mutter. Mrs Hardy got in the other side and patted her. "Not even a coat — no, I know it's not cold for the time of year, but that doesn't mean you can't catch cold." I started up and drove towards the Tump. "Oh Mrs Venables, this is good of you. I don't quite know what I would have done. I don't think we could've walked back."

I flashed her a smile in the mirror as I negotiated one of the bends. I felt almost elated by this turn of events, and at the same time, guilty. Poor Mrs Stevens crouched within the circle of Mrs Hardy's arms, and muttered her distress. Mrs Hardy said, "There, there, love. You'll be all right. Mrs Venables is going to take us to her house and make a nice cup of tea, and then I'll come back with you to that lovely bedroom of yours and put you to bed. How does that sound?" She lifted her head and spoke to me. "I haven't been to work till today — it's like a madhouse at home. Then they asked me if I would go in and sit with Mrs Stevens tonight, and when I got there she'd . . . gone for a walk." She made it sound perfectly normal. I thought how marvellous it would be to be looked after by Mrs Hardy.

We bumped over the kerb and on to the drive, and I unlocked the door and put on lights. Between us we got Juniper Stevens into the living room and by the fire. I lifted the coals with the poker and put on some wood. It crackled and flamed, and Mrs Stevens stopped muttering and watched it.

I said, "She's tired out. Stay with her while I make some tea." I touched Mrs Hardy's shoulder on the way out. "It's good to see you."

While the kettle simmered into life I opened a packet of biscuits that Mrs Hardy had brought with her before Della died, and washed up half-a-dozen mugs. The kitchen was a mess; I'd been home all day and my kitchen was still a mess. I felt the usual pang of housewifely shame. Then I put mugs and biscuits on to a tray, made the tea and took it all back into the living room.

They were sitting side by side on the sofa facing the dark window. The curtains were undrawn and Mrs Hardy was pointing out the lights below. They were brighter now, so the fog must be lifting.

"See?" Mrs Hardy's voice was blessedly familiar, and reminded me how much I had missed her. "Those coloured ones are going down the pier. Then the white ones are along the prom, and you can follow them right up to the cinema . . . see?"

Mrs Stevens peered out of her bundle of clothes and made a grunting sound of assent. Mrs Hardy took her hand in both of hers and rubbed it gently. "You can see them from your new room, you know. Just the same. When I was a little girl we used to come up here just to look down and see the village all lit up. I used to think we was like the shepherds on the hillside looking down at Bethlehem."

Mrs Stevens and I both turned from the window to look at her. She shook her head, embarrassed. "I've always been one for make-believe," she said.

Mrs Stevens spoke hoarsely but very clearly. "I remember you when you was a kiddie. You was little Hildie Wendover. Your dad worked for the squire hedging and ditching an' your ma was at the laundry. They did say you was small cos all your strength went into your hair."

Mrs Hardy smiled. "I could sit on my hair," she said. She reached for one of the mugs and held it for Mrs Stevens, then drank her own.

I looked at her curls and stocky figure, and could almost see little Hildie Wendover. I wondered whether Mrs Hardy still had Hildie's imagination.

"I'll tell you something." She was looking at Juniper Stevens, but I knew this was for me. "I nearly didn't marry Hardy. Almost forty years we been married, and I nearly missed it all because I didn't like the sound of Hilda Hardy." She laughed. "Little Hildie Wendover sounded just right to me. But Hilda Hardy?" She laughed properly, clutching her midriff against a stitch.

Amazingly, Mrs Stevens joined her. And then she spluttered, "Well, I never married my first sweetheart for that very reason, and ain't I glad I din't! Juniper

Jinks! You ever 'eard anything so daft in all your life? Juniper Jinks!"

Mrs Hardy opened her eyes wide at me. Then she shook her head again. "Well I never! I didn't know that! We're having quite a conversation here, aren't we?" She stared into Juniper's empty mug. "Whatever did you put into this tea, Mrs Venables?"

I, too, shook my head. "I don't know. But I might as well admit that I am Viv Venables . . . well, you knew that, of course." The fire fell in and I crouched to feed it, and then turned on one knee to look at them. "Everyone uses forenames these days. Will you call me Viv? And may I use your names too — Juniper and Hildie? They are lovely names."

Juniper suddenly wailed, and then said, "Oh . . . my dear Lord. I've done it again. Bin and wet myself!"

Mrs Hardy — Hildie — was stricken, even though I made light of it without difficulty. Silently, she sponged the sofa cover and put a clean towel on it to dry it. Meanwhile, Juniper was grimly capable, taking herself into the bathroom and stripping off her underclothes, and letting me wash her down and fetch clean knickers from my bedroom.

"This was what my daughter could not manage," she grunted sadly. "That's why her and her husband got me into Tall Trees. I can't seem to do nothing about it. I'm that sorry. And you been so kind . . ."

"Juniper. Stop apologizing. You were right to go to Tall Trees. They will sort you out so that it won't worry you. Listen, I'll come and see you. And someone will help you to visit me, too. Try not to think of it as the end of everything. It's a new beginning really . . ." I heard myself saying all the usual things. Truisms. They were called that because they were true.

Juniper's daughter, who turned out to be older than Mrs Hardy, appeared soon after, and sat with her mother, holding her hand until two nurses from Tall Trees knocked on the door because they could not see the bell. They had a wheelchair and we swathed Juniper in the car rug and walked back up the hill with her. Mrs Hardy — Hildie — decided she could do no more, and came back with me, and for another hour we sat by the fire and talked about Juniper, and how odd it was that she and Jinx had had some kind of relationship.

"When he spoke to you he could not have known that she was going to be coming to Tall Trees," Hildie mused. "I wonder whether it was his devious way of trying to get back in touch with her?"

"I'm glad she didn't marry him. She seems much too nice."

"Yes." Hildie sighed. "I'd better be going. Hardy will want supper. He's been in Cheltenham all day, loading Tom's stuff." She shook her head. "We've brought more back each day. There's so much needs cleaning up. I meant to phone you but it were always so late when we got back . . ."

I patted her hand and made reassuring sounds. "What about Joy and Michael?" I was determined to name them from the outset.

"Still in hospital. They need to put on some weight. They're so tiny . . . how Della would have coped . . . well, we shall never know. Sometimes I wake up and think none of it has happened and then . . . it crashes in all over again." She put a hand to her head, and I patted her shoulder awkwardly, and she half-turned to give me a smile. "It's all right, Mrs Venables . . . Viv. I'm so busy I don't have a chance to dwell on it. I've been doing out the back room for the kiddies. We had the box room made into a bathroom back in the seventies, and I've got the washing machine there, so it will be next to their nursery. Luckily we had that dormer room put in the attic at the same time. It will be just right for poor Tom. He can work up there if he needs to." She sighed again. "I don't know how he's going to cope. He's still got no idea of the amount of work from one baby, let alone two."

I thought of our spare bedroom; it was full of David's books and clothes. I hadn't been in it since . . . then. Could I transfer the books into the dining room? And what about the clothes? I squeezed my eyes shut, and opened them to find Hildie standing up and taking gloves from her pocket.

"I'll take you home," I said. "Really. I insist." I ignored her protests and fetched my coat and car keys. The fog had definitely lifted, but there was still no moon or stars, and the street lamps made small and isolated pools of light only.

When we got down to the river she said, "No light. He's not back yet. Come on in and see what I've been up to."

I followed her into a long narrow passage ending in stairs. A door on the right led into a big living room, a table at one end, armchairs and a sofa at the other.

"Hardy took down the middle wall, gave us a bit more room. Tom wasn't keen on working in his room. All that studying . . . he could do it better with us around and the telly on — or so he said!" She laughed, and I said something about him doing all right anyway. She nodded. "He did that. Poor lad. This is the first really bad thing that's happened to him. Anyway, come on upstairs and see the nursery."

It was a dream: one side pink, the other blue, the ceiling yellow, the cots white. "I got them in the charity shop. Not quite matching, so I painted them white. You got to get special paint in case they try to eat it!"

I was full of admiration. "It's just lovely." I looked at her. "Oh Hildie. They are so lucky. Coming home to this, and to you and Hardy."

"Well, actually, they're coming home to Tom. I know that sounds obvious, but officially, they will be living with him and we will just happen to be around!" She laughed uncomfortably. "It's to do with the Social Services and Della's mother. Apparently."

I looked at the identical mobiles clipped to the end of each cot. "Are you all right with it?"

There was no need to ask, really, and she just smiled and nodded. "These are new. I got them from that big baby shop in the Mall." She pressed a switch on a mobile and it went round, displaying birds and butterflies and playing a nursery rhyme. "You can have them without the music. And you can have the music without the movement. Hardy reckons I bought them for myself, never mind the babies!" She laughed again, and I realized how nervous she was.

"Hildie, please don't forget that I can help out at any time. Really."

"I know. And I know you mean it. But what with Tom being shell-shocked, and all the chit-chat from Social Services . . . I can't help feeling a bit nervy. It's daft I know —"

"No it's not, because ultimately you will bear most of the responsibility. But I do want you to know that I'm there, and I should be honoured to have them." She laughed again, and I said soberly, "Hildie, there are plenty of people in this village who would not countenance me as a childminder. They think at the best I am a careless driver, and at the worst —"

She grabbed my arm. "Don't you dare even say it! I know what that old goat Jinx said to you."

"There was nothing wrong with the car, Hildie. I lost control, and it could well have been my fault. I was in a bit of a state at the time —"

"I think they missed something, Viv. It was obviously an accident, so they didn't have one of those specialist police teams on the job. I've said it all along — there was something the matter with that car. Nothing to do with you being in a state." She looked up at me. "It was not your fault," she said slowly and emphatically.

I tightened my lips against sudden tears, and nodded just as slowly. At that moment I believed her.

Even so, when I got home I still avoided looking in the hall mirror.

CHAPTER
NINE

Tom fetched the twins on Monday morning. It was 18 December, and everyone else was thinking of Christmas.

The journey home was difficult, and their arrival was chaotic. The babies had not enjoyed the journey, and had complained bitterly from their individual car-seats. Tom tried them with the radio, but the noise they made completely drowned it. By the time they crossed the river and turned right alongside the terraced cottages, he was using a technique he had learned when Della's mother had ranted at him, after Della's death, when everything had become insupportable. He tightened his muscles until his whole being was compressed into a grim stoicism and he became nothing but an efficient machine.

His parents were bewildered by both the noise and Tom's strange behaviour. As the car-seats came into the house, and the neighbours came out of theirs, they admitted to each other, much later, that they felt invaded. Invaded by their own son and their brand-new miraculous grandchildren. It made no sense at all. Tilly-next-door shouted above the cacophony, "They'll settle soon enough, don't worry."

Hildie whispered to Hardy, "How soon is soon enough?"

And Hardy whispered back, "Not soon enough by half, I'd say."

Tom took off his coat, lifted both babies on to the sofa, unwound blankets, unpopped Babygros, and used wet wipes with a kind of grim determination. The twins were both, in turn, momentarily taken aback, and their nerve-twanging whine became sporadic.

Tom said, "Leave the car, Ma, we can unpack later. Can you make up a couple of bottles of that milk stuff? I'll feed them now. They've been like this the whole journey, so they should sleep."

Somehow, they struggled through that first afternoon and evening. Tom looked cadaverous; Hardy not much better. Hildie thought about the long night ahead and the even longer day after that. And the funeral. Della's funeral, which was on Thursday.

She said brightly, "I'll phone Viv in a minute and ask her to come to tea tomorrow."

Vivian's story

It was Monday. I went to see Juniper Stevens in Tall Trees, and wheeled her down to the Tump to look at the misty sea and the pier, and to ask her how she was.

"I'm resigned, I suppose." She looked up at me from the chair. "Don't suppose I'd ever have got one leg over the railings, let alone the whole of me, but just for a minute or two it seemed such a good idea." She grinned; she had her teeth in and seemed pretty well with-it. "I reckon I've passed my sell-by date. If you're not needed by someone or something, then you can't help wondering what you're doing taking up space someone else could use!"

She didn't sound bitter; but she was serious all right. I replied just as seriously. "I know what you mean, Juniper — I know exactly what you mean."

"No, you don't, my lovely. You was a teacher, everyone knows that. You gave it up after the accident. Well, you're fit now, and you haven't gone back to it. But you know you could. You might feel useless, but you could change all that."

No one had spoken so straight to me before.

She said, "Let's go up to that seat, then you can sit down and look me in the eye and tell me to mind my own bloody business."

I wheeled the chair up the rough road, put the brake on again, and almost collapsed on to the slatted seat. Wheelchairs are like supermarket trolleys and have minds of their own.

She said, "Go on."

I said, "How do you know . . . all that stuff?"

"Tisn' a very big place. Old Mr Venables had a good job at the museum, then came to live here. Very respected he was, too. We didn't know your David that well, but we was pleased to find he'd married a nice girl and wanted to live locally. We wasn't that particularly curious. But we was interested." She looked at me; she had cloudy blue eyes, and somewhere in their depths I could see something . . . sympathy?

I said carefully, "What else do you know, Juniper?"

124

She did not answer for some time. Her gaze went past me to the indistinct horizon. She said at last, "Some people say you did it deliberately."

"Why would I have done that?" I held my breath.

She gave a tiny shrug. "To kill him? To kill yourself?"

I let my breath go. "I had no reason to do either, Juniper."

She shrugged again. "John Jinks did put it about you wasn't sleeping together. Maybe your man looked somewhere else. Happened to me and my Charley."

There was so much information there, I couldn't take it in at first. I said lamely, "Married couples have difficulties. They work through them." What had Jinx been *saying*?

"That's zackly what I said to him, my dear. He's a trouble-maker, he is." She was triumphant, and my heartbeat decelerated. "I had to do just the same. Work through it. My Charley, he had a fling, too. And it was after that I fell for my little one. Just like you. Only, praise be, I did not lose her." She sighed deeply. "Don't worry, Vivian Venables. You're still working your way through it. Think like that, and it won't be so bad." She saw my expression, and added, "That was your name, wasn't it? Vivian?"

I wanted to shout and laugh. Juniper Stevens thought David had had a fling — was that what she was saying? If only . . . if only it had been that. I nodded to my name.

She was off again. "When you get to my age, you understand how things happen. And once they've happened you can't put the clock back, so you just got to get on with it. Some folks just sit on it, push it right away and say they've forgotten all about it. I'd rather deal with it like you are. Work through it."

She obviously had not heard about my running. I wondered what else she knew. I tested her out.

"You and Jinx . . . you were saying last night about not wanting to marry someone with the same initial . . . you were actually going to marry him?" I tried to make my voice incredulous and teasing at the same time.

Her chin wobbled, as if she might be trying to toss her head. "He wanted me to. He said I drove him mad. We met at one of the dances in the war. I was eighteen and he was a bit older — he says he's the same age as me, but he was born just after the Armistice so he's four years older. And he knew a thing or two. Turned my head right round the other way, he did. We used to meet down by the lake — watch the moon on the water, that sort of thing. He tried it on one night and I pushed him in!" She cackled with laughter, then sobered. "I didn't know he couldn't swim. He was floundering about — it's over twelve feet deep in places. Anyway I knew something about that lake. That's where I was begun . . . what's the word? Conceived. That's where I was conceived, and my mam always took me down when the lake was dredged, to see what she called our family crest." She shook her head. "A door knob. An old-fashioned brass door knob. Can you believe it? Apparently the man who was my father worked on that lake, and the night I was begun — conceived — he drove a great hole in the wall of the lake and cemented in a door knob. He told my mam that one day it would open for someone . . . when it was important enough. What d'you think of that? It was very romantic for an ordinary everyday mason, wasn't it?" She cackled again. "Luckily I knew exactly where it was because there's a mark on top of the wall. I just laid on the wall, took old Jinx's hand when it came up, and put it right on that-there door knob. And he heaved himself up. Reckoned I'd saved his life, so I'd got to marry him. I almost believed him, but then when he went back off leave I met my Charley, and I knew straight off he was the right one. Even when he was all dazzled by Jeannie Watkins from the haberdasher's, I knew he was still the one. And I was right. He was."

She became conscious of my stare, and frowned. "I haven't been and shocked you, have I? Talking too much? I thought it'd help to know other people have had your problems and learned to live with them." She looked away morosely. "Anyway, it's supposed to do me good to talk."

"Yes — yes. Don't stop. I'm surprised, but I'm not shocked, not in the way you mean. Keep going." She sucked in her lips stubbornly. I said, "Tell me about your mother and . . . and the door knob. When you said about it opening . . . is there a door behind it?"

She laughed. "No, course not. No secret passages behind, neither. He meant when it pulled out it would mean something . . . not that it will ever pull out until the whole lake is broken up. It's like part of the rock itself, you should test it yourself some time."

127

I had of course done just that, and could vouch for its total firmness. Yet it was at the moment lying on my kitchen table.

There was such a long pause I thought she really had dried up, but then she sighed and started again.

"The bloody door knob was the reason I didn't have nothing much more to do with old Jinx. It reminded me of what Mam had said when she warned me about the American soldiers and told me to keep my knickers on." She cackled her laugh. "We had a good old row that day. Ended up with me yelling at her that if she'd kept hers on I wouldn't be cooking and cleaning up at the gatekeeper's, then back home doing the same thing for her. And she reminded me about the door knob, and how it was the most romantic thing ever happened to her, and my dad was the only man she'd ever really loved, and though it had been hard having me without him around she never regretted it . . ." She sighed. "They would've got married. Or so she said. He was drownded a day later, when they opened the gates and let the sea water flood into the lake. They reckoned it would take three or four high tides to do the job proper, like. But that high tide was the highest we'd had for twenty years, and it came over the top of the wall like Niagara Falls, and he was there checking the gates, and his foot got caught on the lever and held him down. They dived and dived, but when they brought him up he was dead. Poor Mam. She never got over it. Neither did I. Not really. It was another thing I had to get on with. So I decided the door knob was telling me

128

something that night. It saved Jinx's life, I suppose, and it warned me . . . it warned me . . ."

I glanced at her, and saw she was going through her memories as if they were a series of photographs. I did not doubt that she had had to put up with taunts in those good old days, when the village had been really small and everyone had known that she was . . . illegitimate. What a word to use about an innocent child! Possibly the Second World War had done away with a lot of bigotry, but not all of it. I, too, sat there and let a few of my own memories filter back, and thanked God that Jinx hadn't told Juniper everything.

I wheeled her back to Tall Trees and into her room; for the moment she was staying out of the main rooms. Hildie Hardy had told me that new arrivals were allowed to keep themselves to themselves for a while. "No one expects them to take it all in at once; bad enough that they've had to give up their homes. Let them have some privacy," she had said. I helped Juniper out of her wheelchair and into a recliner next to the window. As I walked back to the Tump it occurred to me that she probably did not know that her old flame was in the same building.

The message machine was flashing as I walked briskly down the hall — not looking in the direction of the mirror. It was Hildie.

"Viv? Funny, I can't think of you as anything but Mrs Venables yet! Listen, Tom has fetched the babies. They're here! We're all at sixes and sevens, but I do want you to meet them properly as soon as possible.

129

Will you come to tea? Tomorrow? Just sandwiches and cakes. I'd like you to be here right at the beginning. I thought we could put them to bed between us. Let me know."

I felt diffident, to say the least. Tom did not know me, presumably he was in a bad way; it was difficult enough to have to rely on his parents, but a strange woman thrust into the tragic scenario seemed . . . unnecessary. I rang to tell Hildie how I felt.

She said flatly, "Viv . . . it's Della's funeral on Thursday. I was hoping . . . I know it's a lot to ask. If you come to tea tomorrow you could see if you were able to face a day with them. They are noisy. Tom was all prepared to take them with us, but what between the weather —"

I interrupted gladly. "I'd be so happy to come and be with them, Hildie. We've talked of this. If Tom agrees, then . . . of course."

"Then come to tea tomorrow, and get to know the ropes, Viv. Besides, I would like to see you. Everything seems so odd. It would be good to have a nice ordinary chat."

I smiled into the receiver; did we really have nice ordinary chats? It was a comforting thought. I said of course, of course, and then that I would make a cake and arrive about three o'clock so that I could help with the sandwiches.

I made two cakes, because the first one was flat. I had no jam in the house so had to take the car out to the garage shop, and they only had marmalade. A marmalade Victoria sponge. It was different, anyway.

I had been going to run that evening — facing my own memories as I sat by Juniper on the Tump had been incredibly difficult, and I had promised myself that as soon as I got home I would change into jogging pants and trainers and just go. But then there had been Hildie on the phone and the Victoria sponges, and the drive out to the M5 for marmalade, and then, frankly, I was exhausted. I ate a piece of bread and marmite and went to bed. I woke at seven thirty and felt refreshed. Perhaps I should stop jogging and take up baking.

It was ideal Tuesday morning weather, breezy, clouds moving along briskly to show some weak sunshine, but by afternoon the clouds were incessant and the breeze was bitterly cold. I brought the washing in and folded it for ironing. Then I drove down to the river and Hildie Hardy's terraced cottage and found that both sides of the road were nose-to-tail with the cars of people using the nearby pub. I drove on almost a quarter of a mile, and parked in the forecourt of the Rod and Creel, and walked back with my cling-filmed cake clutched in front of me. I hadn't brought a hat or gloves; my hands were frozen, my face blotchy red, my hair escaping unattractively from its ponytail. I took a bet with myself that Tom would open the door. Thank God I lost. Hildie looked comfortably domesticated in blue jumper and skirt, covered with what she called an afternoon apron. She took the cake plate with exclamations of delight, and led me in to the big living room, which had been taken over almost completely by a twin buggy; both armchairs were full of packets of nappies. Mr Hardy looked nervous, sitting at an awkward angle at one end of the sofa. The two babies, surrounded by cushions, slept peacefully at the other end. Hildie said, "We're going to put the kettle on, Hardy. Don't move. Keep an eye on the babies in case they try to roll off." Mr Hardy moved fractionally, and flashed me a quick smile.

Hildie put the cake on the table amidst plates of sandwiches, and edged round into the kitchen. I followed.

"He needs a definite job," she said, angling her head in the general direction of her husband. "Tom's gone for a quick walk, to get some air. You know." I knew. "I don't want Hardy to feel left out. Can you cut and butter the scones, Viv?"

So I was allied with Mr Hardy. And Tom had been sent for a walk. I asked after Tom.

Hildie stopped assembling her best china, and stared through the window at the long narrow garden. "'Tis such a terrible business. And the funeral being delayed cos of the autopsy. Still, Tom's all I care about. I don't think he knows what to feel. He's now saying he can't go to the funeral — couldn't leave the babies, he said!" She rubbed at some teaspoons and clattered them on to saucers. "I told him about you. I said the three of us would be going, and that was that." She glanced at me, suddenly anxious. "You will be able to manage, won't you, Viv? You'll have to come here. There's so much stuff with the two of them, it will be easier for you down here."

I swallowed, but nodded quickly. In my imagination I had seen myself wheeling the babies to the top of the

Tump to show them the view . . . young editions of Juniper Stevens. And even that cosy pipe-dream had taken place in an unspecified future. Suddenly everything was upon me. I could barely look after myself, and on Thursday I had to look after two other human beings. In two days' time. I was struck by a very real terror.

"It will be easier when you've got the place to yourself. We're all bursting at the seams now. I haven't sorted out their stuff yet, and that blessed buggy needs a room for itself. But once we're out of the way you'll feel properly in charge." She gave me that anxious look again. "They really are good babies, Viv."

"I can see . . ." I tried to smile reassuringly.

She poured sugar into a bowl. "If you could just start them off . . . Tilly-next-door is home by eleven in the mornings — she does office cleaning — and she'd take over if you had problems. I'll leave you her number. Tom wanted to phone an agency. He can afford it. I just thought they should start to become part of . . . us. Soon as possible."

I rallied somehow. "Sorry — did my nerves show?" I smiled again. "Listen, of course I'm going to be nervous, surely we're all nervous? We've got to learn how to do this and the only way is to . . . do it!" I put the final scone on top of the pyramid on the plate. It occurred to me again how wonderful it was that Hildie Hardy was trusting me with her grandchildren. She knew about my troubles and my running; she had bathed my scratches that terrible night in the autumn. Yet she had chosen me above Tilly-next-door and a professional agency. It occurred to me then that she was doing it for my sake as well as the babies.

Tom did not join us at the table. He took his father's place on the sofa, and his mother brought him a plate of sandwiches and scones and cake. He ate some of it.

He did not look much like the young man who had run through the waiting room four weeks before. His hair was still on end, and he appeared to be wearing the same sweater, but there was an air of exhaustion about him that I recognized in my own bones. His perpetual motion was essential to him, but he was tired out by it.

He barely looked at me. His mother introduced me. "This is Viv Venables, who I told you would help us out with the babies sometimes. Viv, you will have gathered this is Tom, our son."

He managed to take my outstretched hand for a second, but his attention was on the twins, who were making tiny waking-up noises, and as soon as he could he reached over and lifted one of them on to the towel spread over his knees. And then came the other one. He put them head to head so that their legs could kick freely either side of him.

Hildie said, "I'd never seen this way of feeding babies before, have you, Viv?"

"No. It's very practical."

Both twins were working up to a full-throated protest. Mr Hardy had moved some of the nappies, and was sitting in his chair; he got up briskly as the sound crescendoed and went into the kitchen. Tom put a hand on each head and gently massaged the fluffy scalps. "There, there," he said hoarsely.

Hildie said proudly, "Tom has been to baby-care classes and knows how to feed them, change them and bath them."

They did not appear to appreciate the massage: their legs catapulted upward as if pulled on the same puppetstring, the noise got worse.

Mr Hardy reappeared holding two bottles; Hildie shook some from each on to her wrist and smiled congratulations. "Just right, my dear," she shouted. "You've mastered it, all right."

Tom took a bottle in each hand and presented them to the babies. There was a little kerfuffle as the rosebud mouths found the teats, then instant peace.

I said wonderingly, "It's so obvious when you see it happening, but I never fully realized that twins were fed together, with their heads actually touching!"

Tom registered my presence properly. "Apparently this is the way you do it if you're breast-feeding. It makes perfect sense when you think about it."

Hildie said quickly, "You don't have to do it this way, Viv. So long as they both get fed it doesn't really matter."

Tom removed one of the bottles to let air fill a temporary vacuum; the response was instant, and almost as noisy as before. He said ruefully, "Actually, it does matter, Ma. If you feed them in turn the last one protests constantly."

I was fascinated by his efficiency. He caught my eye. "I'm a fast learner anyway, but I had to be very fast about this." It should have been said with a smile, but Tom Hardy had very little to smile about.

I insisted on clearing away the dishes on my own. Hildie sat by Tom and winded one baby, while he patted and joggled the other. He was not really interested in names — I rather doubted whether he had seen the babies yet as people. Hildie said she was cuddling Mike and he had Joy. He made no objection to "Mike" but raised his brows slightly at the name "Joy". I covered sandwiches and scones with cling film and arrayed them along the dresser, then carried out the crockery and cutlery. It was all beautiful bone china and silver-plated spoons and cake forks. I washed, rinsed and polished them, and Mr Hardy came and put them away while I wiped down the sink and draining board.

He said in a low voice, "It will get better. It's all so . . . new."

"I know . . . I know." I murmured back.

He cleared his throat and said, "When I'm up on the Tump next time I'd better take your loppers for a sharpen and clean, Mrs Venables. And after the winter flowering stuff is over, perhaps you'd like me to prune it right down. It's getting in the way of your view, I expect."

"That would be really nice." I smiled at him.

I was even more grateful when he walked with me to the Rod and Creel: it was a starless night and there seemed to be a lot of teenage boys about. Some of them were wearing hooded sweatshirts with the hoods pulled right over their heads. I said apologetically, "I never used to be nervous at night. I don't quite know why I am now."

He took my arm as we stepped off the kerb. "You were like our Tom, weren't you? Sort of dead inside. And now . . . well, perhaps you're coming to life again. D'you think that's it?"

He got into the passenger side and I drove the car carefully between all the others parked on either side of their narrow road and dropped him outside the cottage. Was I coming to life again? I had no idea.

When I got home, I'd intended to walk down the hall and into the kitchen, eyes front the whole time. But after I'd switched on the light I turned slowly and looked into the mirror.

My own reflection looked back at me. There I was, straggly ponytail, student duffle coat which came out just before Christmas every year, jeans and trainers . . . I was forty-one. I would never have children now. My eyes filled and the reflection became blurred. That was why it looked so much like David.

I started to cry. I'd done rather a lot of crying lately because of Hildie; now it was because of me. It was all such a waste. Such a terrible waste.

CHAPTER
TEN

The twins did not "go through the night" as the hospital had promised. After the morning bath and feed they slept for a precious hour. Hardy took the van out on to the road and loaded it ready for work. Tom walked to the health centre to talk to their GP about the new situation at the riverside cottage. They left Hildie hovering over the cots.

She had had worse nights. Sometimes at Tall Trees she had sat all night long holding a gnarled hand, and still put the washing on as soon as she got home. She had not even got out of bed last night; Tom had absolutely forbidden it.

"They need the same person to deal with them, Ma. If they gradually learn that there are three of us ready to leap out of bed at the first murmur, then they will see that as the norm."

So she had stayed in bed and listened to him creeping about changing nappies and administering boiled water. She was exhausted. She had not realized she was weeping until Hardy's arm came around her.

When Tom came in he made her leave the babies and have coffee. "Dad's gone to work." She wailed something about sandwiches, and he went on, "He's going to finish early. About two-ish. I'll take the babies out for a walk and let you have an afternoon nap. He can have a sandwich then."

"Oh Tom. It's cold and so grey. Surely they shouldn't go out in this?"

"They live in good old England, Ma. Got to get used to it some time." He forced a smile. "Listen. Give your Mrs Venables a ring. I'll go up there and have a look at her place. If she's offering to babysit now and then we need to check everything is safe."

"Oh Tom . . ." She thought of the steep hill and poor Mrs Venables, probably put off for ever by yesterday's tea party. Viv. She must remember to call her Viv. "I ought to tell you about Mrs Venables."

"Not now, Ma. I can see she is a responsible woman. That is all I need to know."

She looked at him. Haggard; that was the word for her son now. He looked haggard. It was his wife's funeral tomorrow.

Then he smiled and took her hands in both of his. "I'm sorry, Ma. But you know what you've always said. 'There's nothing that time can't scab over.'"

She smiled back.

It worked out well. They had a sandwich lunch, Tom fed the twins and packed them into the long, unwieldy buggy and left.

Vivian's story

At three o'clock the next morning it all became unbearable. I hadn't slept. At first I had given in to the

139

bouts of terrible weeping; then I had stared into the darkness at some kind of void. I could not have borne the radio, I felt I could bear nothing any more, not even running. Yet I got up automatically, threw on jogging stuff, rammed the door knob into one of the pockets, and left the bungalow. I want to remember that; I was not running away this time. I was running towards . . . something.

It was still foggy so there were no visible stars; the street lamps were aureoled again. I lifted my knees high to avoid tripping. It occurred to me I was running like an ostrich. David would have delighted in lampooning me in a cartoon. His ostrich would have been undeniably me; I couldn't think of a caption. Something to do with legs, of course. I pushed my upper half backwards and pouted my mouth into a beak and lifted my legs still higher. Still couldn't come up with a caption. But . . . at least I was remembering David as he really had been, wasn't I? He had always seen human beings as so . . . *fallible*. Vulnerable. And he had protected them by — by lampooning them. Was he still trying to show me that life — everything — was one big lampoon? The door knob. That bloody door knob. Was that part of the lampoon? Did it make the unbearable . . . bearable?

No. The answer to that was no.

I stopped at the first hairpin and looked towards where the sea must be, and I wailed aloud, "Oh God . . . I miss you so much . . . and I want to tell you I love you . . . I want you to be here — now!" I dropped my head to my anorak, lifted it again and sucked in air. If

140

only he had had "a fling" like Juniper's Charley. How simple that would have been, how easy to forgive! For the first time I wondered whether I had tried to kill all three of us that day last year. I tried frantically to remember . . . but I had run too fast and too far. Memory was . . . unreliable. After all, that was why I was writing this down.

Slowly at first, and then very fast, I started to run again. And my feet, thudding rhythmically, became the only reality. If only I could go on for ever.

I found myself at the lake. At last I stopped and clung to the wall.

I knew that something was going to happen; something important. I couldn't see a thing. The digger could have still been there, buried in the black night fog which had settled and solidified in the deep cavity below me.

I took a deep breath of the freezing fog and grappled the door knob out of my pocket. I rolled it between my palms, and then against my damp face, and then held it to my chest with both hands. The wall, cutting into my waist, stopped cutting. The coldness pressing on to my head and through thinner bits of fleece became fluid. Physically, I opened to whatever was outside, so that the outside became the inside. And the other way round. And I was becoming part of something huge, enormous. Eternal. My physical self was dissolving. But the door knob was there. It was pressing into my chest and hurting. So my physical self was still there. I cannot explain it. I will simply write it down. I was there and then . . . David was there. How could I see him when it was so dark, when the fog swirled everywhere? But I saw him. He was there. The hood of his sweatshirt covered his face, yet I saw his face. The sleeves covered his hands, yet I saw his hands. And I heard him. I heard his voice. He spoke to me. What he said barely made sense, then. The words of an old Beatles song. Made trite by the song, yet . . . not trite.

I am thankful I am writing everything down because I know it will fade. I know I will doubt my own memory. I could have written that I saw a ghost, and it was David's ghost. But the word ghost did not cross my mind until much later, and all I can say with absolute certainty is . . . it was David. The words he spoke were not the sort of words David would have said in life, unless he had said them ironically, or as an example of human absurdity. But he spoke them. It was David, and he said those words. I might doubt it later, but not then. Then I knew it, and now, as I write, I still know it.

I turned almost immediately and ran back home without panic. When I had warmed up I went into my usual steady rhythm, consciously breathing in time with the length of stride and the lift of leg. It was still dark; I ran on the spot while I fitted the key into the lock, glanced at the clock in the hall and saw it was four twenty. I had been outside just over an hour. David was not in the mirror. It had all happened in an hour.

I slept until midday, and then lay still for some time wondering how such a marvellous, dreamless sleep could come after . . . that.

142

Two hours later the door bell ping-ponged. I answered it almost eagerly, certain it was Hildie Hardy with plans for Thursday. I would not tell her about David's words . . . not yet. But one day I would, and she would be solemnly pleased. There would be no bewilderment or dissatisfaction. But then she had not known David as I had. Had he been mocking me in some way? I needed Hildie's simple acceptance . . . perhaps I would tell her now.

Tom Hardy stood just outside the porch; inside, taking up all the space, was the twin pram.

I tried to look welcoming; he did not respond to my faltering smile. It was not yet three o'clock, but already darkness was waiting, and the fog was still around, and that hill was steep enough without having to push two babies and a buggy up its length. I recalled the evening I had helped one of the staff from Tall Trees push Jinx's wheelchair around the hairpin bends.

"Is — is your mother all right?" Something surely had to be wrong.

"I made her rest." He reached for the handle of the pram; he wanted to come in. "She tried to phone you, but there was no reply." He joggled the front wheels on to the slatted boot-scraper; I moved back, opening the door as wide as it would go. I looked down the hall. He'd never get past the coat stand, telephone table, that chair piled high with books and papers . . .

I said, "I'm so sorry. I slept late. Didn't hear a thing."

He got the front wheels over the shallow step; he would now have to do a sharp left turn, and the buggy was long. He coped with that.

"Good wide front door. Shallow step. Decent access."

He spoke as if to himself, then glanced down the length of the hall. "If you could get rid of that chair . . . I'll move the coat stand behind the door . . . yes, we can manage very well like that. Where do you spend most time?"

"The living room. Straight ahead." I squeezed my eyes shut for a second; was it Thursday already? I couldn't have slept for over twenty-four hours.

He pushed the buggy past the telephone table and through into the living room. Luckily I had been in the kitchen since I got dressed, so I hadn't had time to make muddles elsewhere, and no one sees them in that room because their eyes go to the windows and the view of the sea.

Not Tom's eyes. He swept the big square room with a single glance, and parked the buggy right in the middle of the elderly carpet.

"This is fine," he pronounced. He pushed back the hood slightly and peered inside at the babies. "Still asleep. I'll say one thing for that female Hitler back home who calls herself a health visitor. She knew what she was talking about when she said: 'If they won't settle after a feed, walk them.' "

I had to work out that "back home" meant Cheltenham. Our village-cum-town hadn't been home to Tom Hardy for a long time.

I said, "But that hill . . . you could have stayed on the flat and done the sea front."

He straightened and looked at me, surprised. "I had to inspect your place some time," he said. "Ma said it was fine, but the Hitler woman told us what to look for. And with twins, easy access is very important." He dropped his head, checked the babies again and added, "Not good at the cottage. And we don't know where to put this damned thing." He indicated the buggy.

"There's the garage, of course." I held on to the back of the sofa; there was something surreal about everything.

"Dad keeps his tools in there. Works in there, too."

"Surely, just for the time being . . . and it's warm and dry . . ."

"Yes. That's true. If we moved the work bench slightly. Yes. We could do that. In fact Ma and I could probably do it before Dad got in from work." He paused, looking thoughtfully down into the pram. "I'd better get off." He glanced at his watch. "Half an hour to get here. Probably fifteen minutes to get back?"

"Takes me ten to get to the level, probably another ten to walk along to the river."

"Right." He was already starting a three-point turn with the buggy. "Can I see your kitchen on the way out?"

My heart sank. I opened the kitchen door and looked through at the remains of my "breakfast" on the kitchen table. Milk bottle, bread, marmalade pot, it looked horribly sordid. The sink was full of crocks. My gardening boots had fallen over by the back door. A bucket of stuff to go down to the compost bin . . .

He said, "Marvellous. Room for the buggy in here if necessary. Warm. You'll need to disinfect things. I'll bring up some stuff in the car."

He went on down to the front door. We jiggled about as I got past the buggy to open up. I was breathless and suddenly full of anger. I spoke very clearly.

"I thought I was coming down to your place. Your mother seemed to think it would be easier."

"Oh yes. Tomorrow. The funeral. But if you are going to take the babies occasionally, we need to make sure of the environment."

All right, I had offered. But . . . but . . . the sheer cheek of the man! He turned right and wiggled the buggy over the step and on to the scraper and into the porch. Then he turned and forced his saturnine face to smile. "It was very kind of you to offer. Ma was appreciative."

I waited for him to say he too was appreciative, but he turned and walked to the gate. Then he was gone.

I stood there at the open door, still startled by his coming and going. He had not used my name nor any names for his children. Neither had I. It seemed so very . . . strange.

I cleared up in the kitchen. Dealt with the chair, which I had shoved into my bedroom out of the way, then got a bucket of hot soapy water and a floor cloth and got down on my hands and knees. David's words seemed a long way off now. As I scrubbed, rinsed, wiped, changed the water and scrubbed again, I thought about David's appearance, looking for a meaning, trying to believe that it had all really happened. Hildie had believed in the door knob as a symbol, and had made me believe it, too; but the door knob was real, it was tangible, it had held me to the earth . . .

I finished the floor and went into the living room, holding that precious, tangible object to my chest again. In spite of the heating it was cold in the big square room, and I slid my talisman into my pocket while I struck a match and lit the fire. I wished I'd done it before, so that Tom Hardy could have seen the room at its best. And then knew that he would only have seen a danger point; I made a mental note to find the spark guard. Then I sat and gazed out of the window and held the door knob in both hands.

Absolutely nothing happened. I watched the darkness creep from the east and cover the little town, and then, as the invisible sun sank into the sea, engulf everything that I knew was there. My world. Sometimes beautiful, sometimes cruel. Not absurd.

I stood up and switched on the lights. I was tired. In spite of that long sleep, I was bone-tired.

I made tea in my pristine kitchen and took it back to where I knew the sea was below me. I thought of those words again.

David had not been a fan of the Beatles, yet he had said very clearly and distinctly, "All you need is love."

I spoke the words aloud, trying to make more of them. I knew they contained . . . everything. And as I looked down to the blackness that was the sea, I knew something else, too. They were the only words I would

147

hear from David. I was almost sure . . . I *was* sure . . . that I would not see him again in this life.

For a moment, only a moment, I wanted to cry out with pain. But there was no pain. So I made no sound.

CHAPTER
ELEVEN

Hildie had intended to ring Viv and warn her after Tom left with the buggy, but she forgot. She took it out on Tom when he got back.

"It's no good you criticizing! She doesn't see the muddles. No point in putting things away when you're going to need them again next day. No one else to worry about." She told him about Viv and David Venables and the gossip that had surrounded the whole dreadful accident. "And you take the twins up there to inspect her premises!" She snorted indignantly. "That girl has not been interested in her surroundings for a long time. Not unlike someone else I know." She stared at him significantly. She had waited until Hardy had gone into the garage to work on some window frames.

"Maybe I was taking a bit of a liberty. But it had to be done some time, Ma. If she's going to be childminding for us, then we have to check out that her house is safe and warm and hygienic."

"Well?"

"It was. A very pleasant yet odd bungalow, stuck into the side of the hill like that. The living room was chilly, but that's soon remedied. The kitchen was warm. She's not a tidy person, but of course she'll learn fast.

Especially when they begin to crawl. That home-care woman told me a thing or two about keeping anything precious at head height once they begin to crawl."

This little speech placated his mother slightly. She repeated, "Mrs Venables has had more important things to think about this past year. Especially since September."

"What happened in September?" Tom was not really curious.

"Her husband . . ." Hildie stopped, then tried to pass it off. "She felt very close to her husband just then. It helped her."

Tom looked at his mother. She was peeling potatoes, and she nicked her finger with the knife. He took it from her and tore off some kitchen roll.

"I'll do that. Hold the paper over it, stop the bleeding." He pushed her into a chair and returned to the potatoes. "Do I gather that Viv Venables conjured up a ghost?"

"Don't you dare laugh, our Tom. It can happen, you know. When two people are very close." She squeezed her finger till her eyes watered. "It can happen."

Tom said nothing. She wondered whether he might think Mrs Venables was crazy; too crazy to look after his babies. She said, "If I died first I'd try to get to your dad somehow. If that's what he wanted."

Tom looked round at her and smiled. "He'd want it, Ma. And I reckon you could do it, too."

She sniffed, then said, "So you're all right with Viv coming down here tomorrow while we three go to Cheltenham?"

"Of course." He looked surprised. "I thought it was all arranged." He put the saucepan on the hob and swilled his hands. "Did you think I might be put off by a ghost or two hanging around the place? I reckon there's a few hanging around me, don't you?"

"Oh, Tom . . ."

Mrs Hardy went to the back door and called Hardy in for his supper. She was glad she had opened up a bit about Viv. Tom had scoffed rather than scorned. He might even be slightly curious.

Vivian's story

I did not think I would write any more. The things I wrote about, they were necessary. They had to be recorded before my memory of them faded or changed in any way.

That was done. That precious night was recorded in my biro pen inside a pad of A4 paper, and I put it into the small case with my marriage certificate, David's death certificate and the deeds of the house.

But then I got it out again on Thursday night, after Della's funeral, because I realized that it had become more than a record of David. It was a record of the Hardys and what was happening to them. And that was not over. They had a future because of the babies. And somehow I was a hanger-on to that future. I needed to go on recording for a little while, at least. Perhaps just what had happened that day . . . or the next. I don't know.

Anyway, Thursday, 21 December. The day of Della Hardy's funeral.

I arrived at the cottages by the river much too early. Mr Hardy opened the door to me in his shirt-sleeves, a tie held between finger and thumb with distaste. He stood aside for me to go past him; the incessant baby wails made it pointless for either of us to speak. I went into the big living room, where Tom Hardy was sitting on the sofa trying to feed the babies. They were both rejecting their bottles with a kind of irritable panic; it was a far cry from Tuesday's tea party, when Tom had managed the whole thing like an expert. I had been nervous before; unable to sleep and unable to run. I badly wanted to turn and run right then and there.

Tom flashed me an upward look that held relief. He placed the feeding bottles on the table in front of him, then gently moved one twin then another, and stood up. The noise crescendoed.

"Sit in that space," he said, close to my ear. "See if you can position the babies on your lap . . ." He eased me into place. "Now the pillow and the towel. That's good."

Mr Hardy had gone. Hildie appeared and tried to help me, and Tom brushed her away. "She has to do it alone after we've gone," he said loudly and slowly.

"You go and get ready!" Hildie said. She gave him a shove when he didn't seem to hear. He looked at me dickering about with one of the feeding bottles, and went into the hall. I flashed a grateful smile at Hildie. She grabbed the other bottle and massaged one of the tiny heads. Her baby settled, and the decibels halved.

My baby — I knew it was Michael because he had a blue cardigan on — was red with anger. I waited until he drew breath and said gently into the silence, "Come on now, Michael. A good breakfast is a good start to the day." He had already squeezed his eyes tightly ready for the next howl of rage, and then, without warning, he took the teat and sucked on it with enormous power.

Hildie said, "It's as if they know what today is. Do you think that's possible?"

"Yes. I think anything is possible." The sound of feeding babies was instant balm.

"Poor little things. But . . . do you think you can manage?"

"I don't know. But I'll find out, won't I?" I grinned up at her. Both bottles were in my hands, now, and I was managing. I said, "You look really nice, Hildie. I hope you will be all right."

"Yes." She straightened, her eyes still on the babies. "I'll be all right. So will Hardy. And . . ." She sighed. "So will Tom."

Those two words, "all" and "right", did not mean much, except that everyone would go through the motions. I smiled wryly and she smiled back.

I was still feeding the babies when they left.

David could have got a strip cartoon from my day at Number 1, Riverside Cottages. The fact that the babies cried whenever they were awake made quite ordinary activities completely chaotic. I left them safely entrenched in cushions on the sofa while I took out the bottles and put them in a sterilizer, but before I could take the baby wipes and nappies back in they were crying bitterly, and by the time I had cleaned and changed one of them — it turned out to be Joy — the other one, Michael, was apoplectic, and I was trembling all over.

Variations on that theme happened most of the day. I remembered what Tom had said about walking them, but the buggy was nowhere in sight, and in any case, had it been right there in the living room, it would have taken hours to install the twins in it, then jiggle it down the hall and steps to the pavement . . . I quailed at the thought. The best I could do was to put Joy on my lap, so that she could drum her tiny feet against my chest, and get Michael on to my shoulder and rub his back. That was their favourite thing; the back-rubbing.

They took it in turns until lunchtime, then we had a battle with bottles for nearly an hour before resuming the massage. And then Joy stopped kicking and quite suddenly was asleep. Michael grizzled on for a while, and I slid him down by my side and tucked his blanket around him and leaned my head against the back of the sofa and . . . smiled. It was two thirty and Hildie had said they would be home before dark. Another two hours to go, maybe. I opened my eyes and stared down at them, because I could not hear them breathing. They were. And then Michael pursed his lips and gave an experimental suck on his tongue. And Joy smiled. I knew it was wind, and prayed it wasn't bad enough to wake her. She stayed asleep. At first I had to consciously keep still, but then I relaxed gently into the cushions and went on looking. They were so beautiful.

Not a bit like Tom or his parents. So they must look like their mother. The thought was unbearably poignant; I tried to tell myself she would live on in them, but the fact remained that they would never know her.

David's words came into my head again. "All you need is love."

And they had nothing to do with triteness or cynicism. They stated an obvious fact.

Tom's car drew up half an hour later. The three of them crept in, respectful of the silence. They crowded through the doorway, and stood looking down at the twins as if they had not seen them before.

Hildie whispered, "Is everything all right?"

"Yes."

"Have you had any lunch?"

"No." I looked up and shook my head. They exclaimed quietly. "I forgot. They've been like this for nearly an hour, and I could have made tea or something. I just forgot."

Unexpectedly, Mr Hardy spoke. "Sometimes you can't stop looking at them, can you?"

"No."

We smiled, first at Joy and Michael, and then at each other. And I giggled.

"What?" asked Hildie.

"Us." I was spluttering. "We're like cartoon people."

Nobody else laughed. They were just back from the funeral of Tom's wife. I stopped laughing abruptly. Hildie turned to Tom.

"Viv's husband was an artist, and he did a lot of cartoons for — for —"

"A syndicate," I supplied. "I'm so sorry. Let me — let me make some tea."

Mr Hardy said gently, "I'll make it. We're full of tea, actually, but I bet you could drink six cups straight off."

He was right. But the others did well, too. They moved around, taking off their coats, emerging from the kitchen in slippers, Hildie wearing an apron. The house settled around them while I drank tea and "minded" the babies. I was suddenly very tired, and it seemed to me that the Hardys were perfectly coordinated in their movements. It was as if they had choreographed getting a meal on the table: first they boiled the kettle and bore in the teapot, covering it with a cosy, putting spoons in saucers and milk in cups and positioning the tea-strainer — and then I was ushered into a chair and provided with food. There was no barging into each other, no conversation; each person's personal space was preserved at all times. As Tom carried out the empty feeding bottles, and Hildie emerged from the kitchen holding a tray, he lifted his arms and she bent her head beneath them. It was just . . . perfect; I only just stopped myself laughing again at witnessing such harmonious living. All done without a word of direction.

Hildie poured more tea and indicated the sandwiches she had cut for my lunch.

"Dig in. We'll have something hot later. You can't drive home on an empty stomach."

I ate. Never had cheese and pickle sandwiches tasted so good. Tom was saying that he could not thank me enough. Later he drove me home in my car, assuring me that he needed a walk and it was all downhill anyway. He put the car away, while I opened up and switched on lights. It was amazingly different doing this with someone else. I was so used to it on my own.

He stood by the door. "We'll have to think of some way to repay you."

I was aghast. "Don't talk like that — please. Hildie — your mother — she has literally saved me . . . so many times."

He said with a smile in his voice, "She is very insistent." And then, "You've been here, like this, on your own, for a year?"

"Yes." I didn't want his pity. "Are you coming in? The heating is leaking out."

"No. I must get back for the evening feed. Thank you again, Viv."

He was gone.

CHAPTER
TWELVE

The next six weeks passed in a blur. At the beginning of February, Hilda Hardy said of them: "They wasn't so much a nightmare as a blizzard. I din't know whether I were on my base or my apex. As for Christmas . . . well, it came and it went again." She smiled at Viv Venables to show there was no tragedy there.

Viv laughed. She did not know whether she had actually enjoyed Christmas or not, but she hadn't run, so she would at least remember it. For almost a year she had run so successfully she scarcely remembered anything; certainly last year's Christmas had been just a black hole.

This year she had loaded the car on Christmas Eve with as much traditional food as possible: a cooked turkey with all the trimmings, prepared vegetables, a pudding and some tinned custard. She had driven down to the Hardys during the evening and watched Hildie feed and change the twins while she herself laid the table for tomorrow's Christmas dinner. Hardy had come in with a box of crackers and a miniature tree. Tom had been at the supermarket "getting in the drink" as he put it.

158

No, she had no idea whether she had enjoyed it, but at least she had been part of it. Last year she had not known it was Christmas; this year had been different.

Hildie, struggling through her blizzard, hoped that the worst part of this tragedy was over. Della's funeral had been awful. Just awful. The nurses who had looked after her were there; a woman in a navy-blue suit who on closer inspection turned out to be Della's doctor. She it was who had discovered that Della was carrying twins and would need an urgent Caesarean operation. At the back of the church, behind a pillar, had been another woman in the same kind of suit, and when they were going home in the van Hardy had replied briefly to Hildie's query about her. "Elisabeth Mason," he had said. Hildie had felt distinctly queasy. Her imagination had seen a vulture waiting in the wings ready to snatch Tom the moment the other predators left. But Hardy had taken his hand from the steering wheel for a moment to pat her knee and say gently, "Nice of her to be there for Tom." And she had swallowed, then nodded.

At least the hovering Elisabeth had kept behind her pillar. Not like Della's mother, who had wailed throughout the ceremony, and then had rounded on Tom on the way to the cemetery and told him he had "taken" Della and then killed her. It had been an ugly scene. Tom had received it in silence, as if it were his due. Hildie had held his arm and felt the inner tremor through her gloved fingers.

It was the funeral director who finally quietened the screeching as they drove through the gates of the cemetery. "Now then. Now then, Mrs Leach. Think of how it will look if it gets in the evening paper." And Della's mother had suddenly been silent, hard as iron. As the car drew up by the open grave, she had said acidly, "I'm going to live with Della's brother in Perth. That's Australia. He left home when he was eighteen and hasn't been much help since. About time he was." She looked at Tom with such malevolence Hildie had clutched his arm tighter still. "So, if you want to live in Cheltenham, you are welcome. I certainly won't be running across you or those babies. Ever again." That had been something to be thankful for. And Hildie was; very, very thankful.

So the funeral had been over and Christmas upon them, and through it all the twins had cried, been fed and winded and changed, and even then had probably cried again. Hildie's blizzard always included sound. Loud sound. And muddles. She had seen Viv Venables's muddles as a sign of grief, and had felt things were looking up after Hardy had tidied the hedges and conifers and Viv had started eating proper meals — even if they were nearly always boiled eggs and bread and butter. But Viv's muddles had never been as bad as the ones in the riverside cottage. If you counted the twins — Joy and Michael — there were five people living in a house originally used to three. And for the past ten years the three had usually been two.

160

Hardy, who was neat with his tools, lost his favourite screwdriver for two days. Hildie found it at the bottom of the clothes basket. At the back of the counter in the kitchen was an array of bottles taking up much of the work space. The sterilizer was where the bread bin usually went, and she could never remember where it was now. Packets of disposable nappies were everywhere: behind the sofa, in the nursery, even in the van.

Meanwhile, life racketed on. They couldn't have managed without Viv; Hildie said this often in front of Tom, whose attitude towards the tall skinny school-marm was still cautious.

From two days before the funeral, when Viv came round for the first time, it became routine for her to take the twins for an afternoon walk. Michael and Joy. Joy and Michael. She made such a point of using their names, and she could always tell them apart. Before she tucked them carefully into their buggy she would lift each one high so that they could look down into her face and see her laughter. When she inveigled the wheels over the doorstep and back into the little hall, she did the same. She would settle them on the sofa cushions while she unbuttoned them, and sing silly jingles at them. "Michael and Joy, Michael and Joy, one is a girl and one is a boy." They knew it was supposed to be funny, and laughed to each other, raising rigid arms and clenched fists as if cheering her on.

Hildie was supposed to put her feet up while they were out, but usually she was preparing the evening meal or "finding places for things". Viv was there, never late, never over-staying her usefulness. She was there when Hildie broke down just once, and told her that Tom was like a zombie, a wonderfully efficient carer, but hardly a daddy.

What had really upset Hildie was that when she told Tom to relax a bit and just love the babies, he had said, "They are here because of me. They will never know their mother, because of me. I am working on the bonding, Ma. But my priority at present is to keep them alive and well." His smile had been wintry. "Anyway, they will learn the truth soon enough, and it will be very hard for them not to blame me for their mother's death. Probably best to keep a little distance." The words had come from his mouth like bullets from a gun, and Hilda had flinched at each one.

Perhaps Viv guessed at the depth of Tom's feelings, because she had wrapped Hildie in her long arms and said simply, "Poor Tom. It must be so hard."

By February Hildie's blizzard was abating gradually, and Tom had taken on locum work at the local health centre, and had made his attic room into an office, and was well into a stratagem for training the twins to sleep through the night. His attitude remained that of a physician, at home as well as at the health centre. During her spare minutes, Hildie worried about how distant he was, and wondered whether she and his dad had kept him at arm's length as a child. Had Della overwhelmed him with unwanted love when they were married? And the extra-marital relationship — what had happened to that? Hildie frowned, remembering the name. Elisabeth Mason. She had been at the funeral, but as far as the Hardys knew there had been no further contact, so that must have died a death, too. Perhaps Tom could not manage a proper relationship with a woman? And then a thought occurred to her. Might he be able to relate to a woman who also carried a huge load of guilt within her? He was thrown into contact with Viv, whether he liked her or not. But he trusted her with the twins. And he had seen some of her husband's paintings up at the bungalow and remarked on their "clarity".

"What does that mean, son?" Hardy had glanced at Hildie. Meaningfully, she thought.

"Not sure. Their wide-openness." Tom smiled slightly and shook his head. "Seems out of place when you have anything to do with that buttoned-up woman."

Hildie was not sure what Tom meant. Was he sorry for Viv? He had started off by being sorry for Della, and that had been a disaster. But Viv was different.

There was a big age difference. That was true. Maybe ten years. But perhaps that was good, too. Might Viv care for Tom as she cared for his babies? Tenderly and thoughtfully.

There was the business of that dratted door knob, of course. But there had been nothing of that for a long time now. Viv was busy every minute of every day, what with getting that bungalow up to scratch, and taking the twins for long walks, and visiting Juniper up at the home. Viv Venables might . . . could be . . . the one.

And then what Hildie called the "blessed bug" hit the little town, and whole families took to their beds for two or three days, and struggled with an aftermath of weakness and exhaustion. Hildie was the first to go down with it in the cottage, closely followed by Hardy. Tom was doing outlying house calls, and was hardly ever there, and Viv arrived at seven thirty each morning and looked after everyone until he returned at night.

February behaved just as the old rhyme prophesied. "Fill dyke by name, fill dyke by nature," Hildie commented, blowing her nose and dabbing her eyes.

Hardy nodded. "The rhines are overflowing on the Levels. No wonder everyone's picking up this germ. Good job Mrs Venables is all right."

Viv stayed all right until the last day of the month, and then was hit by it very suddenly during an afternoon walk, in-between storms. When Tom collected the babies he immediately opened his case and took her temperature.

"This later strain lasts just twenty-four hours," he said. "I've had a spate of them this morning, too. You should be fighting fit in a couple of days."

She mumbled something, and he said tersely, "Possibly you could cope with them, but possibly not." He looked at the thermometer. "Definitely not. Listen. I'll get hold of a professional. Send her up to you tomorrow morning. Stay in bed till she comes — I'll give her your spare key."

He did not ask if this would be all right. Michael started to cry. Joy did the soprano part. Viv was thankful when they all left, and she could shut the door and collapse on the sofa. At some point during the evening she poured lemonade and chipped some ice out of the freezer. She drank deeply, swilling down two paracetamol. She was so hot and swimmy, yet strangely cold inside. She made up the fire and fetched pillows and a duvet from her room. Just a nap, no need to undress.

She heard the key in the door, the tentative: "Hello?" The door closing again. The voice coming nearer, saying calmly, "It's the nurse." A pause while whoever it was looked into the bedroom. "Ah. I take it you're up . . ." and then the living room door opened.

Viv remembered everything. The spare key . . . the professional carer . . . She felt light-headed but perfectly normal. She said, "I'm all right now. I've had a wonderful night. Tell Tom I'll be down for the twins after lunch . . . or is it after lunch now? I'm not sure. The clock stopped in the night, perhaps."

The voice, as light as her own, not exactly lilting but certainly not a monotone, said, "No, I don't think it has stopped. It's almost midday, and, believe it or not, it's not raining!"

Viv heaved herself up and looked languidly over the back of the sofa.

"I stayed here all night. Much better. I wanted to get really hot. And it's done the trick."

A young woman stood just inside the door; she smiled. She was small and attractive and looked totally competent.

"Hello. I'll go straight into the kitchen, shall I? Tea and thin bread and butter?"

It was exactly right. "I can do it," Viv protested, then immediately sank back into the pillows and duvet.

The woman said, "My name is Elisabeth Mason, and I was a colleague of Doctor Hardy's in Cheltenham. We'll soon have you feeling on top of things again."

She disappeared back down the hall to the kitchen. Viv stayed where she was, gazing at the ceiling. Hildie had mentioned Elisabeth Mason. She had been at Della's funeral. She was the Other Woman.

CHAPTER
THIRTEEN

Hildie had to admit that Elisabeth Mason was next door to being an angel. A late snow at the beginning of March made the Tump almost inaccessible. The staff from Tall Trees walked and slid up and down the hill to and from their work; the residents did not go out, and no one visited them. Elisabeth made an effort to drive her Ka up to Viv's bungalow, and ended up sideways across the road. She managed to reverse very slowly to the first of the hairpin bends and park on the pavement. She then struggled into her backpack, which was full of soups, bread, milk and barley water, and climbed to the top, hanging on to the retaining wall of the garden.

She let herself into the bungalow and found Viv in the kitchen making a cake.

"I made a sort of Victoria sponge for Hildie not long ago, and I'm trying the recipe again." Viv put the tins in the oven and swilled her hands. "It takes about ten or fifteen minutes. We can have some . . . if you can stay that long."

She sounded diffident. She had no idea that the road was almost impassable, but she guessed Elisabeth would have her hands full with both Hardys ill and the twins invariably needing things at the same time.

Elisabeth pressed a hand to her own side. "That would be great," she panted. "But why are you up and doing? You should be keeping warm. Let's get you back on that sofa."

She chivvied Viv back into the living room and plumped pillows efficiently.

"We used to have a cleaner . . . after my mother died — when I was still at school." Viv felt light-headed. She knew it was because she was weak, but it was rather marvellous, too, and she smiled blindingly at this young woman, who had Hildie curls and a round, schoolgirl face. "She wasn't friendly, really. I used to make things out of cardboard boxes . . . model theatres and things. And, like my mother had, she would throw them away because she thought they were rubbish. But in my head I always thought she was my nanny. I wanted a nanny."

Elisabeth did not look surprised. "You think I would make a good nanny? I do need to be one for a few days, because of the twins." She tucked the duvet around Viv's stick-like legs, looked up and met the smile. She blinked.

Viv said, "Do look through the window. The snow makes everything look different. When you came yesterday you must have noticed the fig tree. It was stark naked. It's not any more."

Elisabeth went to the window obediently. It was indeed very beautiful.

"I can see now how the shrubs are sculpted into a perfect whole." She looked over her shoulder. "Did you do that?"

"Yes. I started on the garden last autumn. Just after David pushed me into the lake and then chased me over the hill."

"Oh my God." Elisabeth came back to the sofa, eyes wide. "Sounds terrifying. Who is David?"

"My husband. I killed him. He was angry. Just before it happened he said he hated me. But he's not angry now." Viv put her head back on the pillow, she was suddenly exhausted, and wondered whether she had said too much.

Elisabeth stared for a moment, then went to the log basket and made up the fire. Sparks flew up the chimney. She replaced the guard carefully.

"There. That makes it the perfect nursery, wouldn't you say?" She gave Viv a nanny smile, then glanced at her watch. "I'll get out the sponges, shall I? Where do you keep your jam?"

"There isn't any. I put marmalade in before. That's on the bottom shelf. Pantry." Viv closed her eyes.

Elisabeth stood for a moment, her back against the spark guard. She looked down into Viv's closed face and registered the blue-veined eyelids, the coif of hair. Tom had said this woman was about forty, but she looked nearer to fifty. And she had been coping with Tom's babies and running a sky-high temperature; plus, she was very near the edge. Elisabeth went and found the marmalade; turned the sponges on to

169

greaseproof paper because there were no wire trays in sight, and spread them lightly.

When she went back with cake and coffee, Viv was properly asleep. Elisabeth replenished the log box from an enormous stockpile in the utility room. Put the coffee in a thermos. Switched on several electric heaters, and wrinkled her nose at the smell of the dust burning off them. She opened a can of soup and poured it into a saucepan, then laid a tray for lunch. From the living-room sofa came the sound of coughing.

"It's all right . . ." Viv held up a hand as Elisabeth entered. "I tried the sponge and a crumb stuck in my throat." She smiled again, but not blindingly by any means. Elisabeth thought she was frightened. "Sorry. It's not really sweet enough, and the marmalade doesn't help like raspberry jam would."

Elisabeth poured coffee from the thermos. "Sip this. Have you had your pills today? OK. Two paracetamols then. I've done a jug of barley water. Try to get it all down before this evening. Tom will look in. He's got chains on his tyres."

"Is it that bad outside?"

"Pretty much. I've left the car lower down."

"Oh, I am so sorry. You've struggled up with all that stuff . . ." Viv surveyed the loaded tray . . . the barley water and glass . . . the thermos and the cake. "I really am thoughtless. Have another slice of cake. It will help you get down to your car." She looked at Elisabeth. "Please," she added.

Elisabeth found herself eating the cake, and preferring it less sweet and slightly bitter when it came to the filling. She said as much, and added conversationally that she had bitten the inside of her cheek yesterday, and the cake was very easy to eat. Viv smiled vaguely. Elisabeth told her there was soup in the kitchen and plenty of bread for toast. Viv just nodded; her eyes were almost closed. Elisabeth stood up. "I'd better go. Mrs Hardy is much better, but not as well as she thinks she is! She will probably be up here in a couple of days. She's really worried about you." She hesitated then went on, "I know about the car crash."

"Yes. Of course you do. I told you just now."

Elisabeth did not argue. "Mrs Hardy said the car was faulty, but you still blamed yourself. A bit like Tom and Della." She took Viv's coffee cup from her, and said in a determined voice, "These things happen. We have to accept that they happen."

Viv looked right at her, and said very suddenly, "I was pregnant, you see. And I wanted to get rid of the baby. It wasn't David's baby. I had to get rid of it. But I got rid of him as well. He said he hated me. He wanted me to stop the car. When I wouldn't — when I went faster still — he grabbed the wheel . . ." She looked at Elisabeth with sudden surprise. "That's why he pushed me into the lake. Of course it was. He was angry with me about the baby. And then . . . somehow . . . he wasn't. Not any more. That's why he said that all you need is love. And that's why he won't be able to see me any

171

more. Because it's all right. It — it's settled." Both women stared at each other, then Viv smiled properly again and said, "Thank you, Elisabeth. Thank you."

Elisabeth could think of nothing more to say. She gathered up her gloves and fixed the backpack over her padded coat.

"I'll see you tomorrow. Please ring if there's anything . . ." She could no longer face the smile. Viv heard the door close after her.

More snow fell in the afternoon. Viv watched and saw the softness of it, the gentle obliteration of everything familiar.

At first . . . just now . . . when she had said aloud those words . . . the words David had said over a year ago: "I hate you", she had felt smitten, riven, as if an enormous axe had cleft her in two. She was devastated that his words — his exact words — suppressed for so long — had been remembered. The cause of the "accident" had been remembered. David had twisted the steering-wheel out of her hands, and the car had simply leapt off the road. She had done something unspeakable and he had known . . . of course he had known; he had always known what went on inside her head.

She said aloud, "I must not think of that. I must not think of David knowing." The pain she had inflicted on him seemed worse now than it had during those terrible days. But . . . he had said that all you needed was love.

172

Tom was exhausted when he got home. Hildie noticed how quickly he recovered as he watched Elisabeth feeding the twins. She was pleased about that, of course. But disappointed, too. He had got so much in common with Viv; they could have helped each other.

Hildie sat with her back against the radiator, a blanket wrapped around her from beneath her armpits to her ankles. The slippers below and the bed-jacket above were both Christmas presents from Hardy. They were edged with matching angora, and were the sort of items Marilyn Monroe might have sported. Hildie loved them, though she told Hardy he must be mad, and he should stop wearing his rose-coloured specs.

He had graduated to doing odd jobs in the kitchen, and was cutting sandwiches to eke out the soup for their evening meal. Hildie shuddered to think what her kitchen must be like these days. At least Hardy had some vague idea of where things went, but this Elisabeth, efficient though she was, didn't have a clue.

Tom had hung his wet things in the hall, and now sat at one end of the sofa and took Joy on to his shoulder to wind her.

"Everything looks very organized here." He grinned at Elisabeth, and she gave a small self-deprecating smile.

"It won't be that for a while, I'm afraid." She glanced at Hildie. "I'm sorry if I've put everything in the wrong place. You probably won't be able to find anything when you're well enough to take over."

Hildie was amazed that their thoughts had run so close. She shook her head. "It's been like that ever since Christmas, my dear. We're all new at this."

Elisabeth widened her smile. "One thing. I can't find a bread bin. That's why the bread is wrapped in a tea towel and left out. The bin must be somewhere."

Hildie felt her jaw drop. Hardy, coming through with the sandwiches, and putting them on the table, chuckled. "We can never put a hand on it, can we, my maid? I did wonder — if we put that-there sterilizer thing on top of the fridge, could we put the bread bin back in its proper place? What d'you think?"

Hildie felt a rush of love for him; for everyone. It was such a small thing, to reinstate her bread bin, but in the context of losing Della and taking on Tom and the twins, it was a sort of turning-point.

Michael burped loudly, and the towel which Elisabeth had put over her shoulder was not big enough. Her cashmere sweater was soaked. She laughed, and patted Michael's back. "All right now?" she asked.

Hildie said, "Give him to me and go and change. We might be able to sponge that out."

But Elisabeth shook her head. "I don't mind if it stays there for the rest of the day. Please don't worry about it."

And Hildie, who, normally, would have worried very much, subsided against the comfort of the radiator. Her back was soothed. She decided to "sit up" for her meal. Tom put the babies to bed. They gathered round the table. Elisabeth served the soup. And Hildie asked about Viv.

"Well . . ." Elisabeth smiled across the table. "I was a bit anxious. I think she was confused." She turned the smile on Tom. "I knew you wouldn't have considered her as a baby-minder if you'd had the slightest doubts about her." Hildie's heart sank.

Tom said soberly, "She feels some . . . responsibility . . . for the death of her husband. That is natural enough." He raised his brows, not wanting to liken her situation to his own.

Elisabeth said, "I understand that, and we know that it takes time to accept these things. She did in fact say that she had killed him. But then she seemed to remember something quite different. And then . . . she told me her husband had pushed her into the lake — tried to drown her. When I picked up the car, I drove back that way. There's no water in the lake." She cut the crusts from a sandwich and looked apologetically at Tom's father. "Do you mind me doing this? I'm not usually so fussy, but I've got a sore mouth."

Hildie immediately offered some pastilles she had in the bathroom cupboard; she hoped the conversation would move away from Viv.

Tom said, "Mum? Has Viv spoken to you about this?"

"She told me she fell in the lake and scraped her legs and feet. Ages ago, when it had water in."

There was a small silence. Elisabeth wished very much she had not mentioned anything about Mrs Venables. She said, "Actually, Tom, Mrs Venables really

175

was delirious when I arrived. It seems to be the way this particular infection works. And she may well feel her fall was some kind of punishment."

"She's so at risk when she takes those runs of hers." He picked up a crust from Elisabeth's plate and chewed on it thoughtfully. "That's been one good thing about her looking after the twins. No time for running."

Elisabeth smiled at Hildie. "Actually, Mrs Hardy, may I go and look in the bathroom cabinet? I've just bitten the inside of my cheek — again!"

There was a flurry while Hildie tried to stand up in her cocoon of blankets, and Hardy and Elisabeth held her down. Elisabeth went off to the bathroom.

Tom said, "I've worried about Viv taking on the babies. Now I see them as a godsend, and wonder how she will cope when she doesn't have them."

Hildie said comfortably, "Well, there's at least four years before they go to school, Tom."

Tom looked at his father, then reached for another sandwich.

"Ma. I thought you realized . . . I can't stay with you permanently. Surely you didn't imagine I would plonk myself back into the nest and wreck it for the two of you?"

"You wouldn't wreck it —"

"We've already wrecked it, Ma. But certainly not for always."

Hardy put his hand under the table, and gripped Hildie's knee through the layers of blanket.

"We knew it were just temp'ry. Didn't we, my maid?"

176

Hildie stared at him. "I suppose . . . we didn't think about the future. It was too awful to think poor Della would not be part of it, so we tried not to think . . ." Her voice trailed off. She felt ill again.

Elisabeth came back in, sucking furiously. She looked at the Hardys; they were both staring into space.

Tom smiled at her. "You found the pastilles. Good. We'll make some tea in a minute. Mum and Dad would probably like to watch the news. We'll clear up. And then bed. How does that sound?"

She returned the smile, nodded, then pointed to her face. "I can feel it working already, Mrs Hardy. Thanks so much. It's one of my many failings — biting the inside of my mouth. Used to drive my husband crazy."

Hildie's head came up like a shot. "We didn't know . . . you're married?"

"I was. We're divorced. Actually, we're still sort of friends. My daughter is with him at the moment."

These two bombshells were almost too much for Hildie.

She stammered something incoherent. Tom actually laughed.

Elisabeth reproved him. "You should have told your parents about me, Tom." She looked across the table. "I'm so sorry to bother you with it, especially as you are both under the weather. It seems, looking back, very simple. I married Peter when I was nineteen. We had Maisie. He fell in love with someone else, tried to fight it, couldn't. Luckily she was marvellous when it came to looking after Maisie. So I applied for a place in a training scheme for nurses — especially designed for women with children. Margaret stood in for me when necessary. Then, once school kicked in, it all worked very well."

Hildie stared at her. She reached for Hardy's hand on her knee and covered it with her own. She was conscious of Tom, sitting there, waiting for her first reaction.

She coughed and said, "Maisie. What a pretty name."

Elisabeth smiled widely. "She's ten now. I've told her about the twins, and she's longing to see them."

Hardy said stolidly, "You could have brought her with you."

"I'm supposed to be looking after you!" Elisabeth actually laughed.

"Ma. I'll make the tea, shall I?" Tom pushed back his chair. "Sorry I haven't got much across. But you get the picture now, don't you?"

Hildie said, "Just like your father. And you haven't finished. Not really. If you en't staying here, where are you going?"

"There's a job still waiting for me in Cheltenham. Elisabeth and I will buy a house."

Hildie managed a smile. She was glad that, in the midst of everything, Tom had still been concerned for Viv. Poor Viv. Poor Elisabeth. Hildie felt her chest fill with tears. Hardy tucked her into a corner of the sofa, which smelled of Michael's regurgitated milk, and settled next to her. They watched the news and drank their tea, and in the kitchen they could hear Tom and Elisabeth washing-up like an old married couple.

CHAPTER
FOURTEEN

No more snow fell, and by the next day melting lumps of grey slush were collecting in gulleys, sliding off roofs and dustbin lids.

Hardy telephoned Viv, and told her that Elisabeth's sore mouth seemed to be spreading to her throat. "Hildie thinks she should go home, but she says no — she can handle the twins. We're all right now. Tired and weak, but no worse than that. The three of us can manage."

"What about Tom?" Viv felt her usual irritation with Tom's ability to avoid domestic life: after that first burst of efficiency when he had inspected the "situation" he had been quite happy to delegate.

"He's up your way. At Tall Trees. Old Jinx en't too good. Tom says he'll call on you on his way down. Give you the once-over."

"No need. I'm so much better."

She knew he would come, and sure enough just before she had decided to heat up the rest of Elisabeth's soup, the front doorbell ping-ponged — and there he was.

"Elisabeth gave me the key, but I thought I'd warn you first."

He came in and stood in the hall, taking off his boots. She wished it could have been Elisabeth. Elisabeth had somehow dislodged the truth. That had been no accident.

They went into the living room and he checked the heaters and nodded.

"She told me she had switched on everything she could find. You must keep warm."

Viv wanted to say something stupid like, "Who's she, the cat's mother?" Instead she went to the grate and loaded on another log. "I'm perfectly all right, you know. Enforced rest, of course. But rest, all the same. I'm really sorry to hear about Elisabeth. If you will bring the twins to me, I can manage them while she is ill." She felt a longing to ask him where Elisabeth was sleeping. She said aloud, "None of my business."

He looked at her and frowned. "Of course it is your business."

She said, "I didn't mean . . ." It was all too difficult, and she said honestly, "I thought you might not trust the twins with me any more."

"Don't talk rubbish, Viv. You know that's not true. All the family — all the family except the twins — have got this virus, but there's four of us down at the cottage and only one of you."

She held on to the mantelpiece; her legs felt spongy. She nodded. Had he included her in his family? He said, "Elisabeth said you were delirious yesterday. But I have to say you seem perfectly normal today."

They must have discussed her. She straightened with difficulty.

"Did I say anything to Elisabeth? I can't remember what I said yesterday. I was out of it." She glanced at him, and then away. "Do you want some tea or coffee or soup or something?"

"Nothing." He hesitated, slightly bent over the radiator by the window, warming his hands. "Listen, Viv, if you've got a lot of stuff on your mind, why don't you try to write it down? Apparently it clarifies things."

She gave a scornful crow. "Good Lord! You're like the woman from the bereavement group! And I did write some things down, because that's the only way I could believe they had happened." She sat down suddenly on the sofa. "I'm not doing that again. Like going into an invisible confessional and talking to an invisible priest. Ridiculous!" Tears were in her eyes, and she blinked them away furiously.

He moved away from her, closer to the window, waited for a moment, then said, "What a bleak view today. The fig tree is dripping."

She said nothing. She remembered exactly what she had said to Elisabeth the day before, and how the other woman had heard her words and been entirely non-judgemental. Her tears were for David, who must have known . . . everything, and had then hated her. She pulled a long strip of tissue from the roll tucked under a cushion, balled it up, and pressed it against her leaking eyes. Tom glanced at her, and then turned and walked out of the room.

When he came back she had composed herself, fiercely.

He set down a mug of tea on one of the tables, then sat on a low stool the other side of it and clutched his knees. She took in the jack-knifed legs, the big hands clasped around them, the dark complexion and curly hair — which made him look Italianate. She thought his strong stocky shape might thicken into middle age before it should if he stayed with Hildie and ate her enormous meals. He was probably twenty years younger than David, but physically they could have been contemporaries.

He said, "You could write it in the third person. As if it was someone else completely. Easier that way. Perhaps."

It occurred to her, suddenly, that someone had suggested he should do this confession thing himself. She could just imagine how he had responded to that. Her silence was scornful. He waited, and when nothing happened, he blurted, "You could start by saying that she — this other woman that is yourself and not yourself — was pregnant, but not by her husband."

Her eyes opened wide. She gasped with the shock. Yet surely she must have realized Elisabeth would tell him?

When her heart slowed slightly she took a deep breath. "Did she tell you in front of Hildie?"

"I take it you mean Elisabeth? She did not tell us very much at all. Certainly not that. I already knew."

"Jinx," she said dully.

"Yes. It made no difference to my trust in you. I sort of figured that it would make Joy and Michael even more precious in your eyes." He paused, then added,

"What worried me was this ghost business. The door knob. That made you sound . . . unbalanced." He saw her face, and said quickly, "I don't know how else to speak of it, Viv. To you it has been an enormous experience. Perhaps a cathartic one. To me . . . it's way out of my league." He picked up the mug and thrust it at her.

She took it and sipped; it was much too hot.

"Listen. If you want to talk to anyone . . . I could ask around."

She stared at him through the steam, and almost laughed. "A psychiatrist? What would I say?"

"A counsellor, probably. She — or he — would encourage you into a place where you would tell them about your childhood. Perhaps that would lead to talking about the father of your baby. And why you were unfaithful to your husband." He leaned forward and tried to look encouraging. "You must know that you have a lot to discuss."

"Actually, no. It's all very predictable. I don't need to talk about it, or write it down. I was abused by my father after my mother died. It started when I was eleven. David and I couldn't have children, officially because I was screwed-up. But also because he was impotent. I loved him for that, of course. That was the attraction. And he loved me for taking the blame."

"You poor little sod."

"Let me tell you, Tom, your bedside manner stinks."

He rocked back against his locked knees and laughed. Then sat and looked at her while she drank her tea. Then said, "It's over, Viv. Don't you see what

David has been trying to tell you? It's all . . . gone. It's irrelevant. The sky and the sea and space are wonderful. Our feeble attempts to deal with each other are . . ." He waved his hands.

"Absurd," she supplied, and managed a small smile.

"Sometimes. Not always."

She put down her empty mug and nodded. She stared into the fire; so did he. The silence was not difficult. She waited for him to ask about the father of that baby. The baby she had intended to kill. If he wanted to know, he would ask. She had no doubt about that.

He spoke suddenly. "Elisabeth. She's not married to her husband any more. His name is Peter. He's married to someone called Margaret. Elisabeth's daughter Maisie is with them at the moment. She's ten now. A really nice kid. They all get on all right, and Maisie knows about the twins and is dying to see them."

Viv stared at him, amazed not only by the flood of information, but by the way he had delivered it. She said at last, "And you? Do you get on all right with them?"

"I'm working on it."

She nodded slowly while silence settled again. Then she said, "OK. Here's my piece. I'm somehow bound into the love story that surrounds that bloody door knob. I don't know how. Maybe it's there for all lovers. To open a door in the mind . . . it could be anything. It happened. I wrote everything down about it because I knew I would discount it myself later on . . . or simply forget the details. That was the reason. I am not going

184

to write about the past, Tom." She managed a smile. "Thank you for telling me about Elisabeth. If it matters to you, I have to tell you I liked her very much. The fact that she, too, has had a difficult time makes me admire the woman she is now. So . . . we have swopped some information. Let it end there."

He stared at her, surprised by her considered confidences. Then he smiled at the idea that they'd simply exchanged information.

"OK. I accept that. It's a nice story. Juniper told you? About George Jackson, who built the lake and cemented the door knob two feet below the water line?"

"Yes. I'd never heard it before. And David didn't know it — we used the lake quite often when we came here first, and he would have enjoyed going into its history." She paused, and added with wry humour, "He didn't know then. He knows now, of course. Jinx thinks it was a love-token."

He stared back into the fire, then said, "Will you be all right today?" He glanced up, saw her smile, and added, relieved, "I'll have to bring Ma up tomorrow, maybe Dad as well. I rather think you must be the daughter they never had!"

Her smiled widened and dazzled him. She said, "They are my first real friends, Tom. You too, in a prickly sort of way. And I think — if she is willing — Elisabeth." Ruefully she turned her smile downwards. "I never thought I could be close to anyone until I met David. And even then, we weren't like other couples. Theatre trips, dinners, we always did them alone. We didn't have any close friends. Perhaps it was because we were both tainted in various ways. No, it was more than that. It was because we were so wrapped up in each other. I threw it away, of course. I knew I would."

"You threw nothing away. You must believe that by now."

She stood up. "You'd better go. Thank you."

He leaned forward to peck her cheek.

"You'll have to write it down, Viv. Seriously. You need to look at it. Not to live it any more. To look at it as David looked at his paintings and his cartoons."

She ignored that.

"Tell Hildie to stay in the warm. I'm absolutely fine. They keep ringing from Tall Trees to ask if I need shopping. Everyone is very kind."

He passed her in the hall, bent to put on his boots, straightened and said, "Except you. You've never been kind to yourself, have you, Viv?" He pecked her again to take the sting from his words, then let himself out.

The smell of slush, watery, nearly icy, filled her nose.

She reheated the soup and took it back to the sofa, and ate it straight from the saucepan with the wooden spoon. She wasn't unhappy. It was frightening the way the whole wretched mess was being exposed, but Jinx had still kept some of it to himself, and no one would ever prise that bit out of her. Eventually . . . it would sink beneath memory, even her own. She almost smiled at the thought of writing it down. If she did, it would mean she could never forget it.

The solid comfort now lay in Tom's implicit acceptance that she was part of the Hardy family: the salt-of-the-earth family with no real idea of who she was, and what she had done. She looked out of the window, and wished the slush would melt right away so that she could run. But she was so tired. And probably not strong enough yet to run, anyway.

She lay down and pulled the blankets over her. She knew she should feel exquisite relief in the knowledge that she had not been directly responsible for David's death. But, of course, the fact that he had known, and had wrested the steering-wheel from her, and sent them ricochetting between the beech trees, revealed more than his words that he had hated her; he had hated the baby that was not his; he had hated himself because it could not be his. Writing that down would be facing the fact that she had betrayed David. Her dearest friend, her blessedly sexless lover. Betrayal was so much worse than murder.

She brought down the usual shutter inside her head. The soup and the heat from the fire did their work, and she slept.

CHAPTER
FIFTEEN

Two days later, Viv got the car out and drove to the
service station on the motorway, where she filled up
with petrol and bought the groceries on the list Hildie
had phoned through the previous night. Hildie had
said, "If you get down to the supermarket when they
first open there will be no one there." But the staff were
all local people. And she was sure the staff at the
motorway services knew nothing about her. Their
customers were anonymous, too. Itinerant shoppers. As
she pulled in she smiled at the thought. She
remembered the itinerant agricultural workers down on
the Levels. Why not itinerant shoppers? Why not
itinerant human beings?

There were no trolleys, just wire baskets. She filled
two of them, and drove back on the southbound
carriageway, and went straight to the cottage by the
river. Hardy opened the door and the sound of crying
babies filled the day.

"Let me take that." He reached for one of the plastic
bags, and she deftly avoided him and went past into the
hall.

"I'm back to normal, Mr Hardy. Close the door,
there's a wind getting up."

188

"Well, tis March. Always a windy month." He patted her arm. "Good to see you. I'd rather you called me Mick. It's what my friends do."

She must still have been pretty weak, because his words made her tear-ducts flow. She squeezed down the hall and into the kitchen.

He followed. "Before you ask how we are — we're what my old gran used to call 'bad about and worse up'. Tom's got it, though he says he hasn't. Doctors en't allowed to catch things from their patients. But Elisabeth idn't no doctor and she's real bad." He handed her some cheese and a bottle of milk. "Tis gone into Hildie's back, so if you can manage the twins tonight we'd be real grateful. By tomorrow we should be on the mend."

She nodded and continued loading the fridge. "You might think you are, but it's the weakness. It undermines everything. Let's see how it goes. If I can manage the twins, and you can manage Tom and Elisabeth, we ought to be back to normal in two or three days. Tomorrow is too soon." She closed the fridge door, and glanced at him. "Let me make some coffee . . . Mick."

He grinned. "That'd be nice. I'm sick of barley water."

She put on the kettle and they went in to see Hildie. She was sitting with her back against the radiator, and Tom was on his knees in front of the sofa changing nappies. He looked terrible. Viv patted Hildie's shoulder, and knelt by Tom. "I'll do Joy." She slid off the nappy and used a handful of wet wipes. Joy stopped yelling and cycled her freed legs crazily.

Hildie said, "She's well named. Leave her be a while, Viv."

Tom clinched velcro fastenings, and Michael's protests subsided into grumbles. Tom said he sounded like old Jinx, up at the nursing home. Hildie said, "Nothing like. These two set each other off. Crying or laughing. One starts, the other follows. They're friends already . . . they trust each other."

Hardy brought in the coffee, but Tom shook his head as he staggered to his feet. "I'll have to lie down for a while. I'll get myself some barley water and take a couple of paracetamol."

"What about Elisabeth?"

"I'll take up enough for two." Tom smiled feebly at his mother. "Perhaps this is a test for how we'll cope when we're old."

Hildie made no comment. Hardy said to Viv, "We didn't want her going back home and giving this to her little girl."

Viv said, "Maisie. Such a pretty name."

Hildie said, "Yes. I said just the same thing." She called into the hall, "Rub some of that ointment on your feet."

"It's a vapour-rub, Ma. Chest, not feet."

"Everything starts and ends with the feet. I read about it in my magazine. Rub it on your feet, Tom. There's a good lad." She looked surprised when Viv sat back on her heels almost collapsing with laughter. Tom stuck his head back through the door. He was laughing, too. Hildie said, "See? It's working already!"

Tom disappeared, closing the door after him. Joy punched the air with clenched fists, Michael gurgled. Viv said, "This is nice. It's good to see you again. I'll keep in touch on the telephone."

Hardy said seriously, "Listen. Tom is set on making them go through the night. If they cry, don't pick them up. Just stand by them with your hands on their heads and wait."

"For how long?"

"'Tis usually about fifteen minutes."

"No boiled water? No soothing chats?"

"Just the hands on the heads."

"And then I go? But they'll start up again straightaway."

"Yes. They do. But that won't go on for ever."

"Oh my God."

Hildie said, "We know. Tom hasn't had one night's sleep since he brought them home." She sighed. "Do what you think best, Viv. Boiled water sounds fine to me."

Viv took them to the bungalow. It was two journeys getting the car-seats and all the other equipment back. And they woke at midnight and again at one o'clock and four o'clock. She gave them the water and talked to them gently. She did not take them out of their car-seats until four, when she winded them one at a time and changed their nappies. They woke at eight and seemed delighted to see her still in her pyjamas. She lifted them from their cots on to the bed, wedged them in with pillows, and got in beside them.

"Well, that wasn't too bad, was it?" She stroked their tiny faces. "Those heaters are marvellous . . . we didn't feel cold . . . we didn't feel thirsty . . . and we didn't feel lonely." She tickled under their chins and both babies chortled and kicked. "Now. If I take your nappies off and pop a big towel under you, will you do your exercises while I make breakfast? You will? Come on, then, let's give it a go." She suited actions to words, and then went into the kitchen opposite the bedroom door. When they chortled, she chortled back. She whipped around, making up their bottles, making herself a thermos of tea and adding a long straw. She felt stronger than she'd felt since this bug had hit them all. She called over her shoulder, "We can do this, Michael! We sure can, Joy! We're the indefatigables!" She laughed, and they laughed back.

It didn't last all morning, of course. They slept until a very early lunchtime, and then grizzled while she ate hers. She longed for a nap herself; the rest of the day spread unendingly before her. Then the bell ping-ponged, there was the sound of her spare key in the lock, and Hildie and Mick cooeed their way down the hall.

Hildie was cocooned in coats, scarves, and a woolly hat that practically met beneath her chin.

"We know this is the time they need something extra — just when you haven't got it to give! So Hardy piled me into the van, and said it could be our first outing.

192

We'll play with them while you have a nap. Don't come out of your room until we come in with tea!"

Hardy smiled at her and the babies. They scooped up a twin each, and herded Viv out of the room. Through the bedroom wall she could faintly hear them going through nursery rhymes. She looked at the rumpled duvet and fell into it, kicking off slippers as she went. But as she lay there, hearing life in the other room, she knew that the "blessed bug" had left her, and her strength was coming back. She closed her eyes. She wouldn't sleep, but she would make the most of this breathing space, for Hildie's sake.

The very next instant she opened her eyes to a knock on the door, and in came Hildie with a tray. She had slept for an hour. The best sleep she had had for a long time.

Hildie was bent over the tray, but smiling. "There's some of your marmalade sponge in the tin. Shall we finish it up?"

"What about the twins?"

"They can't manage the peel in the marmalade." Hildie's brown eyes twinkled. "No, they're lying on the floor in front of the guard, watching the fire. Stay put. Hardy's keeping an eye. And I want to talk to you."

So they drank tea while Hildie tried to tell Viv how she felt about Elisabeth Mason. Viv sipped her tea and listened, and eventually held up her hand.

"Do you know what I think?" she asked rhetorically. "I think you were hatching plans to pair off Tom and me."

Hildie was flustered. "Not really. Not like that, anyway. But I thought . . . well, you both need a friend —"

"But we are friends. Now. We weren't at first, but since Elisabeth's arrival we're . . . all right. I honestly think we're all right. And if we are, then it's because of Elisabeth." She put her mug back on the tray, and looked at Hildie. "She's nice. A nice woman. And exactly right for Tom."

Hildie thought about it. "Yes. You're right. It's just that . . . our Tom doesn't seem very good about women. And after Della . . . it all seemed such a mess, so I thought she — Elisabeth — would be another mess." She tried to smile. "You seemed just right for him. I didn't mean to try and make a match."

"Of course not. There's ten years between us. And I'm too old to be a stepmother. Whereas Elisabeth is just the right age. And with a ready-made sister for them."

"And a lot of problems of her own." Hildie smiled ruefully. "I'm not pleased about that, but it might make her more understanding of Tom's."

Viv took the tray into the kitchen and cut the cake, and they joined Hardy and the babies in front of the fire. Hildie wanted to go on talking about Tom and Elisabeth. "It's barely four months since Della died . . . But then of course they had already been together before that . . ."

Viv noticed how skilfully Hardy turned the conversation. "You done a real good job out there, Viv," he said. He nodded through the window. "Everything looks good. Snowdrops is late, though."

She went to the window. "That little cluster around the witch hazel is out. And look at the verbena and jasmine."

Hildie joined her and looked down the windy, wet garden sadly. "I almost forgot about the world. It still keeps turning."

Viv held her arm, and gently rubbed her back through several layers of clothing. "People thought I was still in touch with nature when I did my runs. But I rarely noticed a thing."

Hardy said, "Not surprising. You ran at night, din't you? A wonder you didn't break a leg or worse." He turned and looked down at the babies, who were now studying their own feet. "We ought to go, my maid. Tis getting dark."

Viv walked with them to the door, and noticed how awkwardly Hildie got into the van. She went back to the twins, made up the fire, and talked to them about the importance of keeping well. They made small staccato sounds in reply. They turned their heads when she brought in the carrycots and warmed the sheets. She smiled at them, knowing that they were watching her. When she left them to make up their feeds, they cried. The crying accelerated when she began the laborious business of positioning them, but then, magically, ended as they began their evening feed. It all took so long. Viv realized that without Elisabeth's professional help it would take all three Hardys to feed, clean, wind and change these two small babies every three hours. She put them down at eight o'clock and carried each cot into the bedroom. Then she went back to the living room — and just as she collapsed on to the sofa, they started crying.

She simply could not face standing over their cots with her hands on their heads, so she brought them back in with her. They were so surprised they stopped wailing. She switched on the television without the sound. The fire flickered, the picture flickered, the twins were mesmerized. Two or three times during that night she got up to add another log to the embers; the babies made small animal sounds, but they did not wake until the window was full of grey light. Then Michael opened his eyes and examined the inside of his cot. Then he shouted a greeting to anyone who might be around, and Joy returned it.

Viv looked down at them from the sofa. She grinned. "D'you realize we've broken every rule in the book, and it's worked!"

They clenched their fists and shouted. But they did not cry.

CHAPTER
SIXTEEN

The slush cleared, and the overhanging icicles dripped and ran down the windows. Viv took the children over in turn to trace the rivulets with tiny forefingers. She ran two inches of warm water into the bath, and supported them while they slapped it with wide-spread hands. Then she soaped them gently, swilled them off, lifted them on to warm towels and rolled them up.

"Sausage rolls! Two for a penny!"

She carried them in by the fire and patted them dry. Joy was already making efforts to roll on to her tummy. Viv gave her some help and watched, fascinated, as Joy lifted herself into a press-up position, and pushed one knee forward, but then slipped back.

"Sausage rolls just roll . . ."

Joy persevered rather too long, and ended up crying with frustration.

"Listen, little sausage." Viv cuddled her consolingly. "You're only four months. Too soon to be crawling."

She dressed them and propped them deep in the sofa, where they could see across the room and through the window at the melting world. She was expecting Juniper for coffee that morning, and hoped they would delay their nap until Juniper had seen them.

Sure enough there was the familiar ping-pong at the front door before Viv had cleared the bathroom, and there was Juniper's usual nurse — Belle — at the handles of a wheelchair, and Juniper looking like a member of a Turkish harem, swathed in clothing that revealed her eyes only. There was much laughing as they got her down the hall and into the living room, and then pandemonium as the beautifully presented babies burst into wails of alarm at the sight of the chair and its contents.

Juniper was annoyed; she tugged her face free of scarves and said loudly above their yells, "Enough to make anyone have a fit! Snow's all gone, but we still got to dress up like Eskimos." She leaned forward. "Hello, my beauties. Tis only old Juniper again. Forgotten me already? Your gramma brought you to see me two or three weeks ago." She sat back, overwhelmed by the volume of distress. Recognizing this as a victory, the twins stopped crying; Joy first, and then Michael.

Viv said, "Took them a minute to recognize you. But they've got it. What is it you sing to them?"

Juniper chuckled, and then chanted, "Peas in a pod, peas in a pod, I'll give one a shake and give one a nod!" She proceeded to do so, and then stopped in delight as Michael shook his head in return. While she tried it again, Viv ushered Belle to the door.

"How long can she stay?" she asked.

"Not long. She'll want to get back to see her boyfriend." Belle made a rueful face. "She's spent the last three months making his life a misery, and now he's ill she has to admit to herself that she thinks a great deal of the old goat." Belle stopped by the front door to push her feet into shoes. "This is just what she needs to take her out of herself. I'll be back in time for her lunch. About an hour, probably."

"Thanks, Belle."

Viv went back to the kitchen and made coffee. She could hear Juniper still at it with her peas in a pod. The old girl looked up at her as she took in a tray.

"It's a special rhyme, just for twins, see. A way to see one from tother."

"Have a rest now. Here are those custard creams you like. And have more sugar if you need it. I'll put the children in their cots. They stay in here for their rest, is that all right?"

"Course it is. Glad to hear you're doing something so sensible. I did keep my baby girl by me at all times. Tis easier with just one, mind you. That's why I walks lop-sided. Had her on my hip for three years."

Viv wrapped them into sausage rolls again, and put them down where they could see the water running down the windowpane.

Juniper said, "You got a way with kiddies. Pity you lost yours. Great pity."

"Not really. It was . . . not viable."

"Dunno what that means, Viv. But sounds a funny thing to say about a baby. Never mind, we can't change nothing. Tell me how Hildie Hardy is doing."

They talked about the Hardys, and Viv told Juniper about Elisabeth Mason. Juniper lapped up the information like a cat laps milk. Then she drank the dregs of her coffee, brushed crumbs from the front of her cardigan, and sat back, replete.

"It's good to see you now and then. Them babies is an extra treat. Life got to go on . . . never even pauses, not for man nor beast."

Viv moved the tray. "Belle told me that poor old Jinx is not so good."

"Poor old Jinx be blowed! You did ought to hear some of the things he says to me. Latest is, he wants to go down the lake and look for that there door knob! D'you remember me telling you about that? My old mother's wedding ring that was — she didn't get nothing else out of George Jackson!" She sank her head into her shoulders. "I know what Jinx is after. He hasn't changed. I know 'e did well — keeps telling me as much — but exams idn't everything. District engineer he might have been, couldn't get a wife, could he?"

Viv went to the fire, leaned over the spark guard, and placed another log. She said carefully, "He's a bit of a gossip, I gather?"

"Dun't know about that. He likes stirring things up. Specially with some of the ladies. The more particular ones." She chuckled, then stopped. "Well, he did before he got ill. He called it flak. Like in the war. He did say if they couldn't take a bit of flak they couldn't take anything. Always giving them flak, he was."

Viv forced a small laugh. "I know. I got some of it."

Juniper nodded. "I did, too. I gave him some of it back. With interest. He weren't so keen on that." She

began to button her cardigan up. "Since he bin ill, he's
. . . different. He's mentioned you once or twice."

Viv walked to the window and checked the babies;
they slept.

"Said as he reckoned you couldn't help what you
did."

Viv kept her back to the wheelchair.

"Said you was dramatized. Something like that."

"Dramatized? Does he mean I made it all up?"

"Don't think that were it. You couldn't of made up
an accident, could you?"

Viv turned and came back to the fire. The relief was
amazing; Jinx hadn't told Juniper. She felt physically
lighter, and sat down.

Juniper turned her mouth down. "He's gone soft. I
don't like it. It's as if he's given up. I've tried to
ginger him up again, but he just grins at me and
says he knows what I'm trying to do. D'you know
what he said to me just this morning when I took
him in his cup of tea? He said I hadn't changed. I
was still beautiful. I told him he was a silly old fool."
She sighed. "Then he went back to that door knob.
He seems to think if he could get a-hold of that
door knob all his dreams would come true. Can you
believe it?" She snorted. "District engineer, indeed."
The front doorbell ping-ponged. "Here's that Belle
again. She's a good girl, but she's no good with
wheelchairs. If there's a pothole in the lane, she'll
find it. My backside can vouch for that."

Viv laughed as she went down the hall and opened
the door for Belle. It was a genuine laugh. Jinx, it

seemed, was determined to take her secret with him. She led Belle back to the wheelchair, and wrapped Juniper carefully in her mackintosh and head scarves, while Belle hovered over the carrycots and wondered in a whisper how anyone could tell the difference between the twins. As they manoeuvred the chair down the hall, Viv tried to explain that Michael was the realist and Joy the optimist. It was ridiculous. The theory of the absurd, David would have said.

She watched them set off up the road towards the gates of Tall Trees, then closed the door and leaned her head against it. Traumatized. That's what old Jinx had said. He had told Juniper that Viv Venables was traumatized. Not dramatized. Traumatized.

She wondered whether he was right. And she wondered, too, why she had been so certain that he hadn't told Tom. Everything. Just because Tom had been — for once — too discreet to mention it, perhaps . . . perhaps . . . why wouldn't he have told Tom? After all, Tom was a doctor, and bound not to talk about anything the patient told him in confidence. And if Jinx truly believed she was traumatized, and Tom was a doctor, then he might have seen it as his duty to confide in Tom. Poor Tom was not a psychiatrist, he was a general practitioner, but he had done his best.

"Write it down. You could write it in the third person —"

She turned her head and looked at the row of coat hooks where her anorak hung from its hood. She could grab it, thrust her feet into trainers and be gone. She could pound her escape back down to the lake. Perhaps David would be there again, and forgive her again. And again. And again.

She hung her head. It was so good that David had forgiven her. But she could never . . . never ever . . . forgive herself.

From the living room came Joy's small cry of delight as she woke from her nap. Almost immediately came Michael's grumble.

She went quickly to them, and crouched by the carrycots. They recognized her; she knew they did.

She said, "D'you know what I'm going to do after we've had lunch? I'm going to wrap you up and put you in the buggy, and we'll have a walk. I think the sun is coming out. It will do us all a lot of good."

She did not get as far as the lake. Her legs felt wobbly, and she had to save enough strength to push the pram up the hill again. But she was right, the still, icy air seemed to expand in her lungs, and she had a sense of being cleansed.

As she wheeled the buggy back into the house she looked up to where the trees hid the old Elizabethan manor house. Then went indoors. The door knob was on the kitchen table.

She said aloud, "Hang on in there, Jinx. I'll bring it up to you. I reckon it's the least I can do."

The phone was ringing, and she lifted the receiver on her way to the living room. It was Hildie.

"We're all on the mend, Viv. Elisabeth is making us a stew right now — there was beef in the freezer and

Tilly-next-door got her some vegetables — it smells that good, Viv. I could eat it all by myself!" She paused for breath, and rushed on, "It's all down to you. If you hadn't taken the twins like you did, we'd be dragging around the place like I don't know what!" She took another breath. "How are you doing? We could fetch them this minute. Hardy and me, we went for a walk this afternoon and are quite capable of —"

"We've been out for a walk, too!" It seemed like an enormous coincidence. "Leave them with me for a while longer, Hildie. That is, if you are still all right with it. They seem to be settling. We haven't had a real crying session since you popped in yesterday."

"We'll drive up tomorrow, then," said Hildie. "If you're sure. Certain sure. If you change your mind, just phone —"

"I won't," Viv promised. Although, even as she spoke, Michael let out a sudden bellow of rage at the delay.

"Have to tell you this, Viv. We ran into Mrs Bartholomew — d'you remember, she used to look after the swimming in the lake?" She did not wait for an answer. "Well, she asked after you. Said how sorry she was about David, but they were always a funny lot. Don't know what she meant by that. Anyway, she said if ever you wanted to talk about it, you were welcome to get in touch with her."

Viv barely paid attention; Michael was getting into full flow.

Hildie heard him, and said, "Is that Michael yelling? Sorry, Viv. I'll let you get on. Don't forget — give us a ring if you need us. Please. Otherwise see you tomorrow."

The phone clunked off. Viv went on into the living room and gathered the twins on to the sofa.

CHAPTER
SEVENTEEN

The "blessed bug" left its legacy of weakness for two or three weeks, and April was half-way through before their rather odd lives fitted back into any kind of routine. The clocks had gone on, Easter was over, Elisabeth was back in Cheltenham, and Tom and she were seriously house-hunting.

It was unexpectedly difficult for Viv to return to the afternoon walks, and eventually she worked out that it was because of seeing Tom so regularly. They had parted on such good terms that slushy day at the beginning of March, swopping confidences as if they were business deals. But she was aware that he already knew most of what she had told him, and was intelligent enough to fill in the gaps. And as the days went by, and he was necessarily hurried and therefore terse, she convinced herself that he must know the whole story — every detail. And that for her was unbearable. She went over and over her conversation with him, and then similarly the one she'd had with Elisabeth, until her head ached.

After Easter she started driving down to the riverside cottage and leaving the car there while she pushed the buggy through the village and down to the beach.

She was planning to do that on a Thursday in late April; it was windy but sunny and the big hood on the buggy would protect the babies. They loved sitting up and watching the sea. She thought how marvellous it would be later on in the summer to carry them on to the shingle . . . perhaps she and Hildie could dabble their feet in a high tide. She dared not try to imagine next year. Tom would have moved them to Cheltenham by then, and life would change again. She wondered whether she would be able to return to running . . . it would be difficult to maintain the isolation she used to have. People spoke to her now, when she was wheeling the twins. What was even more difficult was that they spoke to the twins themselves. They pushed their heads beneath the hood and said things like: "Your daddy made me better, and he told me all about you . . . Now, who is Joy and who is Michael?" Automatically Viv found herself repeating Juniper's jingle. Michael knew what to do and nodded vigorously. It made everyone ecstatic. She could have been less responsive, but she was so proud of the twins.

She was clearing away her early lunch things when she heard the car. She was at the door immediately; it could only be Tom, as dear Hardy was working in a nearby village. It was Tom.

"Is everything all right? You are very early."

She went to meet him, assuming the babies were waiting to be unloaded.

He said, "It's all right. Don't panic. I've been on a call at Tall Trees. Let's go inside." There were no babies in the car. Just his bag.

She led the way quickly down the hall and into the living room.

"Is something wrong?"

He made a semi-humorous face at her. "Where on earth do I begin to answer a question like that?" He held on to the back of the sofa. "I've been some time with John Jinks. I don't think he'll last the day. Will you go up and sit with him for a while?"

She heard his words and tried to work out something — anything — behind them. "He doesn't like me, Tom. Juniper is the one he needs now."

"Yes. And she's doing her best. But now she needs to sleep. And he needs to talk to you — well, say a few words."

"The twins . . ."

"We'll manage today. I promise."

She was silent, knowing she had to do this.

He said, "Have you eaten today?"

"Of course. Breakfast and lunch."

"Then . . . there's nothing to stop you going now."

"Is it . . . that soon?"

"Could well be." He was speaking briskly in his doctor's voice. "I could take you up the drive."

She looked at him. "Don't be silly. You don't have to check me in. I'll go. Just let me do it in my own time." She jerked her head sideways. "Go on home now, Tom, you look all in."

He hesitated then nodded. "OK. I'll phone about fourish. Mum's making scones today, I think."

She watched him stride to his car and drive off without a backward glance. She hesitated by the open door, wondering whether he might reverse back on some pretext. But he did not appear, and she straightened her back suddenly, closed the door and went into the kitchen. She picked up the door knob and pushed it into her pocket, gathered up shoes, fleece scarf and gloves, and sat on the edge of her bed while she got herself ready.

An unfamiliar staff member opened the door to her ring.

"Ah. You must be Mrs Venables. Doctor said you would sit with Mr Jinks for an hour or so. I'll lead the way, we've moved him so that he is next to the staff room."

That was a sign poor old Jinx was seriously ill. Also, it was not reassuring that she was instantly recognizable by someone she did not know.

The old manor house was typically Elizabethan, with a long gallery running across its breadth, a magnificent view in every one of its diamond-paned windows. Two wheelchairs were parked in an embrasure, a small table containing tea things between them. Both occupants were asleep. Viv's guide smiled over her shoulder. "They love to sit here on a windy afternoon, but after the first five minutes, they drop off."

Viv smiled, too. She revised one of her ideas, and wondered whether so much napping in "homes" was due to contented relaxation. They turned into a narrow panelled passage which opened out into a glass-domed area rather like a dining room. A round table full of books and papers was beneath the light; there was a desk with three telephones and a computer, and tall filing cabinets around the walls. "This is the nursing station." The guide stopped by a door and held the handle. "Mr Jinks is in here. Most of us are dealing with visitors until five, but there will be someone in the staff rest-room if you need any support." She nodded across the table at another door, then turned and led the way into Jinx's room.

It was so calm, so sunny, Viv felt as if she were stepping into another world. She realized that in spite of all the secondary glazing to back up the old windows, the front of the house was buffeted constantly by every passing breeze; and the April breezes were more like gales today. This room, looking out on the sheltered courtyard with the old stables to one side, was completely protected, and the afternoon sun slanted into it and lit up the primrose-coloured walls and the white surfaces.

Jinx was propped up in bed, apparently asleep. Viv was shocked by his appearance. His face had fallen in, so that even his nostrils looked pinched. His eyes were lost in their sockets, and his mouth was puckered inwards. What saved him from seeming already dead was the bed-jacket. It was pale blue and very beribboned. Viv guessed it belonged to Juniper.

He made a strangled sound and the nurse went immediately to the window and adjusted vertical blinds. "Sorry, Mr Jinks," she trilled. Then, to Viv, "The strong sunlight hurts his eyes."

Viv might have guessed there would be something he did not like.

210

She picked up a chair from a small stack in the corner, and brought it forward. The nurse touched her shoulder. "I'll leave you now. The staff rest-room is immediately opposite and you can always ring the bell — it's on his pillow."

Viv smiled thanks; the door closed; she was alone with Jinx — and it was obvious from Tom's insistence that this was a final visit. She swallowed and drew her chair nearer to the top of the bed. Since her mother, she had never been with anyone so clearly dying. Her father's heart had given out while he slept; and David . . .

She leaned forward. "Jinx. It's Viv Venables. David's wife. I thought I would . . ." She cleared her throat. ". . . pop in. The doctor told me you were ill, and I had something for you so —"

His eyes appeared in the dark sockets; they gleamed as if with a kind of cynical amusement. He picked up on her words. Raspingly, slowly, he said, "So you popped in. Good of you to pop in. Better than the telly. See Jinx peg out. Eh? Eh?"

She was shocked at first, then almost reassured. He was still there, Jinx the Irascible. She leaned closer still and mimicked his sarcasm. "I like the bed-jacket. Blue for a boy."

His face moved, as if he might be trying to smile. "It's hers. I got her in the end."

She thought it better not to question exactly what he meant. But she smiled at him, and said, "I've brought you something you might like to give to her, actually. She told me it saved your life once."

His eyes appeared again, his mouth took shape, he took a short, trembling breath. "That day. You came to see me. You put it on the table. I wanted it. But it was yours. It's still yours." It was as if his vocal cords were grinding each word.

"No. Not any more. I rather think it belongs to anyone who needs a love-token. You found it once. I found it once. Perhaps it saved both our lives. Then it was given to me. Now I give it to you." She wriggled the door knob out of her pocket, took his skeletal hand in hers, and fitted the two together. She held them there for a long a moment, and felt him tremble inwardly. Then she released them. Very slowly, with great effort, he brought his other hand across the turned-back sheet and clasped two hands around the door knob. Viv had an enormous sense of something coming to an end. She waited.

After a while she thought he was sleeping, and began to withdraw her fingers across the sheet and on to her lap. But then his head moved infinitesimally, and she saw that gleam from his sunken eyes again. She leaned forward so that he could see her face.

"Are you all right, Jinx?" What a ridiculous question. Yet, so unusually for him, he did not deal with it as such. He knew what she meant.

He nodded, once, twice. "Thank you." The rasp was a whisper. "The most romantic thing in the world."

She whispered back, surprised. "Yes. I suppose it is."

She put her hand back over his and stared down at them. Three hands clasped around a Victorian door knob that had been cemented firmly into a wall and then released. Three very odd romances.

He made a ghastly choking sound, and she clutched him and looked up again, terrified he was going to go then and there.

But the cough had cleared his lungs for an instant, and he spoke almost clearly. "I've told no one. I never understood it. But I've liked you . . . respected you . . . if you thought it was right, then I trust that. He was my best friend, I loved him. If it was his fault, then he was sorry. I know he was sorry."

She had no idea whether her tears were for Jinx, or for David, or were simply tears of relief that her secret was still hers. For ever, now. She hung on to the back of his gnarled hand, and lowered her head, and watched her own tears fall on to the immaculate turned-down sheet. It could have lasted like that for a few minutes or an hour, there was no sense of passing time, until, prosaically, she had to blow her nose. Then she saw that his eyes were still open and — she was almost certain — were smiling.

He met her searching gaze, and whispered, "Ask her to come to me." She nodded and put away her handkerchief, stood up. He made the choking sound again, and she waited. He added, "Try to live again. Don't hold it by yourself any longer."

She stood up and shook her head, though she did not understand. Then she touched his hand again, saying goodbye, to him and the love-token, and she crossed the nursing station, opened the opposite door and said to the two nurses inside, "Can you tell me where Juniper Stevens is? Jinx would like to see her now."

They both stood up; one of them was Belle. She took Viv's arm and piloted her gently back through the narrow-panelled passage. The other nurse went straight to Jinx.

Juniper seemed to be expecting a summons. She was in the large sitting room downstairs where, not that long ago, Viv had first shown Jinx the door knob.

"I said to the doctor — Hildie's boy — I said as how I thought he would go today, and he wanted to see you before he left." Juniper tried to get out of her wheelchair and fell back. Belle put a hand on her shoulder, and turned her towards the door and the lift. Viv walked by her side.

"He is very weak but he's making sense. Good sense."

"I could've told you that, my lovely. He's gone back in time. Before the nastiness got him." Juniper looked up. "You go down to Hildie, now. Have a nice cup of tea. Tell her what is happening."

Viv watched the lift doors close on her, and then went to the side door and let herself out. There was the enormous view of sea and sky again; the tiny piece of the universe that made them all seem small and puny. Absurd.

She walked down the drive to the retaining terrace wall, and stared out at the view, realizing again how beautiful and vast David had made his paintings. She knew that somewhere out there he still existed; maybe the beauty of the skyscape lay in the fact that it was composed of essences of humankind. She rested her arms on the wall, and let random and insignificant ideas and thoughts float through her. Somehow David had managed to separate himself, perhaps assemble himself, from all this beauty in order to make contact with her; perhaps with great difficulty. She had known for certain that the time by the darkness of the lake, back in December, had been a farewell and a forgiveness for both of them; a universal forgiveness.

She was crying again, great gulping tears. She let them drain from her eyes and through her body like a baptism. A literal immersion. Then she blinked fiercely, scrubbed at them with her sodden handkerchief and turned towards her home and — perhaps later — Hildie.

CHAPTER
EIGHTEEN

John Jinks's solicitor was also his executor; he and the funeral directors "saw to" everything. A notice appeared in the local paper in good time for people to attend the service at the parish church, if they wished. It was soon bruited around that, in spite of his many complaints about Tall Trees nursing home, he had left everything he had to them, and as he had never married and had husbanded his money carefully, this was a not inconsiderable legacy.

Hildie exclaimed afterwards about the thirty-four people in the church "not counting the vicar and the undertakers". She was solemnly pleased at such good attendance. "I've been to four or five funerals of the residents," she said to Viv and Juniper. "Most of the congregation were from the nursing home — that's natural, as we've had the closest contact. But I didn't expect Esmé and Winnie to turn up. He loved to rile them, and he usually succeeded. That man from the council — fair enough, Jinx worked for them most of his life. And perhaps someone from that engineering institute or whatever they call themselves. But there were at least half a dozen from both places! Even more doddery than he was. Walking sticks everywhere . . .

they always fall down when they're propped up, have you noticed? Made a regular clatter . . ."

Viv had attended the service but not gone on to Tall Trees for drinks and sandwiches afterwards. She thought that after the bequest such hospitality was probably seen by the owners as obligatory, but Hildie shook her head. "They've had bequests before and never seen the need to do this. The residents just loved it. You should have seen Juniper doing the hostess. And Belle got a marriage proposal!"

Viv laughed and then sobered. "It never stops," she commented. Then, abruptly, "I gave him the door knob for Juniper, Hildie."

Hildie was silent for some time. At last she nodded consideringly. "A good thing to do. She's keeping quiet about it, so it must be important to her." She lifted her tea cup. "Well done, Viv. Does this mean you are letting go at last?"

"I don't know. I really don't know."

"When Tom and the babies go back to Cheltenham, will you go back to running half the night away?" Hildie tried to make it light.

"I don't know," Viv repeated.

"Do you remember when we went to the cinema? Last winter, just before the twins were born?"

"Of course. How could I forget that?"

Hildie smiled ruefully. "So much has happened since then. Well, I thought I understood how you felt that day. I can't remember what you said . . . but I realized that you had had a difficult childhood — and then the accident. But the way you have worked and worked!

217

The way you have stood by me! By all of us." She smiled. "Don't be embarrassed, Viv, it's true. I — we — could not have managed without you. I just hope and pray you won't have to go back to running."

Viv shook her head, denying what Hildie found praiseworthy. She said, "If I do, it will be to connect with everything around me. I'll try not to run away again." She lifted her shoulders helplessly. "You know, Hildie, all the stuff I did in the garden, everything, really, it's just been another way of running away."

Hildie shook her head more vigorously than Viv had. "Don't tell me lies, Viv Venables. Looking after Mike and Joy hasn't been running anywhere. It's been work, and it's been happiness. I've got eyes, you know."

They both laughed. Viv thought of the laughter she had shared with this woman. And with Juniper Stevens. That would go on. That would heal the final memory. There would be no need to run again.

She walked many of her old running routes. Some she simply did not remember, others, along the coastal path, would not take the twin buggy. She had not realized they were all so beautiful. One narrow, rutted lane stopped abruptly at a stile. She put the brake on the buggy and sat on top of the ancient ridged wood structure, wondering how long these awkward old pedestrian gateways would be permitted. Below her the twins talked to each other, punching the air to emphasize various points; they thoroughly enjoyed the bumpy rides. She stared across a field starred with daisies, and remembered the nature walks of her

218

teaching days, when the local children had tried to teach her the old country names of their wild flowers. "Not sorrel, miss. We calls it the vinegar plant. And that there, that's egg and bacon. No, tis all right, miss — you can eat it — when it's fresh like that it's called bread and cheese . . ." How wonderful it had been to spend so much time with children who were not frightened. Who could explore their environment carefully and with interest, instead of looking for hiding places, running down alleys, crouching between pews in deserted churches . . . She got off the stile as Joy began to grumble, and joggled the buggy back down the lane. "Home again, home again, jiggity-jig." She laughed down at them playing their favourite game. It looked like they were pretending they were in a train. They jiggled about and made "choo choo" noises, Mike first, and placid Joy echoing him.

In July Elisabeth brought her daughter, Maisie, to meet the older Hardys, and Mick relaxed his rules and loaded everyone in his van so they could visit Viv and her bungalow.

Maisie did not look like her mother; she was just eleven years old and was already taller than Elisabeth. She was as lean and gangly as Viv, her white-blonde hair in a long ponytail, her blue eyes rather apprehensive as they unloaded the babies and all crowded down the hall. She smiled and shook Viv's hand very formally, but said nothing. Then she went into the living room and was confronted by the steep fall of the garden and then the sea and sky.

She reached for her mother's hand. "You didn't tell me this," she said. She looked at Viv. "It's like an eagle's nest. Like we could take off. Like we could fly."

Viv laughed, nodding. Elisabeth said, "I looked out of the window before, of course, but I don't think I actually saw anything except the snow."

Maisie was transformed. She had to hold Mike, then Joy, and point out everything: from the fig tree to a container ship apparently floating above the sea. Viv tried to explain how often the horizon melted into the sky. She said, "My husband was fascinated by it, too, Maisie. He tried to paint it."

"Can I see?" Maisie propped the twins expertly into the sofa. "I'm, like, going to be an artist when I grow up. Daddy thinks I've got a good eye. So do you, don't you, Mum?"

"We should have brought your sketch pad and stuff," Elisabeth said.

Viv said, "Well, let's have tea and cake. Then perhaps I can find some old sketches . . ." She caught Tom's eye and petered out.

He said, "You've got a couple of those skyscapes in the dining room. May I show Maisie?"

"Of course." Maisie followed Tom out, skipping occasionally. Viv did not follow. She felt helpless. "Shall I put the kettle on?" she asked the others.

Hildie and Mick were settled either side of the babies. Elisabeth said, "I'll come and help. I loved your kitchen that day I was here, before the dreaded lurgy got me, too!" She laughed and followed Viv down the hall. "I thought I'd got my usual sore mouth. What a time that was!" They went into the kitchen, where the trolley was laid ready. She said, "Oh, Viv. You've got it so — so —"

Viv said quickly, "I had to sort things out properly. Because of the twins."

"But you've kept the warm feeling. You wanted me to be a nanny. And you've made yourself one. The house says it all, so secure and stable."

She was laughing, but Viv said soberly, "You told me it was your role then. And it became mine."

Elisabeth passed the tea caddy. "It helps to have a role, doesn't it? It's the way I juggle things, too. Half a nanny, half a mother, half of a relationship."

Viv heard the sadness behind the flippancy. She said, "That's too many halves by half!" She put the cosy on to the teapot. "But you're right. It is good to have a role." She smiled. "You know I wish you all the best — you and Tom and your lovely Maisie, and Mike and Joy . . . mother of a big family! Have you come up here to tell us when it will begin?"

"Not really. We think we've found a house. Maisie has got a place in a good school next September, and it's just around the corner. Not too far from the health centre for Tom and me. But nothing is signed or sealed. Money is tight, and we need an enormous mortgage." She made a face. "You know . . . all the little snags."

"You'll cope with them. Maisie adores the twins, I can see that. Is she all right with Tom?"

"I think so. It's difficult for her, she's used to having two mothers, but not two fathers. How would you have felt if your father had remarried?"

221

Viv said emphatically, "I would have been delighted. Relieved. This role thing again . . . if a child has to take on the role of the departed husband or wife, it becomes too much."

"You were expected to fill your mother's shoes?" Elisabeth saw the shadow cross Viv's face. She said quickly, "It wasn't like that for Maisie."

Viv cleared her throat almost angrily. "She knew that you were alone. Probably upset. She might have felt guilty because she still loved her father. And it sounds as if she and her stepmother get on well, too. More guilt." Viv got one of her Victoria sponges from a tin and fetched a knife. "Believe me, most children are pleased when that awful gap is filled by someone else." She smiled again; her mouth trembled. "Would you cut this cake for me?"

Elisabeth took the knife. "Is it another marmalade sponge? I've used marmalade ever since that day in March."

"Have you?" Viv was grateful again for the way Elisabeth could change the conversation so easily. "Actually I meant to get some raspberry jam. I thought Maisie would prefer something sweet."

"Well, I see you have chocolate biscuits, too." Elisabeth finished cutting and found a place on the trolley for the plate. "Viv, are you going to be all right? You can come and stay whenever you like — I'd love that. I've been too busy to make many friends, and we get on really well."

Viv swallowed fiercely and nodded, quite unable to speak. Elisabeth went on, carried away. "Why don't you try a new life completely, and live with us? I'm sure I could get you a job in reception at the health centre. Or you could teach again. It would be simply marvellous! Why didn't we think of it before? Maisie obviously likes you, and you like her, and you're so good with the twins. That sounds as if I expect you to look after all the children! But of course I don't mean that. Just share them with us."

"Oh . . . oh no. Really. You're so kind — so sweet. My life is here. I have to make it here, until there's a proper base from which to . . . go." Viv fought tears and a sudden terror. She cut through Elisabeth's persuasive protests. "Honestly, Elisabeth. Tom has been very kind but . . . after all, until the twins arrived he did not know me . . . and the two of you need your space. It simply wouldn't work. But the fact that you thought of it and suggested it . . . I will visit, I promise. It took just an hour to drive to Cheltenham when I went last. I could babysit now and then. If you like."

Elisabeth saw she had gone too far, and said that would be marvellous. "But you've got it wrong about Tom. I know he sounds rather — brief — at times, but he thinks a great deal of you, Viv. You speak of guilt. He feels that you and he share a terrible burden of guilt. He can talk about his guilt — to me and to his parents. He says he has tried to get you to talk to him about yours, but you cannot."

"There's nothing to say, Elisabeth. Things have happened . . . nobody could understand unless they had been there . . . experienced these things for themselves." Viv shook her head. "Let's take the tea in, now. And don't worry about me. Please. As a matter of fact, I wrote some things down as they happened — so that I wouldn't forget the details."

"Oh . . . does Tom know?"

"I can't remember . . ."

"May I tell him? He would be so pleased. He has written a lot of stuff himself. In the third person. Says it helps."

Viv said nothing as she pushed the trolley down the hall. She was amazed that Tom needed to write down his feelings. She accepted that Elisabeth knew a different Tom . . . for instance she was fairly certain that Tom had never "talked to" his parents in the way he had to Elisabeth. That was probably why he had written down some of his thoughts. And it must have worked because he had wanted her to do the same thing. Just for an instant she wondered whether it would work for her.

Maisie was shy again during tea. She sat close to her mother and listened as Hildie told them all about Juniper and her romance with John Jinks.

"Don't you think that's romantic, Maisie?" she asked. "He was in love with her all those years, and at the end she fell in love with him, too."

"And then he died." Maisie took her mother's hand. "I didn't like Dad falling in love with Margaret, Mum. But it's awful that David Venables died when he was in the middle of painting space. And now this story about John Jinks . . . such a funny name. I'd rather put up with the divorce so long as Daddy is still alive. Wouldn't you?"

224

Elisabeth looked at her, then tucked her into her shoulder. "Yes. Yes, I would, darling . . ." Her eyes swivelled at Viv apologetically, but Viv spoke to Maisie with wonder.

"Maisie . . . how marvellous that you can see what David was doing! Thank you. D'you know he used to say that everyone reckoned it was tricky to paint water, but it was a darned sight trickier to paint space."

Maisie looked up at her from the safety of her mother's embrace and smiled a wobbly smile. "It's beautiful. That's how he did it. Painting beauty. And then those little pictures of people . . . so funny. You have to laugh."

Viv nodded. "You do, indeed."

Maisie said, "It's like he knew that he must never get too heavy."

"He never did." Viv nodded and crossed her fingers beneath her paper napkin. He had "got heavy" just once. Only that once.

Tom and Elisabeth could not raise the money for the house, but during the school holidays they found a large garden flat in one of the Regency crescents, and spent the rest of the summer scraping off several layers of paper in every room. The three bedrooms were tucked away behind an enormous gloomy corridor, almost underground, windows at head height; the spacious kitchen/living room ran the width of the garden, with huge sash windows looking out on to a stone-flagged semi-circle scooped out of the garden. Later, the twins would be able to play there safely.

Elegantly curved shallow steps led to a walled garden with an apple tree.

Elisabeth gave Viv and the Hardys a guided tour as soon as the sale was confirmed.

"This was where the cook and maid worked and lived." The original shallow sink was still in situ, a coal range on one wall. "I think we'll have an Aga . . . or maybe one of those eye-level ovens and a separate hob. Not sure yet."

Hildie said nothing, Hardy grunted enthusiastically, Viv said, "That sounds perfect — especially as the twins will soon be walking. It's beautiful. Simple, easy to keep going. What does Maisie think?"

Elisabeth made a face. "Politely nice." She shrugged. "She's used to a lot of room with her father and Margaret. And, of course, when she's with me she's really got the whole house to herself."

Still Hildie made no contribution. Hardy cleared his throat and said, "Reminds me of when Tom was at home. He always liked to do his work downstairs. Telly on, Hildie nattering, cooking."

Viv said, "I would have liked that, too. It's proper family life, isn't it? Going out of fashion now." She had Michael on her left hip; Hildie cradled Joy.

Elisabeth nodded thoughtfully. "Certainly, Maisie hasn't had that sort of family life. Perhaps that's why . . ."

Hardy said, "I could fix up her room. Make it into what they call a bed-sit. So she's always got her — her —"

Hildie furnished, "Own space. That's what they say now, isn't it? I must have my own space. As if they're scared of sharing anything any more."

Viv and Hardy both reached out to touch her. Elisabeth nodded. "That would be great fun for her, Mick. If you're sure you can spare the time."

He gave the impression of rolling up his sleeves then and there. "Get it stripped down. Walls cleared. I can burn off most of the old paint. The wainscoting is grand, so are the doors. You've got room to keep that sink — vegetable preparing and suchlike — and we can have a new kitchen starting from here . . . you'll have a good time choosing that." He whipped out an extending measure and went towards the range. "We'll have this out and in one of those Victorian auctions. Then I'll get started. Maisie's room first, and then this space." He looked around admiringly. "I'll get Elgar to help out. He's got an eye for old houses."

"Elgar?" Elisabeth and Viv spoke together.

"Named after the composer, yes." Hardy nodded. "He — the composer — came to the village, you know. Elgar Tompkins was named after him."

Everyone laughed. The twins shrieked their joy. Elisabeth was visibly reassured. She confessed that she had thought they might disapprove of her and Tom buying a flat. "We wouldn't have got this one," she said. "Except the owners insisted on vetting would-be buyers, and they were hoping for a family." She said musingly, "So, three children, a doctor on call during the night, and a nurse — well, it seemed it was what they were looking for!" She laughed. "They came here in 1953 — Coronation year — and had a family of four, and they never wanted to leave. But the basement was broken into twice last year, and they were scared. It was quite a business getting the deeds split, but anyway, they did it eventually." She paused and looked around. "I'm so glad you like it. Tom fell for it like a ton of bricks, but when Maisie was so cool I did wonder whether we were doing the right thing."

"Do you like the old couple upstairs?" Hildie said bluntly as she re-settled Joy on her shoulder.

"Oh yes. They're both in their late seventies, but they still play tennis." She pointed to the apple tree through the wide windows. "Montpellier Gardens are just across the road, and they use the tennis courts there. And they swim. One of the daughters still lives in Cheltenham. We've met her — she was one of the vetting committee — and she's really nice. She's often here with her husband. The grandchildren go to Maisie's new school . . . that's another reason Maisie is a bit quiet these days. She's nervous."

Hildie said, "She'll be less nervous with this kind of family background." She smiled, coming to life at last. "Just think of being able to boast a brother and sister who are twins!" She walked through the living area and into the corridor. "You know, this is what interests me. It's so big."

Elisabeth said, "Apparently it's the space between the two load-bearing walls. Plenty of room for trolleys . . . see, there's still the dumb waiter down here." She opened a small door in the far wall to reveal a tiny lift. "It had to be all boxed in for security reasons, but it

228

would have taken food and so forth into the upstairs dining room."

Viv said, "It's fascinating, Elisabeth. Maisie will love all this."

Hildie said, "When you showed us the bedrooms, first of all I thought how good this big corridor was to take you away from the living quarters. Then I thought . . ." She paused for effect and on her shoulder Joy chuckled. "I thought, table tennis!"

Hardy guffawed a loud laugh, and the twins stiffened, startled. He said, "Hildie was champion at table tennis. She won a cup." He looked around. "She's right, there's room for two tables here . . . snooker? We need decent lighting . . ."

Viv loved the way he kept saying what "we" needed.

Elisabeth breathed, "Hildie . . . you're wonderful. There's nothing you can really do with this space. Like you, I thought it would be useful to separate sleeping from living space. But a play area . . . oh, Hildie."

Hildie grinned. "Tell Maisie I'll take her on."

They all laughed. The twins yelled their delight.

As Hardy said as he got into the nearside lane of the motorway, "I think it's going to be all right."

Hildie agreed. "Long way to go, but they've got something really good to work towards."

CHAPTER
NINETEEN

The summer went all too quickly. Viv continued to look after the children most weekdays. When Michael learned to crawl, Joy was just three days behind him. Viv completely cleared the long hall in her bungalow and let them skitter up and down unimpeded. Once in the living room they began to pull themselves up by the chairs. She could imagine how they would love the enormous living area at the flat in Cheltenham. This small single-storeyed dwelling, clinging precariously to the cliff, would become what it had been before. Isolated.

Elisabeth brought Maisie down again to get to know her new grandparents, and when a shopping trip to Bristol was planned, Maisie asked whether she could stay with Viv. Elisabeth brought her up, the twins sitting in their car-seats.

"It will only be for a few hours, Viv," Elisabeth said, standing by the passenger door to let Michael and Joy know they were not being unloaded yet. "Hildie wants to look at carpets. Mick is working up in Cheltenham at the flat . . . Tom is at a conference . . ."

Viv beamed at Maisie, wondering what on earth one did with an eleven-year-old whose life was being turned upside down, and who at this moment was looking anxious.

"I'd love that. How do you feel about it, Maisie? It's quite warm. I've looked out a couple of David's sketch blocks. We could sit in the garden and — and — have a go at painting space."

Before she could offer the alternative of a walk over Becket's Hill or a matinee at the cinema, Maisie's face opened wide with delight. Viv remembered how she had been Maisie's age when she had learned how to look for danger, run, close herself in. That was why she had forgotten so much after the accident; that was why she had started running again. She had gone back into that closed-in state.

Michael was beginning to protest; Joy looked at him and puckered her forehead and mouth in preparation. Viv said, "You'd better go. They'll be fine once the car starts. Give my love to Hildie. Hope she finds something she likes."

She and Maisie waved them off, and turned in unison. Their movements matched in other ways, too: they paced each other down the hall and into the kitchen, Viv filled the kettle and Maisie plugged it in. It made Maisie feel comfortable.

"It's so nice here. You have proper tea like Mum. Margaret and Dad have green tea. It's OK but ordinary tea is homely."

Viv smiled, remembering what Elisabeth had said about nannying. They took vacuum mugs of tea outside and walked down the garden and then back up again, pausing to frame different aspects.

"The thing is, your husband, like, painted *everything*. There's a single leaf at the bottom of the picture in the dining room. It looks a bit like one of those leaves." She pointed to the fig tree.

Viv nodded. "Everything. Yet nothing." She sat on one of the steps leading to the house, and patted a space next to her. "He sat here sometimes. Other times he had a chair just outside the window. Then he might go down to the bottom wall and look over to the sea."

"You mean he changed places for one painting?"

"Yes. And do call him David." Viv stared down at the fig tree. "Do you see, Maisie? It makes sense of his cartoons, too. Everything and nothing."

But unexpectedly Maisie shook her head. "Not quite nothing. If he painted that —" She stretched out an arm to sky and sea. "It was everything. But that leaves us. And we're not really nothing. David . . ." She said the name shyly, and glanced at Viv. ". . . painted us as funny. My art teacher said, 'Don't forget human beings don't always look like they look in advertisements. They often look quite odd, but that's because they're real.' "

"Oh, my God." Viv stared at the small oval face by her side. "That's exactly it. I don't know whether David realized . . . he never explained his stuff. Reckoned if you had to explain something you created, then it wasn't right. But you've put your finger on it, Maisie!" She stared for a moment longer, then looked away. "Sorry. I don't know what to say." For a moment she longed to tell Maisie about the time above the dark hole where the lake had been emptied, where she had become part of the flow of everything and nothing. She swallowed.

Maisie was embarrassed but pleased. "It wasn't actually me. It was my art teacher. And she also said that if you sketched each day you made a sort of diary. And I do that. I've done every room at home . . . the house where I was born. And Mum thinks I should start on the flat, but I haven't. Not yet, anyway."

Viv breathed carefully, and brought herself back to the world of this girl who was about to lose her home and move into a flat with three extra people.

She said, "Are you nervous about moving, Maisie? Would it help if you did a cartoon of yourself? Looking a bit nervous, then a bit more . . ." She laughed to show it was funny.

Maisie laughed, too. "Mum's having to move, too — she keeps reminding me of that. And I can always spend time with Dad and Margaret." She shook her head. "I just don't know what it will be like actually, do I? The twins are great. So is Tom. I think I'm probably much more nervous about starting at St Bede's. It specializes in the arts, but maybe not the sort of art Mrs Morrison teaches." She shook herself all over like a puppy. "I don't know! That's why I wanted to come and look at — at — David's paintings again. Because they make everything seem ordinary." She opened her eyes wide, and looked imploringly at Viv. "Gosh! I didn't mean that like it sounds. I'm really sorry."

Viv laughed. "I know exactly what you meant, Maisie. Listen. Shall I fetch one of David's sketch books and you can have a go out here while I cut sandwiches and stuff for tea?"

Maisie nodded enthusiastically.

It was that evening when she thought about her time with Maisie . . . that was when she knew she had to turn herself inside out in an effort to . . . what was the word Maisie had used? Detox. Get rid of the poison in her own system.

They had eaten the sandwiches in the garden. It was August but overcast — ideal weather for sketching — and Maisie had been unwilling to leave her sketch book. So they had munched their way through cucumber sandwiches and chocolate biscuits and another thermos mug of tea, and Maisie mentioned a special picture she was painting.

Viv asked casually about it. Maisie pursed her full mouth.

"I can't say much yet, because I don't know how it will work out. I tried to paint — like David. But I'm not good enough to — to — like — sort of — join it up properly."

"OK. Wait and see if it works. David threw away loads of stuff to get through to what he was seeing in his head. But he didn't give up easily."

"No. I sort of guessed that." She removed a slice of cucumber from two slices of bread and nibbled it. Then she said tentatively, "Viv . . . Mum hasn't really had time to make friends. I think because Dad fell in love with Margaret she has always felt sort of . . . not rubbish, exactly. Second best. And she says you haven't made friends because you gave everything to David. She'd like it if you could be her friend. What do you think?"

Viv smiled instantly. "I think it's already happened."

Maisie smiled too, happy, relieved. "Oh good." She bit into her sandwich with relish and spoke through it. "And another thing. Is it all right for me to be a friend, too? Tom said that as you are the nearest thing to a sister for him, maybe I could think of you as an aunt. Which is fine. But I'd like a friend, really. Friends talk to each other like we talk, don't they? They don't go on and on about what to wear, and doing homework, and trying not to be shy. They talk about important things. Like what goes on in here." She tapped between her eyes with a sandwich crust. "Mum calls it a detox. You get rid of things you didn't even know you needed to get rid of!"

Viv laughed, and nodded vigorously. "I'd love to have a friend like you, Maisie. Hildie started all this. She was my first friend. I remember we laughed together because she was Hildie Hardy and I am Viv Venables. You can join that particular club, can't you? With a name like yours, you're so obviously going to succeed."

"Maisie Mason? Oh Viv! I just hate it. It sounds madeup and silly."

"It's a name people won't forget. And that's important in the art world."

"Is it? Is it really? I hadn't thought . . . I mean it sounds, like, so bimbo-ish."

Viv rocked back, laughing. "David said that his name sounded pompous. He was never pompous. And you'll never be bimbo-ish."

Maisie smiled hopefully, diffidently. She finished her sandwich and listened while Viv told her the story of Thomas à Becket's assassins, and how they had come here in search of sanctuary.

She breathed, "I *see*. Becket's Hill. Of course." She looked at Viv. "I've been trying to copy David. But I can't paint everything. I have to paint . . . something." She looked past the fig tree. "Becket's Hill is left out of my everything. But it's there." She looked at Viv excitedly. "If I block it in now, I can mix that green when I get home and just . . . get it."

It had been a moment of pure epiphany for Maisie, and as Viv lay in bed that night she knew it had come to her, too, through Maisie. She began to cry, slow hot tears of sheer dread. She did not want to do this. But if she was to "detox", it was the only way. She could not run from it any longer. She could not draw it in a series of cartoons. She had loved David, he had been her best friend, but she had never really told him . . . and she had married him because he was impotent.

She got out of bed and fetched the case.

CHAPTER
TWENTY

Vivian's story

I have decided to do it. How far I can get I have no idea, but I am going to start off in the third person so that I can be an objective observer. Externalize. Or as Maisie might put it, "Like . . . stay cool."

I looked through the small case where I keep my papers last night and saw that I had not only reported the times that David . . . what? Made himself known to me? I had done more than that. I could have started the report down at the lake when he — apparently — pushed me in; and then listed the other times. I clearly felt bound to interpret these times — firstly so that I would find the door knob and recognize it when he brought it to me. And then so that I would know something very obvious . . . love is all you need, and everything else is unnecessary, melts away, even forgiveness.

If I had reported just those times I suppose . . . think . . . I would not have been reporting everything that was important. Perhaps David had already shown me that the universal and the particular had to co-exist to make any kind of sense. That meant I felt bound to

237

report on Hildie and Mick Hardy. And then Della, who was so important in my life, even though I had never seen her. And her twins: Joy, Michael. And Tom Hardy, who, incredibly, had been Della's husband and, it seemed, felt brotherly towards me! There were so many other things: absurdities, real-life cartoons. Juniper who could have been Juniper Jinks. Poor Jinx himself, who had kept my secret to the end.

This report cannot be like that. My contact with David after his violent death had to be in the context of day-to-day life to make it real, to keep me from "losing it" completely; in fact, perhaps to bring me back to sanity. This report has nothing to do with day-to-day life. There must have been a day-to-day life, but it was overshadowed by the separate life. A secret life. I can barely remember going to school, accepting as many sleep-overs as possible yet never making friends . . . It happened so long ago and has very little to do with Viv Venables. It's about Vivvie Lennard.

So here goes.

Before Viv Venables there was Vivvie Lennard. She was nine when they moved into Montmorency House, a block of flats overlooking Hotwells. Her mother called her "my nut-brown maid". Her father was called Dennis, and jokingly referred to himself as Dennis the Menace from a character in a comic. He called his wife his "brown bird" so they — mother and daughter — must have looked the same. Except that brown bird was beautiful and plain and nut-brown maid was just plain.

238

Brown bird's real name was Barbara. She was beautiful and plain at the same time.

Vivvie was an only child, and her school friends were just school friends. Her mother was her very best friend, she needed no one else. The few times she brought anyone home — Janet Atherton or Maria Sykes — her mother laid tea for three in the kitchen, and then said, "I'll leave you to have a chat. Have mine later." Vivvie felt she had wasted precious time with her real friend. She stopped asking anyone to tea.

She said to her mother, "You're my friend, aren't you?"

"Of course I am, Vivvie. You know that."

"Shall I call you Barbara?"

Her mother laughed. "If you like. Why not? I call you Vivvie."

"And nut-brown maid!"

"Too true!"

"I can't call you brown bird."

"No. Better not."

But Vivvie rarely used her mother's name. Until the night her father came home and told them he'd lost his job. He was angry. He said it was only a case of last in first out, nothing to be ashamed about. But he was angry because he was always going to be the last in. Since Vivvie's eighth birthday he had had three jobs.

Barbara was not so sympathetic as usual. She dished up sausages and mash and said brightly, "Vivvie started a new job today, actually, darling. It was her first day at her new primary. Have you forgotten?"

Dennis made an effort. "Make any friends?"

Vivvie wanted to make it all right for him; wanted to show him that if they had each other, the three of them, nothing really mattered.

"I've got my best friend," she said.

He wasn't really interested but said, "Oh? Have I missed something? Who's that, then?"

"Barbara, of course!" Vivvie laughed. She was absolutely unprepared for the stinging blow to her head which sent her reeling on to the kitchen floor. Barbara was crouching over her, gathering her up. "It's all right, darling. Dad reached for the cruet and fell over the table . . . it's all right . . ."

But beyond the comfort came a vicious voice she had heard before, sometimes, in the night, or perhaps in a dream. "Cheeky little cow! Why can't she get her own friends — leave us to have a life of our own? For God's sake stop smothering her — come here, give me a kiss — not like that — come *here* I said —"

And incredibly Barbara let herself be engulfed by him. Vivvie, sitting up and holding the side of her head, not surprised any more, knowing somewhere somehow that this would happen.

A year later. Dennis would not, could not, believe in the breast cancer. He said just once, "Good job it's there. Isolated. Cut it right away. Get rid of it." He said he had never heard of lymph glands. Therefore they did not exist.

He got a job a week before Barbara died. It was a good job, well paid: he drove one of the enormous machines that extended the motorway into the south-west. He did not like not being a white-collar worker any more, but the new job gave him a sense of power he had never known. He was up there in his small cab by himself, with a battered radio blaring forth on the shelf in front of him. He was all-powerful. He thought he could conquer Barbara's illness and she would be grateful, and they would be back to being man and woman. Vivvie, who looked disturbingly like Barbara, would be going to a sixth-form college one day. Barbara wanted her to go to university; he thought it would make Vivvie think she was someone special. But maybe a teacher-training place wouldn't be a bad idea. She looked a bit like a school-marm when she was doing her homework of an evening . . .

When he got home that night, the house was empty and some interfering neighbour came out to tell him that Vivvie was by her mother's bed at the infirmary. He hated that. He should be there. Vivvie always came between him and Barbara. When he got to the ward the night sister told him in hushed tones that Barbara had passed away three hours ago. He did not believe her. "My bird? She wouldn't go without waiting for me to say goodbye."

"We could not contact you, Mr Lennard. And your daughter was with her, of course. She wanted to stay by her mother until you arrived, but we have sedated her, and she is lying down in one of the side wards."

He went and looked at Barbara. She was still beautiful, still his brown bird, but she was no longer inside her own body. He turned almost immediately and said, "I'll take Vivvie."

They woke Vivvie up with some difficulty. She walked by her father's side like a zombie. The corridors went on for ever. The night air was not cold, but she gasped with it, even so. Dennis unlocked the door of the flat and went straight to the kitchen. She heard the familiar sound of a tab ripping from a beer can. She sat in the living room for a long time, but he did not join her. She went to bed. Perhaps she would die in her sleep like her mother had. Perhaps her mother was waiting for her. She closed her eyes. When she opened them it was light and she could hear her father being sick in the bathroom.

After the funeral she gradually accepted that Barbara's death had been her fault. Dennis shunned her, except when one of his explosions of anger needed an outlet. Then he would turn his back on her for a long time while she stayed frozen-still, sitting "doing nothing" — which meant doing homework — or standing at the cooker making some kind of meal. Once the contents of the frying pan caught fire because she dared not move. There was no escape. He would suddenly whirl around, one arm and open palm outstretched. The incident of the frying pan resulted in a visit to outpatients. The sister in charge asked a lot of questions. Dennis seemed unable to speak. Vivvie said, "I was cooking bacon and I forgot it, and when it caught fire I tried to throw it into the sink and — and —" She started to cry. "I fell down and Daddy came in and brought me here."

"Then that's fine." Sister hardly liked to produce a barley sugar for this girl who looked more like sixteen than eleven. "Show your daddy what a brave girl you are. Let's have a smile!"

When they emerged into the weak January sunshine she did her best. "Look at the snowdrops, Daddy. Spring is coming."

Before Dennis could respond, a woman rounded the corner, making for the orthopaedic ward, and smiled recognition.

"It's Vivvie Lennard! Do you remember me? I taught you in reception class."

Vivvie managed a proper smile. "Mrs Lachlan."

"Top marks! And this is your father? Mr Lennard. I'm really pleased to meet you. I meant to write or telephone. I was so very sorry to hear that your wife had died."

Dennis blinked, took the outstretched hand, then let it go.

"You worked away, didn't you? But I expect she told you how well Vivvie was doing. And to get in to Cutler's High is no mean feat! Are you enjoying it, Vivvie?"

"Oh, yes."

"Well, I have to go. My husband has broken his arm, and is having some physio. I am picking him up." She turned again to Dennis, and moved her head from side to side. "My goodness, Mr Lennard. Your daughter is so like her mother. That must be a comfort to you. You have each other."

She was gone, and they walked on to the bus stop. Dennis said nothing until they were in the lift of Montmorency House. Then he said, "Stupid cow."

But that evening was different. That evening he kept turning from the television and looking at her. When she went to bed he said abruptly. "My brown bird loved snowdrops."

She lived in terror of him turning his back on her. He did it more and more. It did not always mean that there would be an explosion of fury directed at her. Sometimes he would bring his fist down on the nearest breakable object. If the object cut him, he would hold out his arm to her and she would bathe it with disinfectant and plaster it up.

When she was almost twelve she began to have moments of being not so plain. She learned to cook properly. He would give her money each week, and she would spend it carefully so there were hot meals each day. Very occasionally he thanked her and gave her a quick hug. One day he watched her finish her own meal then leaned across the table.

"Are you coming back to me, brown bird?"

She looked at him, eyes wide. She knew how unpredictable he could be; she slowly moved her chair away from the table so that she would be out of reach of that whirling arm.

He said in a low voice, not angry, "I did not realize . . . did not know. I can't live without you. You knew that. Yet you left me . . . just left me. It made me angry, bird. So angry. And all the time you — you — you were coming back to me. You always did." He smiled. He had a piece of lettuce in his teeth. He stood up, and Vivvie froze as usual. But then he gathered her to him and just held her and stroked her hair. She clung to him; she cried. She thought at that moment she would gladly devote her whole life to him. She loved him.

It made no difference when she tried to fight him off. She should have done what Barbara had done, and let him engulf her completely. But later, when she learned to do that, it still made no difference. When he realized she was not Barbara he still hit her frantically, accusing her of trying to make a fool out of him. She ran out of the flat. It was dark. Leaves were falling in Cumberland Road and she remembered going to her first school this way. Her feet knew where to go. He was still panting and calling behind her . . . don't be a little fool . . . you're old enough now to know . . . come home this minute . . . He was fitter than she had known, and she could not shake him off. She turned left and ran alongside the river, and turned right again and straight over the footbridge across Coronation Road and into the small streets of Bedminster. Everything looked so different in the dark, but at last she spotted the wall of the playground. His voice was silent. She vaulted the wall and stood close to it — clung to the rough stone — and heard his feet kicking the leaves as he ran. Tears of terror ran down her face and she clapped a hand over her sore mouth in an effort not to sob.

He seemed to know exactly where she was. He stopped and leaned against the wall. She could have sworn she felt his body heat through the stone. She shuddered again and again and now fought nausea.

He whispered, "Vivvie. I'm not sorry. I paid you the compliment of seeing my brown bird inside my nut-brown maid."

That did it. She sobbed and vomited at the same time. He must have heard her yet he continued to speak.

"You're an adult now. You know about love. That was love, Vivvie. And you are a lucky girl to learn about it." He paused, then with an obvious effort he said, "I know it was wrong. It won't happen again. But you will always know that I love you." He said nothing about the beatings. She controlled her heaving body and tried to dry her face on ripped clothing. He listened to her fighting for breath. He said, "I love you. I don't think I knew that before. You are all I've got, Vivvie. And I am all you have got. And now we have this secret. I trust you with it. That is proof of my love, surely? Walk round to the gate, my beautiful girl. I'll help you over it. We'll go home together. Barbara loved meeting you from school and scuffing through the leaves. We'll do that. Come on."

She stood for a moment longer. She had kept the beatings secret because it might have meant Social Services taking her right away from Bristol, and she could not bear to leave Cutler's. She had to keep this secret, too. He had said nothing about the beatings; perhaps he would never mention this again. And he was her father. Of course she loved him.

246

He did not touch her as they walked home. Instead he talked constantly of her mother. She had loved snowdrops in the spring and in the autumn it had been the "chestnut spikes".

And all the time, Vivvie knew it would happen again.

CHAPTER
TWENTY-ONE

Vivian's story

After I got that far I left the whole thing for over a week. I intended to leave it for always . . . nearly burned what I had done. It did not help in any way whatsoever to "confess" in the third person. When I wrote that last sentence I just got to the bathroom before I threw up.

But then Maisie telephoned. She had started at St Bede's, and it was horrible. Her mother had gone down to the flat to paint the new bathroom, so she had phoned me; she did not want to worry her mother, and had told her that everything was going well and that she was settling in. But she needed to talk to someone honestly. Could she have a day with me one weekend?

"I'll collect you on Saturday. I want you to see some cartoons I've unearthed — see them in the context of the everything. D'you remember what we were saying about the everything and the nothing?"

"Of course." But Maisie's voice was small. Things had got in the way of her understanding of David's work. She could only cope with one thing at a time, and the enormity of her new school had swamped her.

I said, "I'll pick you up early and we'll be back here in time for coffee. That gives us until about six or seven in the evening — depending on your other plans. In that time we can rearrange the whole world. St Bede's first and then the universe." She laughed reluctantly. I said, "Will it be awkward?"

"No. Tom's got a day off, so he and Mum are meeting Hildie and Mick at the flat. They reckon we can move in at half-term." She sounded unenthusiastic.

"Right. Settled. What shall we have for lunch and tea?"

Her voice lifted slightly. "Steak and kidney? And one of your sponges for tea?"

"Jam or marmalade?"

"Well . . . I'd prefer jam but it wouldn't be one of your specials, then. So marmalade, please. And Viv . . ."

"Go on."

"Don't tell Hildie and Mick I asked you to invite me down."

I didn't ask why. I said, "OK."

On Saturday I left the house at eight o'clock. Elisabeth had telephoned me and thanked me so much for asking Maisie to come for the day. "She was going to come with us and help with some painting, then changed her mind. Quite honestly, Viv, I think she's having a hard time at the new school. I'm really glad she's not going to be sitting at home all day brooding."

I was with her before nine and we were back in the garden with mugs of coffee at ten thirty.

She told me about the absolute "foreigners" at her new school; the cleverness of the girls; the cliques that had already formed and excluded her; the little smiles when she told the art teacher that she wanted to paint everything.

"They thought I meant everything. And of course I meant . . . *everything*." She made a face. "I might have to do still life next Wednesday. Still life." She looked gloomy. I had to laugh, and then she looked hurt.

"Maisie, I'm so sorry. But just because you admire David's sky and seascapes, you mustn't think he never painted a still life. He went to art college, for goodness' sake. The skyscapes and the cartoons evolved as he evolved. Listen, when is the school taking you to the museum again?"

She looked gloomier still. "Next Tuesday, as a matter of fact." And repeated, "The museum! I ask you!"

"Right. I want you to find all the examples you can of still-life paintings. Note the painters. Find out more about them. Internet or encyclopedia. Ring me."

"What about?"

"About still life. About the painters. Your feelings on the two."

She groaned, but grinned too. "I can tell you now. I feel the whole idea of a vase, a dead flower, a scarf on a table . . . too petty for words. Who cares? Who wants to know?"

"Well I do, for one." I stood up. "I have to look at the steak and kidney. No, don't come with me. Here's a pencil and a note pad. Choose one thing — no good coming indoors, because I haven't got any vases with

250

dead flowers and scarves. Stay right here. Choose something — the fig tree, a bit of wall — something in the garden not beyond it. And describe it. In words not pictures. Don't name it. You'll read what you've written to me, and I must know exactly what you are talking about, and I must know it intimately."

I came indoors while she was still spluttering protests. I knew I sounded unbearably school-marmish. And I knew something else, too. I would have to go on writing about myself in the third person.

She chose the straggle of nasturtiums that fell over the wall right next to where we had been sitting. She said defiantly, "You have to know it's a flower, of course. But you must try to tell me which flower. Is that OK?" At one point she read out that it was like the aurora borealis. That threw me for a moment, but when she spoke of it creeping over stones, curious like kittens, I knew. I had seen films of the Northern Lights, and the fingers that swept across darkness were like nasturtium growth on fast forward. That was her way of describing the everything. The kittens represented the paradox. And if she could take the time and trouble to do it, what choice did I have?

So here goes again. No more horrors; no more feelings. It happened.

Dennis Lennard used to say, "Don't look at me like that, it's your duty, my girl, and don't you forget it." Worse still, "You've taken her place, you look like her, you talk like her, you are her." But he must have known the reality of what was happening, because afterwards, his anger knew no bounds. He always blamed her. There were beatings, and then tears, and then recriminations and promises that it would never happen again.

She protected him. She dared not let friends come too close, in case they suspected that her bruising was not a congenital condition, but one of the teachers suggested casually that she might like to board when she began the two-year A-level course.

"I understand you live with your father in the city. A long walk. Would you like the head to give him a ring about it? Boarding would give more time for studying. And of course for leisure."

Dennis seemed relieved by the arrangement, and she felt more protective than ever. In some way it had been her fault. He had always told her so, and his cooperation over the boarding issue proved it. He recalled that Barbara had mentioned boarding at the sixth-form college before Vivvie got her place at Cutler's. "I didn't think that would happen any more." He avoided her eye. "I shall miss you, of course, but after all I'm away in the week. We might go to the pictures or something at weekends."

She said, "It will be all right." She hardly knew what she meant. Definitely no pictures. Her one hope of salvation lay in never seeing her father again. At one point she considered trying to become a nun. But he must have felt as she felt, because he did not try to get in touch. She spent holidays with anyone who'd have her: school friends, fellow students, teachers. And when she got older took live-in holiday jobs. All to get away from seeing him. And years later, when she wrote to tell him she was getting married, his only reply was a printed card congratulating her. She and David had been married two of their precious ten years when she received a solicitor's letter informing her of her father's death. There had been an accident with his crane due to negligence on his part. Even that made her physically sick, and David took over and dealt with the correspondence. He had always been understanding. They kissed. They hugged. And she told him not to worry; she was free, now. But she was not free.

She had opted for teaching because it was what she had discussed years ago with her mother. She felt at ease with children, and she would certainly never have any of her own. She was good at it; excellent at allowing them to discover things for themselves. They liked her, respected her; they would have loved her if she had permitted it. She kept everyone at arm's length until David appeared and simply ducked under her elbow.

She told him before he could get ideas. He said, "Nothing to fear from me, then." She had no idea where the goal posts were. She looked up impotence on the internet. There were different kinds; there were no rules. "You mean we could be friends?" she said.

"Loving friends," he embellished. "Someone to stand by when we have to be counted. Someone . . ."

He hesitated, and she supplied the next line in a nasal twang, ". . . to be there for you."

They both laughed, and she had been certain-sure that it was impossible for it to work. Yet it had. Until . . .

I wrote that single word and then could not go on. I had been so absolutely sure that if any rules were broken they would be broken by David. Never by me. I knew through experience that "men were different". I waited for David to kiss me as a husband and not a friend. We slept in the same bed up until the last few weeks. I never moved close to him consciously, even when there was snow on the ground, but I frequently woke and found my head on his shoulder. I moved quietly away. Just once he said, "Surely you know by now that I don't bite?" I think I apologized.

We were loyal, loving friends. As the years went on I relied on that. Until. And then . . .

I cannot go on, of course. The whole idea is ridiculous. It is half-term next week, and I am driving behind Hardy's van to Cheltenham, where we are moving Tom, the twins, Maisie and Elisabeth into the flat so close to Montpellier. I am going to think about that. Nothing else.

CHAPTER
TWENTY-TWO

Hildie's contribution to the day was a wonderful and enormous casserole of venison. Hardy had done some work for a nearby National Trust property and brought home a pile of venison steaks. Viv took two marmalade sponges and a sherry trifle. Maisie had made toffees for "afters". Her new school friend, known for some obscure reason as Cumber, had helped her and assured Tom that home-made toffee was perfectly all right for diabetic sufferers.

"I'm not diabetic," he said. "Bit worried about my teeth, though."

Cumber sighed deeply. "Medical men always have to find objections to any food. Any food at all." She rolled her eyes at Maisie. "I did tell you."

But Maisie said staunchly, "He's all right. Honestly."

For some reason Viv looked over at Tom, and grinned.

A removal van arrived with carpets and furniture for the bedrooms. Maisie had wanted all her own stuff, nothing new at all. "Home from home," she had said. She and Cumber disappeared into the end room and unpacked the tiny music centre. Music spilled over into the living area and so did the girls, dancing crazily. "We could have discos here!" Cumber gasped, arms flying above her head.

"What about the twins?" Elisabeth asked.

"What about my table tennis?" Hildie added.

Maisie did cartwheels the length of the playroom. "Anyway," she gasped back to Cumber. "It's my home! I don't want that lot at school taking over!"

"Don't blame you. They're pretty rank."

"Rank?"

"Like. You know. Weeds and things."

The girls fell on each other, laughing hysterically. Viv looked at Tom and grinned again.

Later, when tables and chairs and rugs had arrived, and they had eaten their fill and probably more, Maisie and Cumber made up the bunks in the end room, showered and put on T-shirts and leggings, which, apparently, were standard nightwear. Tom and Elisabeth fed the twins and got them ready for bed. The other three washed up and found places for everything. They thought it was time to go: everyone had a bed, and the enormous old larder was full to capacity, and everyone was exhausted. It was definitely time to go.

"Not all at once," Viv said to Hildie and Hardy as she found a small cupboard that would do splendidly for the baby crockery. "I'll go and say my goodbyes, and you can have another hour with them." She thought of the bungalow waiting for her in the twilight of this late October afternoon. Soon the clocks would go back and winter would be upon them; another winter. Two years since . . . the accident. A year since the arrival of the twins and the death of their mother. She shivered. Would she have to start running again?

Hildie said, "Can we come to you first of all, Viv? I've left my cardigan in your kitchen and it's got the key to the garage in the pocket."

Viv looked at her over the top of imaginary glasses; just as she had looked at David sometimes.

Hildie said, just as he might have said, "No, honest! And you could make a nice jug of cocoa for us, then we could go straight to bed. I can tell Hardy is on his last legs."

Hardy was at that moment up a long pair of steps screwing some spotlights into position. "Poor Hardy," Viv commented. And went to say goodbye to Elisabeth and Tom.

Maisie ran after her in her night gear; through the living-room window and across the future play area and up the semi-circular steps to the lawn.

"You didn't say goodbye!" she accused.

"Sorry, Maisie. You and Cumber were back in your room, and . . . why Cumber?"

"It's her name — Miranda Cumberbatch. And we haven't even got into bed yet. We're going to sing to the twins. Cumber plays the double bass at school and she can make the sound with a rubber band and her teeth. She says it will soothe them to sleep." She giggled. Viv giggled. Maisie said, suddenly sober, "It's going to be all right, Viv. The most wonderful things have happened. First, Cumber. And then Merilees Harper. She does Eng. Lit. She knew you at your school. And she knows about David's work. She's going to ask you about a retrospective. Her name was Merilees McKinnon. You didn't tell me you'd got a scholarship to Cutler's. You didn't tell me you'd won the Accolade for 1983."

Viv was silent under this shower of words. When she spoke she said, "Merilees McKinnon. She was beautiful."

"She's not any more. She was in a fire, and she had cosmetic surgery, and it makes her face still on one side."

"Paralysed?"

"Yes. That must be it. But her hands are healed, and she comes to art classes with us to learn to draw and paint, and she's still the most popular girl in the school!" Maisie laughed again, a little uncertainly.

Viv hugged her briefly. "You'll be all right with her. Give her my phone number just in case she's serious about the retrospective. I would like that more than almost anything else."

Maisie glowed at the words and the hug. Unexpectedly — shockingly — she took Viv's hand and kissed the knuckles. Then, covered with embarrassment, she turned and disappeared into the house. Viv walked to the gate, located her car and got into it. Just for a moment she had a sense of a future; it was there, waiting for her if she wanted it. People like Maisie and Elisabeth; the Hardys; even, possibly, the unknown couple in the background — Maisie's father and stepmother Margaret . . . they could be part of it. But she would have to do more than try to forget the past;

she would have to absorb it in some way, accept it. No more running. Acceptance. And then moving on.

She wound down the window and adjusted the side mirror and took a deep breath of the air, with its hint of winter. She whispered into the oncoming night, "Dammit! I'll have to write it out, won't I? Just like Maisie seeing the Northern Lights in those straggling nasturtiums, I have to see something — something — *redemptive* — in what happened." Just for a moment she dropped her head to her chest and closed her eyes. Then she sat up very straight, wound up the window and put the car into gear.

The Hardys drew up outside the bungalow fifteen minutes after she had put the car away and let herself in. Needless to say the cardigan was nowhere to be seen. "It must be in the van somewhere," Hildie said, feigning bewilderment.

"Never mind. I've the garage key on my ring." Hardy sat at the kitchen table; he did indeed look tired. "It's been a good day." He smiled at both women. "They're going to be all right there. That little girl will hold them together. And her friend, Cucumber, she fitted in like a hand in a glove."

"Cucumber?" asked Hildie incredulously. Viv was pouring cocoa from a jug and slopped it on to the table. Hildie marvelled loudly that when the majority of people began to lose their hearing, they did just that. Lose it. Hardy had to be different, of course; Hardy had to add a syllable where none was. Hardy protested.

"She's long. And she's sort of curved — that's probably from playing one of those great violin things — and she's green."

"Green?" Hildie queried again, on a rising note.

"Well, simple, direct. She don't try to act like a twenty-year-old."

Hildie looked at Viv. "He's right. Do you suppose it was Cucumber and not just Cumber?"

Viv's eyes were streaming tears of laughter. She said, "Her name is Miranda Cumberbatch." And they all clutched each other and laughed helplessly.

But the next day was Sunday, and she was due to see Juniper. The weather was good. She pushed the wheelchair to the lane and the wall, and they paused and looked across at the two islands and the Welsh coast. All of it appeared to be hanging in the pearly air a few feet above the sea.

Viv said curiously, "How would you describe those colours, Juniper? The sea isn't grey or blue, and where does it end and the sky begin?"

"Use your common sense, my girl. Them islands come out of the sea, so that's where it ends. And the colours is all different greys. We haven't found labels for all those greys, yet. The colours of the air and water. Them's the colours you're looking at."

"David would spend hours mixing paints to get the colours to his satisfaction. And even then he wasn't satisfied."

"Course not. If he'd been satisfied he would have been God."

"Oh Juniper . . . there's a chance, just a chance, that his stuff could be exhibited."

"Would that please you?"

"Of course. He was so well known for his cartoons. No one knew, or wanted to know, about the other work."

Juniper made a noise expressing disinterest, then said, "What I want to know is, why did you get that there door knob? Jinx did tell me you had it and gave it to him to give to me. That was a nice thing to do. But why did you have it in the first place?"

"I don't really know. I thought it was simply a token. Jinx said it was like carving initials on a tree. You know the sort of thing."

"It was more than that, my girl. It were my mother's wedding lines in one way. She wanted a ring and she got a door knob. But it meant a lot to her, because it was all she did have. Cept me of course." Juniper tried to cackle a laugh.

Viv said, "I've given up trying to work it out." She paused. "You must feel I've . . . taken something that has nothing to do with me."

"That's how it is, isn't it? Dun't matter now, of course, cos it's back where it belongs. And it weren't your fault — I'm not blaming you. Nothing like that. I just wondered . . . well, I just wondered."

"Yes." Viv sat down on the seat, which had lost a slat since her last visit. "What are you going to do with it?"

"Keep it with Mam's things. I did think I might get you to take me down at high tide and lob it over into the sea. But . . . well, it was hers." Juniper sighed. "It will go to my daughter. Afterwards." Viv nodded and Juniper added quickly, "Less you got any other ideas."

"Well . . . I did wonder whether it should go back. Just in case anyone ever needed it again."

"Ah. I thought that, too. But who's going to get cement to set two feet under water?"

"They never filled it. The tide comes over the top and drains out again. I reckon Hardy would do it. Hildie would persuade him."

"An' if she can't I will." Juniper looked very happy at the thought of a fight. She missed her wrangles with Jinx more than anything. "This time next week it'll be dark at half past five. We could all go down with a torch."

"What on earth do we say if the police turn up?"

"Easy. You're burying me alive!" Juniper cackled happily. "There's always something to laugh about if you try hard enough!"

Viv stored this remark away for Maisie, and stood up, ready to push the wheelchair down to the bungalow and coffee. "I've got chocolate biscuits," she said.

"Not allowed them," Juniper objected automatically.

"Oh dear." Viv grinned down at the headscarf. "Never mind. I'll eat yours as well as mine."

"Just cos I'm not allowed them dun't mean I'm going without!" Juniper tilted her head and looked upwards. And they both laughed.

CHAPTER
TWENTY-THREE

Vivian's story

Hardy had changed. I had always known that he understood how things were, that even his silences were full of implicit understanding. But now, he spoke his feelings more often.

He said, "Well, I'm not saying I won't do it. And I'm not saying I don't believe all this ghost stuff — Hildie has dropped enough clues for me to pick up that you bin having a bit of a time of it." He gave me a glance from beneath his brows, as if he expected me to collapse in a heap. "What firms it for me is Juniper Stevens. No one is more down-to-earth than Juniper Stevens — unless it were that John Jinks. I din't know much about him, and I've lived near Juniper most of my life."

He paused for a long time. Hildie and I both started out holding our breath, but had to give up. Hardy believed in taking his time.

Eventually he put his hands on the table and said, "All right. Though if anyone catches us we're going to look right fools." He looked at Hildie. "Do it really matter? Can't you get old Juniper to chuck the damned thing over into the sea? You know you could."

Hildie said stubbornly, "I dun't think that's quite right, myself. But it were given to Juniper's mother in the first place, then — and this is the most important — it were somehow taken out of that wall and landed up on this very kitchen table."

She, too, placed her hands on the wooden top next to her husband's. She said, "I think Viv must have the final say-so."

I had given it some thought, and felt that whichever way we chose would be all right with David. But Juniper wanted this, and so did Hildie.

I said, "I plump for putting it back where it was."

Hildie nearly cheered. She said, "Tomorrow night there should be a decent moon, and it's still dark early. We'll bring Juniper down here for tea and load the wheelchair into the van, and I can stay with her on the little promenade while you two go down with the cement and the tools."

"Juniper?" Hardy and I spoke in unison.

"Of course. We have to be together for this."

I almost laughed, because it was so obvious Hildie was going to enjoy the whole thing as an adventure.

And so it was.

We had tea. Juniper produced the door knob, and we passed it around, thinking our own thoughts. It would probably be the last time I would see it. I remembered it pressing into my chest and hurting that night when David and I had flowed into the air together. Like swans. Like the aurora borealis. Not for the first time I realized how privileged — honoured — I had been. I had touched the everything.

Juniper was as contrary as ever. She looked at the door knob and said dismissively, "Lot of fuss about nothing. Fancy giving that to someone you're supposed to love better than life itself. That's what Mam said, you know. She seemed to think he had chosen to be drownded down there . . . 'Our place' she called it . . . rather than go back to Wales. Dank old hole in the ground. But she said then that he loved her better than life itself. Let it go back where he put it in the first place."

I opened my eyes wide at Hildie. She turned her mouth down, shoulders up. Then she took the door knob in her right hand and passed it straight to Hardy. She said, "It's caused trouble. But it's still a love-token. That's what counts."

Hardy transferred it from hand to hand, feeling the weight, then he dropped it into a bag and said, "Beautiful piece of door furniture, that. Victorians knew how to make good stuff."

It was dark; full moon but often hidden by scudding clouds. The wind was sharp as we loaded Juniper and her chair into the van, and bundled ourselves in afterwards. Ironically I was wedged between a lavatory pan and a bunch of plumbing pipes; Hilda shared her place with the cistern. Such a good example of the absurdities David drew; a small bubble containing suitable words should be somewhere. Juniper supplied them. "My old man said follow the van," she commented drily, as we took the corner and only just avoided a near sheer drop down to the sea. "God help us, Hardy, 'aven't this thing got brakes?"

He replied in similar vein. "I don't dilly-dally on the way, Juniper Stevens. You don't 'ave to come if my driving don't please you!"

She was silent. Nothing was going to stop her now.

We reached the ramp, guarded by the same red and white tape that had been in place almost a year ago. Hardy pulled on the hand brake with some force, shot out of the driver's seat, removed the tape, got back in and coasted us down on to the little promenade. The moon emerged from cloud and we saw a desolate view indeed: the bed of the lake was invisible, the whole thing was an enormous black hole. Impossible, absolutely impossible to imagine my desperate swim . . . David's presence everywhere. As I scrambled out of the back of the van and looked up at the blackness of Becket's Hill, I remembered the even more frightening thud of his invisible feet as he had followed me through the trees.

"Don't mess about there, my maid. Hildie will push the chair round to where the steps are. Let's get going." He passed me a box and the bag containing the door knob. He shouldered his tool bag and hooked a bucket over one arm. We went ahead of the others, past the huts. There had been a rail to help swimmers down the steps; it had long gone. But Hardy seemed to know where it had been and went unerringly down the first two steps, then paused to see me on to the top one. We let our feet feel their way down to the bed of the lake. It

266

was covered in about two inches of slimy mud. Hardy said something under his breath and I echoed him. He whispered, "Don't try to get out of it. Slide through it. Use it to make the going easier."

Hildie said from some way off, "What's up? Is something wrong?"

Hardy made a shushing sound in her direction. Hildie said something to Juniper and there came an answering cackle. We skated through the slime very cautiously; it became quiet except for the occasional clank from the bucket, and the swishing sound of our Wellingtons. It seemed to take ages to reach the opposite wall, and it became darker as the camber took us deeper and away from the moon's fitful light. When we got there Hardy whispered, "Where was it put in the first place?" And his voice went right around the lake and came back to us like a whispering gallery.

I looked at the sky and tried to orientate myself. Hardy produced a torch and we sprayed its beam along the flinty surface without success. I faced the wall and reached past my head and began to pace along its breadth; the beam of the torch wavered, and just as I was about to give up, Hardy breathed, "That's it. Stay there just a minute, maid." He reached past me, holding an enormous masonry nail. "OK. Got it. Relax."

I did so. The palms of my hands recalled that rough surface. I remembered Hildie kneeling by my feet gently stroking on the vinegar.

"We'll soon have this done. Tis upsetting, but you have to see it through, maid. You know that."

I hadn't up until then, but I did now. He took the cloth from the top of the bucket, and I draped it over one arm while he re-mixed the cement with a trowel as if it were dough. Then he upturned the box I had carried and stood on it and wedged cement into the hole I could not even see. Then he got down and indicated that I should take his place.

"The cement will stay wet until morning, so take your time. Just push it in gently, and push the cement against it, as you would when you are planting."

It was excellent advice for a gardener. I stretched my arm above my head and found the big patch easily with my fingers, took the door knob in my other hand, and eased it into place, and then packed more cement round it. Hardy held up the bucket for me to take more handfuls and I did so, spreading the surplus as best I could. The torch beam wavered on it. "Perfect," Hardy whispered. And I could see that the flints and rock pieces had already encased the wet cement. "Come on down, now," he said, in a more normal voice. "Let's go. We'm, done the best we can, and the rest is in fate's hands."

The torch went out. I kept my eyes where I knew the door knob was. I murmured, "Thank you. Thank you, David." Then I climbed down.

Nothing much happened on the way back; I half-expected one of us to slip down on the mud and complete the other half of the evening; the absurd half. But in fact we were into the rhythm of skaters now and Hildie was at the steps with outstretched arm to help us up. Juniper informed us we didn't smell like roses.

268

Hildie said, "Never mind that. Let's get her into the van before she freezes to death." She pushed the wheelchair back up the ramp, and we trailed soggily behind her. Almost there and we heard the wail of a police siren. We froze in our tracks but it went on by, lights flashing. It scared Juniper into an unusual silence. We loaded her in record time, collapsed the wheelchair and wedged it behind the lavatory pan. Hildie swore — also unusually — at the cistern as her elbow connected with the overflow pipe. Hardy closed all the doors and began to reverse out carefully. We got home and spent quite some time cleaning up. "Destroying the evidence", as Hardy put it.

"You're in a good mood," Hildie accused.

"I am. We've done it. The whole thing is done with. Viv and Juniper are . . . well, they are themselves again. P'raps for the first time in a long while. I feel free too — don't you, my maid?"

Hildie thought about it as she washed her hands at the kitchen sink. "P'raps I do. Yes, it could be that I do. Like when the prince kisses the sleeping beauty and wakes her up." She smiled round at us.

Juniper said irritably, "She don't change. Little Hildie Wendover and her games of pretend."

Hildie said, "Go into the toilet with Viv while I cut some sandwiches. Then we'll have a bit of supper before you go back to bed."

Juniper cheered up immediately. "You were right about Tall Trees, Hildie," she called down the hallway. "I've had a better time since I went there than ever I had at home!" She looked up at me as I helped her out of the chair and on to the toilet. "I met John Jinks again, and now I've put him to bed." She cackled, and I had no doubt she was implying innuendo, but I was feeling more than relaxed; I was feeling peaceful. And confident. Tomorrow I would finish my third-person confession and then it would be over.

CHAPTER
TWENTY-FOUR

Vivian's story

It was a very quiet wedding; a registry office wedding, simple and sincere. Two teachers came from school; three of David's friends from his schooldays. And his father. Viv had met Mr Venables twice before; noted his gentleness and his physical resemblance to David, but not much more. David, naturally, called him "Dad" and she called him "your dad". She had to force herself to go that far. The diminutive "dad" meant so many things to Vivvie Lennard: love was there somewhere, but uppermost was terror.

She had no idea whether he knew about his son's impotence. She and David had briefly shared their secrets, and in doing so had somehow exchanged them. She took on his impotence, and he took on her abuse. There was no more discussion. But suddenly she needed to know whether Mr Venables knew David's secret. After the first visit to his cottage in the Mendips she was warmly appreciative of his quiet welcome, but he gave nothing away. He might think of her as the wife of his son, but if he and David had talked together — and she had no experience of fathers and sons — he could very well know that she was his son's loving companion, loyal friend, his "other half"; not his wife.

He came to see them once a week, usually for a traditional Sunday lunch. She grew to trust him. When he heard that her own father had died he was quietly sympathetic. He said, "I understand you had an unhappy childhood, Viv. And now, no father. If I can step into his place it would be an honour." She disguised her shudder, but later, when his attitude changed oh-so-subtly, she thought he had seen, and she tried to make up for it. Perhaps she tried too hard, because when he had his stroke, and it became apparent he could not live alone any longer, it seemed as if he expected to move in with David and Viv. They told him they would talk about it . . . sort it out . . . then they drove home from the hospital in complete silence. The combe, snaking uphill, ground dropping away one side, crowded with beech trees, seemed sinister. An omen. They turned into the lane, and David parked the car outside the gate; they sat looking at the view, still saying nothing. She took a deep breath.

"David, I love you and I want you to be happy. But . . . I don't think I can bear it if your father lives with us."

He stared at her for a moment, then gave a great guffaw full of relief.

"Oh . . . dearest Viv! I thought your sense of duty was going to prevail over anything I might say! You had your nun look. It did not bode well." He hugged her to him. "Darling, I could not live with my dad. He has always . . . somehow . . . belittled what I do. It is only since I've known you that I have been able to paint my feelings, and even now . . . seeing him every week . . . it is —" He laughed, almost ashamed. ". . . shall I say, he inhibits me!"

Viv was amazed. "You're so alike — he's so gentle and kind — it must all be in your mind, David. Seriously."

"Perhaps. I shouldn't have told him about my 'condition'." He laughed, making it a joke. "Men see impotence as a failure. Which it is, of course. But it should not trickle into every other bit of one's life."

So Mr Venables did know. Viv slid her arms under David's, and held him to her. They were interlocked. She realized how right he had been to bulldoze her into this relationship. It worked. It really worked.

He said, "I don't know how I'll tell him that we can't have him. But I'm going to be straight."

"Hang on. Let me do it. It will split you two. And that would be a pity. I'll do it. Lots of daughters-in-law have to make this kind of stand. It would mean me giving up my job, and I'm not willing to do that. I can be straight."

And she had been, and Mr Venables had nodded agreement the whole time. She had thought he was hurt beyond words.

He went to Tall Trees because an old friend of his, John Jinks, was there already and said it wasn't too bad. For a while he refused all invitations to the bungalow, then when he came he brought Jinx with him, and they developed a kind of ironic patter which was entertaining in itself, and provided David with another comic strip called "Dinner with Dad". It looked like a Dickensian etching, with the four of them overlapping each other as they leaned into the table exchanging scurrilous gossip about the nursing-home staff. The dialogue was always contained within a pall of smoke from their cigars. Fortunately only one erudite magazine published this series, and the two men never saw it. David sighed once and mourned, "The only cartoon that Dad would have appreciated, and I cannot let him see it!"

Viv was surprised. "Why on earth not?"

"He'd recognize too much of himself. He might sue me." David grinned.

Mr Venables — Viv still thought of him by his formal name — had two more strokes. They were minor and did not incapacitate him for long. But both times David and Viv had to wrestle with their consciences. David felt bound to go over their circumstances.

"Thank God you got this place here, Dad! You get professional care — several of the staff are state-registered."

Mr Venables smiled and nodded, but still said, "Viv's a natural carer, anyone can see that."

David said sturdily, "Viv leaves the house at seven thirty and doesn't get in until five each afternoon!"

"She'll be retiring soon."

"Dad, Viv isn't forty yet. She might retire early, but not that early."

His father made rumbling sounds in his throat.

274

He and Jinx egged each other on to behave like schoolboys. Both of them asked Hildie Hardy if she would marry them, though they well knew she was married to the local carpenter and handyman. They discussed in very loud voices the possibility of sleeping with various members of the staff. The staff largely ignored them, though Hildie came back at them at times. The female residents weren't so forbearing, and some of them made the mistake of protesting. Jinx could make Esmé Wetherby's face flush crimson just by looking at her, and then spreading his hands helplessly when one of the staff enquired what was going on. Winifred Samson was made of sterner stuff, and told him once that no woman would look at him while Mr Venables was around. It was Mr Venables's turn to redden with embarrassment, and Jinx's to ask pettishly what was wrong with him — he had been in charge of all public works in the area for twenty-two years, while old David Ven had merely looked after dead things. Winifred came back witheringly, "You are coarse, Mr Jinks. Whereas Mr Venables is sensitive." And Jinx had turned purple with sheer annoyance.

He had said cattily, "*Miss* Samson, isn't it? Perhaps you should have been a little coarser a little earlier in life."

Esmé shrieked her outrage; nurses came hurrying. Winifred looked at him with scorn. "I don't usually confide in men, gentle or not. But I will just say this. I might be a spinster, Mr Jinks. But I am not, certainly not, an old maid!"

She and Esmé left the arena and left the men, gentle or not, spluttering.

David and Viv went up to smooth things over. The matron was Marlene Richards, but her name was never used. She was Matron.

She said, "I'm afraid your father is very much influenced by Mr Jinks, and I cannot ask you to have a word with Mr Jinks. It would probably exacerbate the situation, anyway. If you could explain to Mr Venables that they are acting like playground bullies and genuinely upsetting some of our ladies, I am sure he will cooperate and persuade Mr Jinks to moderate some of his more — er — jocular — comments."

They did their best. Mr Venables looked totally crestfallen. "It was just a bit of fun," he said apologetically. "If you'd been there you would understand. We get bored. And the nurses are so distant, not like in hospital. Of course, we're all old. It would disgust them if we simply asked to be hugged."

David grinned. Viv sat as if turned to stone.

The next day she asked David whether he had told his father about her. He was driving her to school because he needed the car: he had been invited to take six pieces of work to a gallery in Bath for an exhibition the following month.

He flashed her a sideways smile. "Well, of course! He knows I don't do my serious work in a vacuum. Of course I've told him about you. I tell him about you all the time."

She said slowly, "Have you told him about my childhood?"

276

"Oh. You mean your father? I told him you had a rough time. No details. Of course not. None of his business. What on earth brought that up?"

"He seemed to . . . know." She caught his eye in the rear-view mirror. "Sorry. Am I being paranoid? When he asked for a hug —"

He interrupted with an explosive sound.

"He did not ask you for a hug, Viv! And yes, you are being paranoid. He said that if — *if* he — probably meaning Jinx — asked the nurses for a hug they would be disgusted. Actually, I have a feeling it's policy these days. Physical contact is taboo. Can lead to being sued in court."

She thought back, and knew David was right. She dropped her head. "Darling, I'm sorry. It's just the — the — dad thing. Mine is dead and yours is sweet and nice and funny — I mean, he and Jinx together must bring the place alive. But somehow . . . I'm so frightened. And the fear disempowers me. Like a rabbit in the road — I'd heard about them being caught in the glare of headlights but until it happened to us that time . . ."

"And what did we do?" he asked quietly.

"You stopped the car, and I got out and picked him up, and put him on the grass verge. The point was, he didn't struggle when I picked him up. He had given up. And that is how I was. And I can see that now — remember it — realize that's how it was. I knew it would happen, and I did nothing. In fact I protected my father. Dad. He was Dad, you see. I loved him."

David was silent; the car moved into the nearside lane to peel off at their junction. There was a roundabout and he negotiated that. Then he spoke.

"D'you know, Viv, for a moment there, I felt such deep envy."

Of all things, she had not expected that. She turned to him, distressed. "Oh, David. My love for you is free and total. We hold nothing back — nothing —"

"Except . . . that."

"It's my stupid fault, David."

"And mine."

There was another silence, and into it she said quietly and with conviction, "Thank God we found each other. We should have spoken like this before now. We have something extraordinary, David. We should acknowledge it, honour it, more often."

They drew up outside the school. It was early. The head teacher's car was the only one in the car park.

David said, "Dunkirk", and she looked a wild question at him. He smiled, "You have just made a wonderful victory from defeat. Worthy of Dunkirk."

She held his eyes for a moment, then leaned over and kissed him. "I shall remember that," she said.

She got out of the car and he shouted at her, "I'll be here at three forty-five."

She waved and smiled and shouted back, "Great! Good luck!"

They both thought everything was back to normal, their kind of normal. Perhaps they did not want to see that David senior was slowly failing. They heard tales from the staff about Jinx's run-ins with some of the female residents, and assumed they included his best friend, David Venables. They visited less. And though on a nice day he was perfectly capable of walking down to the bungalow, he seldom did.

David was requested to do a residency at one of the universities on the south coast and wanted Viv to take a few weeks off and come with him. But it was September; a new school year. The head had asked her to take the reception class and settle them in "properly".

"I know you love your ten-year-olds, Viv." Viv was surprised; yes, she did love them but never demonstratively. What she liked about them was that they were old enough to recognize her respect for them. The head went on inexorably, "I think your professionalism would be good for the tinies. They don't need mums, they've got them at home. They come to school expecting a teacher, and you will fit that expectation perfectly."

Viv was not sure how she felt about it all. One thing was certain, she was committed to it. She explained all this to David. He made a face.

"I'm not competitive, luckily. I wouldn't stand a chance against four-and-a-half-year-olds." He picked up her hand. "Will you be all right? You need not visit Tall Trees, you'll have enough on your plate."

"Of course I'll be all right. What about you? What do you have to do? Actually *do*?"

"It's an open decision. And I've decided I'm doing an adaptation of one of your school projects. D'you remember the junk sculpture?"

"Of course. But they will have done that already. It's a standard primary-school thing."

"The object is to make a maquette. See where it goes from there."

"Techniques."

"Why not? Artists need to be technicians these days."

"What about your imaginative stuff — what about the skyscapes?"

"We'll see."

They bought another car. She missed David even when she was at school and would not normally have been with him. At weekends she was very conscious of Mr Venables at Tall Trees. David had told him about the residency, had told him about Viv's new class at school. In fact there was a great deal to do for her tinies; their "finds" had to be made significant, and she spent evenings mounting acorns and grasses in the small frames David used for some of his cartoons, labelling them carefully and then adding "What? Where? Why?" It had been Marvin Jellicoe, who knew everything before he was five years old because he watched television assiduously, who said, "We'm detectives, miss. Like CSI."

And Sky Smith, whose mother was a left-over hippie, who said ecstatically, "We'm *green* tectives, miss. Cos we'm finding out everything about flowers and stuff."

She had loved them as they came in to school on their first day, hanging on to their mothers' hands desperately. She respected them because they were wise already. They deserved her evenings and weekends.

David's father had the company of twenty-four contemporaries at Tall Trees. She said to David, "I won't be able to visit regularly like you do. These children need me in a way the juniors didn't — I'm not being awkward, David."

He said, "Don't feel desperate about it, love. You're here if there's an emergency. I've told Mrs Hardy the situation — she's got a soft spot for Dad. In fact she's even got a soft spot for that mate of his. Jinx. Sarcastic old blighter. Matron knows, as well. They'll give him some extra attention."

But she felt guilty.

And then Jinx and David senior had some kind of falling-out. Mrs Hardy called in about it on her way home one evening. Viv had been sewing tapes on to the tabards the children used for painting. She had met Mrs Hardy when she and David visited Tall Trees. She was small, plump and cheerful. She was cheerful about this at first, then not so cheerful. In fact her face lengthened, and she sounded anxious.

"Jinx enjoys the whole thing. He's used to being on his own, and waging war with Winnie and Esmé. Your dad isn't like that — as you well know. He needs that friendship." She forced a smile. "Hasn't eaten this week. Doesn't come into the lounge."

Viv was still cringing at that word . . . dad. But he wasn't her dad, so she rallied quickly and said, "I'll go up. This minute."

Mrs Hardy said, "You've only just finished your jobs, I can see that. Have you had anything to eat, yourself?"

"Not yet. But I will do when I get back." Viv smiled, there was something about Mrs Hardy she liked. "I've got some pears. I'll take a couple up and try to get Mr Venables to have one."

"Mr Venables? Ah, of course, he's your husband's dad. He talks about you such a lot I get mixed up."

They walked to the gate together and then split up. Viv thanked Mrs Hardy for letting her know. She thought it would be all right. Awkward, but all right.

He was sitting on the edge of his bed trying to reach his socks.

She said, "I'm sorry. I forgot you all went to bed early. I got these pears, thought we might have one each."

His pleasure was painful to see. She felt mean. His smile was shaky, and she knew for two pins he could cry. But all he said was, "Viv! How's our David getting on? Early days yet, I suppose. Still settling in."

"I think so." She drew a chair forward, leaned down and removed his socks and put on his slippers. Leaned back well away from him. "It's just his thing, of course. And he's got time for his own work, too. Couldn't be better."

She talked about the weather. The fallen leaves in the driveway of the home, slippery underfoot now because of a recent shower. He looked at her. His eyes were asking her something. She peeled and cored a pear and cut it into segments. He ate one obediently, like a child. She told him about her new class: Marvin and Sky. He tried to look interested, but his head fell back on the pillow awkwardly. She lifted his slippered feet on to the bed and leaned over him.

"What's wrong? Why have you quarrelled with John Jinks? David thought you were good friends."

He moved his head from side to side. She waited but he said nothing.

"You're not eating. Mrs Hardy is anxious about you."

"She is such a dear." He smiled for the first time. "She doesn't let Jinx get her down."

"And neither must you."

"He knows." He sighed. "I told him. He was angry, called me a pervert. Can't face him."

She realized the sigh had been a yawn; his eyelids were drooping, the eyes almost unseeing. She had a terrible sense of déjà vu, and jerked back from him with horror. He opened his eyes wide at the sudden movement, and looked at her and said, "You must have known, Viv. It happened a long time ago . . . my first stroke . . . knew I could not come to live with you . . ."

She breathed, "You did not want to live with us?"

"Surely you understood? You understand so much . . . accept so much . . . you accepted the situation . . . did not make a fuss . . . saw as little of me as possible." He turned his head on the pillow. "I know you did not discuss it with David. Thank you for that, too. I love you, Viv. And you have respected that love, and not seen it as perverted. Jinx debased what I feel for you. I cannot allow that."

She did not move a muscle. She remembered that was the best way. If she stayed very still and let it

happen, there would be less violence. She remembered
. . . remembered the voice saying, "I love you" . . . "I
love you" . . .

Time ceased to be; at some point the wrinkled
eyelids closed. She stayed as if turned to stone, daring
to hope that she could stand up and walk out of that
room. Then the voice began again, talking of the past
and the "brown bird", just as it always had done. Pain
was everywhere, it flowed around her like the water of
the lake.

"My wife was very much older than I was. She
wanted a child quickly, before it was too late. After she
died there was a kind of relief, because she had got
what she wanted, and I was free. David's disability was
not diagnosed until he was in his teens . . . it became
my punishment. I wanted him to be a serious artist . . .
cartoons weren't the way. And he met you. And he
changed. His work became . . . different. It was your
doing . . . Saw the sort of love you had . . . wanted it
. . . fell head over heels for you." A tiny smile lightened
his sombre face.

Tears were pouring down her face. Had Dennis
spoken like this? Behind the brutality had there indeed
been love as well as degradation?

The voice whispered on and on. His wife . . . his son
. . . his love . . . the love that was his salvation, and
which belonged to his son. And his son could not fulfil
that love.

Still, she did not speak or move.

". . . wanted to thank you . . . wanted you to know
the joy I have felt . . . it must not be a burden to you

284

. . . a gift . . . unwanted I know, but a gift just the same . . ."

She still did not speak but she moved. Like an automaton she lifted herself from the chair on to the bed by his side. Her arm slid beneath his head, her other arm went around his body and held him to her. She cradled him; Vivvie Lennard, who shrank from intimacy, held her father-in-law tenderly and said, "I did not know. Forgive me. I have never understood."

They lay together for a long time. She was conscious that someone peered through the glass of the door and then went away. Her arm gradually numbed. She moved slightly. He breathed into her ear, "Don't go."

Had it been then, at that moment? There was a point at which she could have left him. And then that moment was gone. She kissed his forehead. "Dad," she whispered back. "Dad." It was not a moment of surrender; she remembered those well. This was a moment of decision.

Her decision. Whatever might be the outcome, she had decided.

"Dad." She murmured the word over and over again. "It's all right. We love you. Your nut-brown maid. She loves you."

CHAPTER
TWENTY-FIVE

The second anniversary of the accident came around. Hildie did not mention it but she did suggest they went to the pictures again.

"It's not Harry Potter, but it's something for the kiddies."

Viv had already looked it up in the local paper. "It's a film about Narnia." She beamed at Hildie. "Is this going to be an annual event?"

"Why not?" Hildie beamed back. "You're feeling good, aren't you, Viv? It's sticking that blessed door knob back where it came from, isn't it?"

"Yes." Viv hesitated. "Also . . . your Tom suggested — ages ago — that it might be a good idea to write things down. I've been doing that. I wasn't going to, but Maisie did something similar and it seemed to help her."

Hildie nodded, pleased. "He's done that, too. Written things down. Sorts it out inside your head." She asked no questions; she had asked them of Tom and he had told her they were inappropriate. She had wanted to say "Why?" but had stopped herself. And Hardy had actually told her later that he had been proud of her!

She said instead, "You and Maisie. You get on well."

There was a note of wistfulness in her voice, and Viv said quickly, "It's because of David. His work appeals to her."

Hildie nodded, then said, "I'll have to get Hardy to go to art classes, then!"

She meant it as a joke, but Viv shook her head. "Hardy is an artist already, and he doesn't need an exhibition to prove it. Walk through the village and you see his art everywhere."

Hildie did not scoff. "I know. Go into the library when you can, Viv. He's made some shelving for the children's corner. Each bookcase has a window in it with curtains. They draw different pictures and slot them into the window spaces, so that when people open the curtains there's a view. It's really good." She was quite pink. "I'm really proud of him."

They went to the cinema just as they had done the previous year, and Viv insisted on leaving her as before. Hardy liked his Saturday sausage and mash and had had little enough of it for a long time. Viv promised Hildie she would make herself a boiled egg. Hildie reminded her that the following weekend they had been invited to the twins' first birthday party. "We'll go in the van because Hardy's made two rocking horses."

Viv had seen the first one — the "prototype" Hardy had called it — and had not imagined he would find time for a second. She also wondered whether there would be room for the horses and herself in the back of the van.

Hildie read her mind. "I've cleared those toilets out of the way, don't worry. And Hardy has soaked the horses in wood preserver so that they can go out on the patio. Elisabeth is fairly . . . tidy."

They parted, and Viv started up the hill and then stopped and turned back. It was four thirty, and there was over an hour of light before the evening set in. She could watch the sun sink into the sea from her windows, but she had spent the last two hours watching a cinema screen and suddenly wanted to be part of things. She certainly wanted to shake away the film images and reinstate her own reality before the evening at home.

She had put her case full of papers in one of the top cupboards in David's work room and was still terribly conscious of it lying there. She had read her first account of contacts with David, and then followed it with the second terrible confession. She had acknowledged its redemptive messages; she knew she would not find the word "dad" horrific again. It reminded her that you could link the absurd . . . the fear . . . the cruel and the sordid . . . into the infinite. David had told her that all she needed was love. She had found it that long evening with her father-in-law. Compassion had reached a point of such intensity that the only way to go had been physical. Love had overwhelmed her. She could actually think of her own father compassionately.

She knew now, with certainty, that her father had ill-treated his wife just as he had abused his daughter. The instant adoration he had wanted had not been there, and he had demanded it with force and then hated himself and had wept. It was almost simple. If his wife had lived, she might have stopped that vicious circle somehow. Perhaps Viv's own removal from it had stopped it. She had never tried to find out. But she had discovered something else. David had shown her what tenderness was. And that was why. That was why. That was why . . . the rest of it had happened.

She walked past the familiar shops, and wondered whether this really was a new beginning. She corrected that thought immediately: she could never begin again, but perhaps she could start again. Not from the beginning by any means, nor from the point of the accident. She had travelled a long way since then. The difference was she had been travelling — running and panic-stricken — away. Perhaps now, she was walking towards. It was still frightening. But not . . . completely frightening.

She left the line of shops; the smell of the sea mingled with fish and chips. Leaves were everywhere. Winter was almost here again. She had somehow survived two of them, and found she was no longer alone.

She lengthened her stride, left the shelter of trees and houses; ahead lay the enormous field where hundreds of years before, the people of the villages had let the sea flood through to make salt pans. The light from the low sun came over the sea wall and made her blink. She would climb to the top of Becket's Hill and look over at the islands and then go home. She started off across the field.

The matron of Tall Trees had asked her whether she might like a part-time job at the home. And Tom had "suggested" brusquely that she might want to go back to teaching. She knew there was always a need, especially in the winter months, for supply teachers. And Esmé Wetherby had suggested diffidently that they were thinking of starting a reading group at Tall Trees, but did not quite know how to go about it.

She reached the amusement arcades and the crazy golf course. She discovered she was . . . excited. The possibilities for starting again were all there. She would talk to Juniper about the book group, she would break through all the scoffing about "going back to school at eighty-five" and ask her for suggestions for the first book. Something funny? Maybe something they had already read. From the war years. An old-fashioned romance? She could imagine Juniper's expression softening.

As she passed the shuttered ice-cream stall, she could hear music. At first just the repetitive bass beat that often came from car radios. She walked on towards the lake and it became recognizable as something she had heard on her own radio. A singer burst into the rhythm of the percussion; she could not make out the words of the lyric. Terse, very modern. And coming from the deep hole that was the lake.

She hurried to the wall. The whole curved area of the little promenade surrounding the empty blackness was highlighted by the last rim of the sun as it lay on the sea. And on the steps down to it a disc player, looking strangely like the head of an extra-terrestrial creature, was blaring forth its insidious beat and its incomprehensible message. And in front of it, a girl and a boy no older than sixteen were dancing. They were facing each other, not touching, gyrating crazily, every ounce of their beings chock-full of energy, every muscle moving as they jumped, pumped their legs and arms, twisted their necks and shoulders. The singer slowed, and they had to adjust their own movements. Viv heard the girl's laugh as she paused a second. The music ended. A voice spoke, velvet smooth, saying something about love.

The dancers, left high and dry without music, were caught in mid-flow. The girl screamed with laughter, and collapsed at the waist, hanging her head to her knees like a broken doll. The boy said, "What are we supposed to do with that? You can't dance to words!"

Viv went on up the path through the woods. The music started again, and she supposed so did the children, and she smiled, imagining them releasing all that pent-up, extrovert energy to their own special music. She wondered how long it would be before they realized, all too clearly, that they danced to words all the time.

The trees ended abruptly, and she was on top of a bald hill, looking down the coastline to where the Atlantic surged into the estuary daily. Below her in the small muddy harbour, the Pill, a boat was on stilts being scraped before the next tide floated it off. The light was fading, and the Pill was in the shadow of Becket's anyway, but it looked exactly like the boat she had seen here last year. And she was standing now where David had appeared that day, a Sunday morning. And she had run away.

She left the path and began to giant stride down the steep grass slope, just as he had done before. She ended up, breathless, just above the boat. She was exhausted, exhilarated, as she imagined those dancing children had been. Like the girl, she bent over from the waist, clutching her sides, laughing aloud. As she straightened, a man ducked from the other side of the boat, and straightened too, looking up at her questioningly. He was holding a bucket and a brush. She could smell the tar.

"You all right, lady? Did you fall?"

She was momentarily shocked at his sudden appearance when she had thought the whole spread of sea and land was hers alone. She clamped her hand to her side as a stitch pulled muscles across her waist.

"No. I sort of slid and ran from the top." She was breathless, panting. "No, I'm fine. Thanks."

They both waited for her to recover; he stood awkwardly, holding the brush over the bucket; she bent again, measured her breathing as she always had done, lifted her head and smiled down at the man.

"I suppose people are always doing that," she said.

"The kids do it. Yes. Dangerous. That's why I told 'em to have their jig or whatever they call it down in the old lake area."

"Oh." She was interested. "I think they would call it a gig. There's a couple there now, practising I suppose." She smiled. "They looked like acrobats." Then she frowned. "What about if they fall into the lake? There's no water."

292

"I got them to sweep it out after yesterday's tide. Still got the big brooms we always used. They thought it was fun. I told them about the acoustics. They'll use the lake bed, see. It contains the noise as well as the kids. We strung up the old fairy lights so they can see what they're doing."

She stared at him, astonished. He grinned suddenly, and nodded. "I know it's still risky, but you got to give them some slack sometimes. Trust them. There won't be any drink or drugs. That was the deal."

"Yes." She was having difficulty in accepting that anyone except herself . . . and the Hardys and Juniper and Jinx, of course, knew anything about the lake.

He said, "I'm Jack. Jack Bartholomew. My mother used to supervise the stuff at the lake."

She felt her face stretch wide. She stammered, "I remember. Of course I remember. It was all coming to an end when we moved here, but when I was a child . . . we came for the day. Picnics . . ."

He nodded. "Lot of Sunday-school treats happened in those days. No health and safety then. The kids scooted down that hill on tin trays."

She nodded, then blurted, "Last year I walked along the path here. It was a Sunday. I think you were here then. Painting your boat."

"I would have been. I put it up in the winter these days." He smiled. "You used to jog a lot, didn't you?" He cleared his throat. "I know about you. I saw you the other night. Juniper Stevens was with you, wasn't she?"

Viv was aghast. The whole thing was going to be dragged into the open. How would they explain it?

He saw her total dismay, and said quickly, "It's all right. I know Mick Hardy. We used to go fishing together."

Viv sat down abruptly on the slippery grass. He made a move to clamber over the rocks. She said quickly, "I'm all right. Embarrassed, of course. I can't explain . . . I'm so sorry."

Thankfully he stopped where he was. She got to her feet. He seemed to be waiting. She stammered, "Perhaps . . . maybe . . . you could talk to Mick?"

He lifted his shoulders. "Nothing to talk about. They're going to fill the lake properly again. No facilities for swimmers, but if anyone wants to use it . . ."

She did not know what to say. There was silence. Into it came a bass beat from around the corner of the hill. She cleared her throat. "Is the gig starting already?"

"More practice prob'ly." He, too, cleared his throat. "Everything's different when you're young. You never think about consequences. What you might have to do to put things . . . level . . . again."

"No. That is true."

He took an audible breath. "There was a lot went on. Always seems to be something going on. But then . . ." Another breath. "My mother's got her marbles in the right place. She could tell you." He puffed a little laugh. "She's told me. Course. But tell the truth, it goes in one ear and out the other. And half of it she makes up. The Jacksons were good at making things up. And she's a Jackson, all right." His laugh was full-blown. He expected her to echo it. She tried.

He said, "Why don't you go and see her? She knows about you. She'd really enjoy seeing you. She lives in that sheltered housing place. Nice little bungalow. Friends around her. Couldn't be better for her. I'll tell her you'll call in, shall I? Would you mind?"

"No. I wouldn't mind."

"You might like to write down some of her memories. You could make a book out of it, really."

"I think I've done enough writing down." But she did not speak those words. She was already moving off.

When she was out of his line of vision, she started to run. She thought, it will never end. So long as I live it will be there.

CHAPTER
TWENTY-SIX

The birthday party was a riot. Joy and Michael might not have known what it was all about, but they soon realized it was in their honour. Until their grandparents arrived, the favourite presents were their baseball caps, one with a blue peak, the other pink. They learned that when they peered out from beneath the peaks with pursed lips they got kisses, and laughter, and applause, too.

When the van drew up, Tom was summoned, and he and Hardy staggered through the garden with the rocking horses and installed them on the flagged patio outside the window. Cumber and Maisie bestrode them and had a twin each in front of them. The excitement was intense. Everybody had to sing a song and every song had a chorus of: "Jig-jog jig-jog jigalong home". Hardy watched them, his face split by a beaming smile. Hildie watched him, and then the twins also, with great pride. Tom caught Viv's eye and put up one thumb and after a second she did the same.

Elisabeth was looking tired. When her ex-husband arrived he remarked on it, and Tom heard him and visibly bristled. Viv took Tom's arm and led him to the kitchen area, where glasses and beakers were piled high in the sink.

"Let's do these." She pushed up the sleeves of her cardigan. "You dry, Tom. You know where things go."

"We've got a damned dishwasher, Viv," he protested. "I think Elisabeth needs some protection from the chairman of Mason Electronics, don't you?"

"Not from you, Tom. She will become piggy in the middle. Your parents will rescue her. And dishwashers need to be loaded and unloaded. We can have this lot done and put away ready for the birthday tea. Actually, that will cheer up Elisabeth, she likes things organized properly." She glanced over her shoulder; Hildie was already standing by Elisabeth. "And actually again, she is looking tired. Bad nights with Joy and Mike?"

"Not particularly. Maisie isn't especially cooperative lately." He took the offered tea towel reluctantly. "Of course Elisabeth doesn't have any time to give her until the babies are in bed."

"Ah." Viv rinsed a glass and set it in the drainer. "I thought Maisie might take over the bedtime thing."

Tom's mouth tightened. "The other evening I overheard her tell her mother she gave far more time to her stepchildren than she did to her own daughter."

"Which is probably true. And will be for quite a time." She glanced up. "Would it help or make it worse if I talked to Maisie?"

"I don't know. You could try. But she thinks of you as a friend. It would be a great pity if that changed." He sighed. "I tried to get her to write things down — you

297

know, in the third person. But you didn't do it, so I can't expect her to."

"I did." She smiled wryly. "I should have thanked you. It helped enormously. I'll never be free of it, of course, but it has allowed me to find certain . . . redemptive . . . qualities. In the whole thing."

He was pleased. "I did the same, Viv."

She nodded. "Yes. Hildie said you had. A useful psychological tool, I think." She picked up another cloth and began to dry. "Leave it with me, Tom. I'll see how Maisie reacts. If it's not good I'll drop it. All right?"

"Thanks. Look how good she is now — thoroughly enjoying herself with the kids on the horses."

"She *loves* them, Tom. That's the important thing." She put the last glass in one of the new cupboards and added quietly, "It's the only thing."

He laughed. "Wise older sister, eh?"

"Oh, Tom." She looked at him, and he saw the tears but ignored them, and said, "Does it sound good?"

"Oh, yes."

"I agree."

He held out his hand and she took it, tea towels and all. She thought he might lean over and peck her cheek, but he held on to her hand instead and said in a low voice, "So be it."

And she repeated, "So be it."

Tea was almost civilized. Margaret, Alan Mason's second wife, arrived hot from some committee meeting and took over the "waitressing" with aplomb.

"Darlings, I had the most enormous lunch at my club. Couldn't eat another thing. And I borrowed this outfit specially for the job, so please don't ruin it for me." She ferreted in her bag, and produced a white cap and frilly apron.

Maisie whispered to Cumber: "She didn't borrow it at all, at least not today. It's what she calls her vamp's outfit, for when Dad is tired or gets cross."

Viv, overhearing, glanced at Elisabeth, pretty and plump and organized and kind, yet still no competition for Margaret Mason. Elisabeth caught her eye and closed one of hers and Viv knew it was all right. Elisabeth was very happy to be herself, almost married to Tom Hardy and with a ready-made family. Of course she was tired and perhaps unhappy about Maisie at the moment, but she knew it was part of the family life she had chosen. Viv decided to leave well alone; Maisie was sensitive where her mother was concerned, and might well think Elisabeth had asked Viv to "talk" to her.

They ate sandwiches and jelly, and Elisabeth and Maisie fed the twins and fielded flying jelly, and laughed together and Viv relaxed and turned to Cumber on her left.

"Hello, Miranda. How's it going? Egg and cress?"

"Oh thanks, Viv. D'you mind me calling you Viv?"

"Not a bit. I called you Miranda."

"I like it. Everyone calls me Cumber except Gramps, of course." She smiled. "He hated Mum marrying Dad, so he pretends I'm called Miranda Field." She giggled. "When I got to know things I thought Mum and Dad weren't married, and I really was Miranda Field. But then I had to have my birth certificate for school and —" She drew her face down and said in sepulchral tones, ". . . I really am Miranda Cumberbatch, whether Gramps likes it or not." She laughed. "He's OK, really. It's just that when Mum and Dad are on tour it's deadly dull living in an enormous house in the Cotswolds with your grandfather, who is a botanist. And though he thinks Mum and Dad should get proper jobs, when he's in charge of me I have to practise on Mattie far oftener than when Mum and Dad are home. Mattie is my double bass," she added as Viv's eyebrows went up.

"So your parents are . . . in show business?"

"Musicians. Both of them strings. They're backing Marvelmen at the moment. But after the German tour they've got something lined up with a string quartet. They can play anything." She was flushed with pride.

Viv said warmly, "How wonderful, Cumber. No wonder you like being called that. No one can copy a name like you've got."

"No, they can't, can they?" She finished her sandwich, and then said diffidently, "Maisie has told me about your husband. Mrs Harper — our Eng. Lit. teacher — would like to meet you. She is going to write to you, actually. Will that be all right? Maisie says you are stricken with grief and I wondered whether you might not want to see anyone from the past."

Viv could imagine these two eleven-year-olds romanticizing the couple who lived on the hill. She could also imagine Merilees Harper's diffidence about

300

getting in touch again. Vivvie Lennard had been practically a recluse at school.

She said, "Of course it will be all right, Cumber. I am looking forward to it." She smiled as she realized how true that was; it would of course be marvellous if Merilees Harper could arrange an exhibition of David's work, but even without that, it would be very good to see her again. Vivvie Lennard had kept herself to herself to protect her father, but she had always admired Merry McKinnon, who had run the school drama society.

Cumber smiled back at her mistily, and said, "It's so great here. Maisie's family. Full of life."

"I take it your parents will be home for Christmas?" Viv asked.

"Not sure. Maisie said I could come and sleep in her bottom bunk if they weren't home, but I couldn't leave Gramps."

"Might it be possible . . ." Viv spoke hesitantly. "None of my business and all that, but perhaps you and Maisie could cook Christmas lunch for Gramps and then have Tom and Elisabeth and the twins for tea."

Cumber's face lit gradually from within. She breathed, "It would be really great. We've loads of rooms and things. And the heating is always on because Gramps has breathing difficulties in the winter. We could play treasure seekers — Maisie could come over and we could work out a trail and write clues and things —"

"Hang on, for goodness' sake! You haven't asked Gramps and you don't know whether your parents will be home —"

"It would be even better if they were! They could play carols, and we could sing and dance — oh Viv, it would be fab. You must come and Mr and Mrs Hardy."

"Definitely not me, Cumber. Really. I'm booked at our local nursing home."

Cumber's face did another quick change. "Oh no! You're ill?"

"I hope not. We've started a reading group there and we're finding extracts from *A Christmas Carol* we can read to the others after tea to frighten them all to death — not quite to death, perhaps!"

"Oh Viv, what a shame. When it's your idea, too!"

Maisie turned and called, "What idea? Tell!"

"Later." Cumber called back. "It's good, you'll like it."

Margaret brought two small cakes in then, lit with a candle each, and everyone gathered around to give their own version of how to blow out the tiny flames. Unfortunately when they succeeded and the wicks emitted smoke, both children burst into tears, and the candles had to be lit again. And then again.

Still laughing, the party began to break up. Hardy, crouched over the television, announced that City had lost their match, and heavy rain was forecast from the west. Hildie immediately fetched coats and gloves. Margaret glanced at the wrecked table and said they would have to make a move, too. Maisie said, "Me and Cumber will put Mike and Joy to bed, if you like."

Elisabeth hugged both girls and called them angels of mercy. Maisie was forced to say honestly, "Not really. We've got something to discuss."

They drove through Bristol because the motorway was heavily congested; it meant going up the combe and passing the spot where David had twisted the steering-wheel and taken them over the edge and into the beech trees. Viv had not come this way for two years, and she waited for at least an echo of that terror to return. Nothing happened. Hardy said nothing, and after they had passed the road sign emblazoned with its zig-zag warning, Hildie turned in her seat and said, "I think Della would have been pleased, don't you, Viv?"

For a moment Viv was unable to understand the question, and when she did relief came with comprehension, because if Hildie had remembered about the combe she would never have asked such a thing.

She said, "I'm sure she would. But don't forget, Hildie, I never met her. I have no idea what she looked like. I know her only through what you have told me."

Hardy cleared his throat. "What a thing to be talking about! Course anyone would be pleased that their families are coping, let alone having parties. Trust you to bring up the subject of dead people!"

Viv released the strap long enough to pat Hardy's shoulder. "Hildie doesn't want to forget her — not on the twins' first birthday."

"I know, I know. All I'm saying is, it went well by any measure. And if half Hildie tells me is right, then Della was there and was enjoying it with the rest of us."

"Cumber is keen to invite them up for Christmas tea." Viv changed the subject tactfully. "Were you planning to have them to stay?"

"No, we weren't. Not again," Hardy got in before Hildie could open her mouth. "I just hope they'll go! Nice change for them, and good for Maisie, too. That Cucumber girl is really nice." He got the laughter he had asked for, and settled into his seat for the long drive downhill to the sea and the village.

Viv said, "I did tell you, didn't I, Juniper, Winnie, Esmé and that nice Lily Croker are going to do some readings on Christmas afternoon — then sing carols?"

"You did. But you will come and have some of our turkey, won't you?"

"Love to. Thanks, Hildie." Viv caught a glimpse of moonlight on water. "And tomorrow, I'm going to see Mrs Bartholomew. Her son was caulking his boat a couple of weeks back. We were passing the time of day, and it turned out he was Mrs Bartholomew's son. He asked me if I would call on his mother. I said I would."

"She in one of the other homes?" Hildie asked. "She must be getting on — older than Juniper?"

"Much younger, I would think. She was still captain of the ship down at the lake when we moved here."

"Was she really? Time is strange. Sometimes long, sometimes short."

They began the climb on the other side of the valley. Hardy negotiated each hairpin bend with great care.

"She lives in sheltered accommodation. A bungalow. On that development behind the Pill."

"I never knew her," Hildie said. "But her son used to fish with you, didn't he, Hardy? Send our regards."

"I will," Viv promised. They drew up outside the house, and Hardy opened the back doors and helped her out. Hildie went ahead, unlocked and walked down the hall, peering into the rooms and switching on lights.

They said goodnight. She watched them back into the drive and turn the van around; a tiny peep on the horn, and they took the first bend and were gone.

She closed the door and looked into the hall mirror. She looked different: she had topped her usual black slacks with a jewel-green tunic in honour of the birthday, and it must be that that was making her glow.

She said, "David, Tom asked me to be his sister. Isn't that something?"

CHAPTER
TWENTY-SEVEN

Becket's Close was a crescent of identical bungalows set around a lawned island of flowerbeds and shrubs. Concreted ramps with safety rails led up to front doors. Outside Mrs Bartholomew's front door, a small car was parked with a note inside the windscreen which said simply, "District Nurse".

Viv almost turned back, imagining that Mrs Bartholomew was at this moment having treatment of some kind, but then she remembered she was expected, and that the car might belong to one of the bungalows on either side. Space was very limited, and she was thankful she had walked down.

She rang the bell, a ping-pong almost exactly like her own, and the door opened immediately.

"My dear, I saw you hesitate at the car, and I was coming to give you a call." Mrs Bartholomew stood aside. "Come in, come in. The note means nothing. I was on the district many years ago, and when I couldn't get a disabled parking ticket, my son thought it was highly amusing to fish out my old calling card and stick it in the windscreen." She indicated Viv to go ahead out of the cramped hall and into the living area. "He's a bit of a joker, is Jack. Keeps me going, I can tell you!"

Viv stood in the middle of the room; it was a glorious clutter of plants and books and shelves of mementoes. The wide window ledge must have held thirty or forty glass paperweights — and a troop of ebony elephants. The window overlooking the rest of the crescent could have offered a peaceful view of the lawned island if it hadn't been blocked by the car.

"I know it's a bit of a muddle in here, but I will get it straight eventually. It's difficult to fit everything in." Mrs Bartholomew did not sound apologetic, and Viv had a feeling that she chose to be surrounded by her things.

"It's great." Viv turned with a smile and held out her hand. "It's your life. All around you. It — it's a happy room! And you haven't changed at all. I remember you so well. In that little office by the changing huts. You look exactly the same."

It was not strictly true. The dark hair was now almost iron grey, and there were lines in the face that had not been there eight years ago. But the black eyes were still bright, and there was a firmness in the handshake that left no doubt she could still take command of an army of swimmers.

"I feel the same from the waist up!" She patted the back of Viv's hand, released it and sat down in a well-padded chair by the window. "It's my legs that give me gyp. Sit down, Mrs Venables. It's good of you to pop in like this. I've been curious about you, I'll admit."

"Curious about me?" Viv settled herself, and noticed the tea things on the table behind the knitting and the photograph albums.

"Well, about your husband, of course. His cartoons. And then about you. Jack has told me how you used to run all the time — he used the word run, not jog."

Viv said nothing to this, but she was surprised that Mrs Bartholomew knew about David. "You liked David's art?" she asked, smiling. "Not many local people knew about it. He would be very pleased."

"I always turn to the cartoons in the newspaper. They often tell you more than the articles and reports."

Viv laughed. "Oh yes. He would be pleased to hear you say that."

Mrs Bartholomew laughed too, then got up, and with the help of the furniture negotiated the table, two more armchairs and a Welsh dresser, and lifted a shutter to reveal a galley kitchen behind a counter. She flicked a switch and a kettle on the counter boiled immediately; she poured the contents into a teapot and brought it back to the table.

"So convenient here, Mrs Venables. Living area this side of the front door and bedroom and shower room the other. Always something to hold on to. No trouble at all."

She set the teapot on its stand, and sat down with a little breath of relief.

"That's better. Now you can tell me why you've come. Then I'll pour the tea and we'll talk it all over. Does that sound about right?"

"Yes. But . . ." Viv was at a sudden loss. "I thought . . . I mean I understood from your son that you would welcome a visit. And the Hardys met you one day . . .

That was why I telephoned. And you suggested today. And I'm here." She tried to laugh again, and faltered.

Mrs Bartholomew fished down the side of her chair and produced a spectacle case, opened it and put on glasses. She peered through them at Viv's face, then took them off and put them away again, obviously reassured that Viv was being truthful and open.

"Well, I'm blessed. I was so sure you knew. I asked Jack, and he said he had no idea but you often came around by the lake." Viv felt her stomach sink; it was that blasted door knob again. Jack Bartholomew had seen them replacing it. On the other hand it did not sound as if he had confided that to his mother.

"You don't know that your husband and me were first cousins, then?"

Viv sat up straight. "I had no idea." She subsided. "And neither did he. He would have said. We came down to the lake to swim, neither of you appeared to know the other." She frowned. "What do you mean, Mrs Bartholomew?"

"Well, he probably didn't know, then. And I saw no point in telling him. My mother and her sister were both dead and the connection between us was gone. He was nearly twenty years younger than me. I was intending to come to see you, however, after that terrible accident. Then I was moving, and Jack said as how Hildie Hardy was looking after you. So I knew you'd be all right."

There was a little silence. Mrs Bartholomew took off the lid of the teapot, stirred the contents and replaced the lid.

Viv said, "I still don't understand. Why didn't David know about you? Why didn't his father tell him?"

"I'm not sure he knew." She poured the tea. "But if he did, it was a sordid little story to most people. He would have forgotten it as soon as he could."

"He wasn't like that," Viv said in a low voice. "He was a decent man. And lonely. He would have been glad to have made contact with his wife's family."

Mrs Bartholomew picked up her cup and saucer and sat back. "I'm not so sure. We're a pretty rough lot." She saw Viv's sudden flush, and smiled. "I don't mean he was a snob. Though he and that John Jinks were thick as thieves, and Jinks was a snob if ever there was one."

Viv did not know what to do. She had come here in the same spirit as she went to Tall Trees, and now she felt condescending. And why on earth was there all this secrecy?

Mrs Bartholomew's black eyes twinkled suddenly. "It's all a bit much, I can see that. Look. Sip your tea and I'll tell you about it. It's so simple, really. Time has made it seem complicated. And the fact that it's in two halves. My grandfather had two families, one on this side of the water, and my mother and aunt the other."

Viv sat very still, frowning slightly, still puzzled. Mrs Bartholomew leaned forward and pushed a cake stand nearer to Viv. She said kindly, "Have a cake. These were two for the price of one."

Viv did exactly as she was bid; Mrs Bartholomew had not lost her touch.

"Juniper told you about George Jackson, the mason who built the lake? He was my grandfather. And her father. Though there's a lot of doubt about that — my grandmother never believed it. Anyway, he came over to do this job — biggest job he'd ever done — leaving behind twin girls, Rose and May. Rose was my mother and May was David's mother." She sighed sharply. "Next thing my poor old grandma knew, he was home for a weekend and telling her he had fallen in love with Nellie Stevens. Proper-like — those were his words. Can you believe it? My grandma never did. Or if she did she thought he'd get over it, and come back home to her and his five-year-old twins." She sighed again. "Then, of course, the day they let the tide into the lake, he gets his foot caught on a lever and he's drowned." She paused and stirred her tea. Viv sat as if turned to stone.

Mrs Bartholomew put her spoon carefully into her saucer and said, "Rose got out of Cardiff as soon as she could. My grandmother never got over her handsome, wonderful George being drowned like that — terrible thing, no compensation then. She had to go out to work, and as soon as it were legal so did Rose and May. Not much of a life, apparently. My mother — Rose — came over here hoping to get something out of the accident. That was 1935. Bit late in the day, but she met up with Jimmy Jinks — John Jinks's father, and got him to fall for her in a big way. He set her up in a nice flat in Clifton and she got a job down in the council offices doing filing. Taught herself to type on the typewriters there when everyone had gone home. And

311

as soon as she got to fifty words a minute, Jimmy Jinks got her a job as secretary to the school doctor. She didn't marry the doctor, but she married his brother." Mrs Bartholomew's laugh was infectious. "Not such a good catch. He couldn't keep a job and was only too glad to be called up in 1940. Went out to Africa a year later and didn't come back. I was born in 1937. Mum was twenty. She got her army pension, another job in the new typing pool, and we got on very well." She paused and looked down the years as she sipped her tea. "Yes, Mum and me got on well. Really well. She lived with Barty and me for years, no trouble. He liked her, too. And when Jack came along he was her boy as much as ours."

She was smiling slightly, reminding Viv of Juniper when she reminisced. This woman was half-related to Juniper . . . it was incredible.

"Poor May didn't do so well." Mrs Bartholomew sipped again and came back to the present. "There's always one in every family who gets lumbered with the elderly. Jack hasn't got no choice, but May had. She could have gone when Rose went. Grandma was floored by what had happened, but she was still strong enough to manage. In a way she would have been better. As it was it didn't take her long to lean on May until she couldn't stand straight by herself any more." She sighed sharply and picked up the cake stand. "Come on, have another one, they'll help you to swallow other things as well." She grinned. "It's not that bad really, is it? Must happen to lots of families —

discovering they've got another one tucked away somewhere because Dad strayed."

Viv said nothing. She took a cake and put it carefully on the china plate that matched the cup and saucer. She wanted to say that George Jackson had really loved Nellie Stevens, and she had had the door knob to prove it. But how ridiculous would that sound? Especially if Mrs Bartholomew knew nothing of door knobs. She bit into her cake.

"When Grandma died, May was nearly forty and properly on the shelf." Mrs Bartholomew took a cake herself, and viewed it suspiciously. "Barty said to me that if it hadn't been for her hanging on to look after Mum, I might have had to do my stint, and we might never have met. So we should help her. He — my Barty — was in charge of all the electrics in Somerset: traffic lights, street lights . . . you name it. He got May the job in the museum when he was doing some special lighting for a new exhibit. David Venables was the curator by that time, years younger than her, of course. She fell for him hook, line and sinker. He didn't stand a chance. She took after her dad — just kept going till she got what she wanted. She was pregnant after their first date — can you believe that?"

Viv almost choked on her cake. She would never be able to share the sheer irony of all of this. She thought of May Jackson. Her mother-in-law.

"They got married double-quick of course. It was 1957. The sixties hadn't even arrived, and they didn't get to the Bristol museum for a very long time." She chuckled. "Might not have got there yet for all I know!"

She swallowed. "The cake's a bit tough, isn't it? Probably past its sell-by date. There had to be a reason they were giving it away."

"It's not bad." Viv finished hers and sat back. She found she still liked Mrs Bartholomew. She liked her matter-of-fact attitude towards her grandfather's perfidy. She saw people as they were, and did not condemn them. Viv smiled, and said, "Thank you for telling me all this. It puts everything into perspective, somehow."

"I'm sorry I didn't get in touch before. I wasn't sure your husband knew anything about the Jacksons. May was funny like that. She probably never told old David Venables that she had a sister — a twin sister, what's more! I think she'd caught some of Grandma's bitterness and shame. And when she died I thought that was the end of it. But I kept an ear open for the two Davids. If they'd needed help I'd have been there. And then, when you young people moved down here into that house on the top of the hill, I thought I ought to do something about it. Every time you came for a swim in the lake I used to look at the two of you and see how happy you were, and I thought, don't start rocking any boats, Maggie Bartholomew. Might muck them up for ever. You just never know, do you?"

Viv shook her head. "You never do."

"And then his dad came down to Tall Trees and was being looked after by Mick Hardy's wife. Mick used to take my Jack fishing and on trips . . ." She smiled nostalgically. "I was down at the lake all summer long. We missed Barty, course we did, but we managed. We

314

got through it. Just like you're getting through it, my girl."

Viv nodded this time.

Mrs Bartholomew said, "Would it have helped if I'd come to see you right after the accident? Would it have helped to know this?"

"I don't think it would. I had to be helped in a different way." Viv smiled. "But it was connected with what you've told me. It was all connected."

"Well, yes. It would be. We're all connected. Thing is, d'you want to be connected to me and Jack? You can be honest with me."

Viv's smile grew. "Do you ever go out in your son's boat, Mrs Bartholomew?"

"Of course I do! And my name is Maggie."

"And mine is Viv. And if I can come out with you now and then I would very much like to stay connected!" She laughed, and so did Maggie Bartholomew.

"You worked that one well, my girl. We'd be glad of your company."

They settled down with another cup of tea and Maggie Bartholomew spoke of the lake in its heyday, and how a few people were asking for it to be tidied up so that it could be used again. Some wanted it listed as being of historic interest. Viv asked how the gig had gone the previous week, and Maggie rolled her eyes and said the youngsters could wrap Jack around their little fingers. "The noise was something terrible, and there've been letters in the local paper."

"Perhaps it will encourage the district council to get the lake filled with water again," Viv suggested.

Maggie described her own childhood visiting her grandmother and Aunty May and swimming at Barry Island. "My idea of heaven, that was. When they were looking for someone to superintend the swimmers over here I jumped at the job. I'd been nursing so I had the first-aid qualifications. And with Barty gone I wanted to get away from illness."

She told Viv about the spring tides that leapt over the retaining wall and half-way up the changing huts, so that the whole area was taken into the sea.

By the time Viv left she felt strangely different.

Maggie stood by the door to see her off. "Will you move back to Bristol eventually?" she asked.

Viv said truthfully, "I could never leave here. I don't know what will happen when I can't climb the hill any more. But I can't live anywhere else, I know that."

She walked back to the Pill and watched Jack Bartholomew as he worked on his boat. When he spotted her he came clambering over the rocks and stood below her.

"How did it go?"

She knew what he meant, and did not prevaricate. "Rather a surprise — a shock, I suppose. But as your mother said, it was so simple. It explains things to me, too. I suppose it makes us sort of cousins."

"I would have liked to make myself known to your husband — or to his father. But Mother said best leave well alone."

316

"I think she was probably right. I'm not sure how David's father would have reacted. It's different now . . . too far away to worry us." She grinned. "Next summer your mother has said I can come out in the boat with the two of you. Will that be all right?"

"It certainly will!"

She went on home wishing she could have told him the whole story. How David would have loved it! She could tell Tom, of course, but she would then have to show him what she had written, half the irony was lost without that.

She rang Hildie when she got home, and told her that it had gone very well with Mrs Bartholomew.

"Her name is Maggie," she said.

"Strange. I always thought it'd be something like Erica or Helga. Strong names. Not feminine and ordinary like Margaret."

"George Jackson fathered girls. All girls. May and Rose and Juniper. May had my David, Rose had Maggie and Maggie had Jack. Perhaps that is short for Jackson. But May wanted nothing more to do with her father, and she let old Mr Venables choose a name."

"Well. That solves that problem, then. I don't mean the names. I mean that you and David were all twined up with that door knob. David was a second-generation Jackson, and you were his love. Simple when you know, innit?"

Viv opened her eyes wide, and looked at her own reflection in the hall mirror and tried to see David.

She smiled. It was enough to know that he was . . . around.

She put the phone down, and it immediately rang.

A voice, low, musical, said, "Vivvie?" and her heart almost stopped, because that had been her name a long time ago. "It's Merilees. Cumber and Maisie are with me. I wanted to ask whether we could visit you . . . some time."

Viv heard her own voice. Joyous. "I'd love it! Come the first weekend you are free."

CHAPTER
TWENTY-EIGHT

The sluice gates were closed before Christmas and the sea gradually filled the old lake. At weekends a canoe club trained on the area beyond the door-knob wall and children sailed model boats in the paddling pool. Sometimes during the bitter months before spring, Viv swam from where the old diving tower had reared up against the background of Becket's Wood, towards the further wall. It was icy cold that first winter, but she always felt better after it. Sometimes she brought Juniper. At others, Maggie Bartholomew would appear, leaning heavily on her stick as they negotiated the steps. She and Juniper did not come together.

Viv calculated that by next summer she would be able to manage the full length and actually hold on to the door knob before turning back. She wondered now how on earth she had managed that desperate night-time swim.

Her life was full. The reading group were often quarrelsome, but when Maggie Bartholomew joined she kept them in order. They managed *Captain Corelli's Mandolin* without too much trouble.

Viv did a week of supply teaching; one of the local teachers would be taking maternity leave in the summer term, and the headmaster asked her to fill in full-time.

Weekends became very special. Hildie announced that weekends must be kept for "the Cheltenham lot". That meant all kinds of permutations: Cumber and Maisie might arrive at the bungalow on Friday evenings, and the Hardys might go back to the flat with Elisabeth. Sometimes Viv went to the flat on her own, so that she could look after the twins while Elisabeth and Tom "did a film".

She eventually let Tom read all her writings. When he did not get in touch with her immediately afterwards she thought he must be condemning her, and her heart sank. Then one late afternoon, already dark, she walked down from Tall Trees and saw his car parked outside the gate. He got out, just a silhouette, but already so familiar. He went to meet her and held out his hands. She took them. He said, quietly, "Thank you, Viv. I thought I knew everything, but of course I did not. If it helps at all, I don't think Jinx knew, either. He may well have guessed, but no more than that."

She led him into the house, through to the living room, stood by the dark window.

"I thought you would be . . . disgusted."

"Disgusted? By an act of love and compassion that was . . . boundless? Oh, Viv."

He stood by her and suddenly held her to his shoulder. Then laughed. "I'm no good at this, but if

320

we're going to be honorary brother and sister, I'll have to learn, won't I?"

She gave a sob and put her head to his.

She told him later about David's mother. "D'you know, Tom, when Maggie Bartholomew told me that her Aunty May had "got herself pregnant" — I think that was how she put it — on her very first date with David's father, I wanted to laugh. Surely that's a sign that I am accepting it all?"

Tom looked up from his teacup. "How d'you mean — I don't get it."

"Come on, little brother! It happened just the same for me, didn't it?" She sobered suddenly. "What does get to me still, is . . . what would have happened, Tom, if my baby had lived through the accident?"

Tom nodded. "What would have happened if Della had lived?" He shook his head as if to clear it. "As Dad said the other day when Ma was doing this sort of thing — we can only play the cards we are dealt."

It was exactly what Hardy would say and after a while Viv smiled.

David Venables's retrospective exhibition has been arranged for late summer at a gallery near the Tate Modern. There is a great deal of discussion about the opening and who will go. So far, Merilees, Maisie, Cumber and Viv will travel by train to London. The Hardys will look after the twins while Tom and Elisabeth drive up.

Viv and Merilees were quietly easy with each other from their first reunion, and both accept that one day Merilees will talk about the fire that scarred her face. Perhaps Viv will reciprocate; she is not sure. It is enough for now that Tom knows everything that has happened.

She discovered quite soon that she was not frightened to take down the files from the top cupboard and read them. They are no longer bundles of extroverted guilt. They have become celebrations. And much more prosaically, they record journeys. Her journey, Tom's journey, and others. Starting over eighty years ago.

Sometimes when she is gardening she stands beneath the fig tree, holds its trunk and wonders whether it is as simple as David tried to tell her. Is love really all you need? There had been a radio programme — very academic — years ago which her mother had enjoyed and her father had mocked unmercifully. One of the learned contestants had often started his answers with the words: "It depends how you define that word . . ." She could almost hear her father's voice sneering, "It depends how you define love."

David's definition had encompassed eternity. She knew she could not understand it, however often she looked at his skyscapes and cartoons. But for an instant, she had been part of it. That must be enough.